MY
SISTER
AND
OTHER
LOVERS

MY SISTER AND OTHER LOVERS

ESTHER FREUD

BLOOMSBURY PUBLISHING

LONDON · OXFORD · NEW YORK · NEW DELHI · SYDNEY

BLOOMSBURY PUBLISHING
Bloomsbury Publishing Plc
50 Bedford Square, London, WC1B 3DP, UK
29 Earlsfort Terrace, Dublin 2, Ireland

BLOOMSBURY, BLOOMSBURY PUBLISHING and the Diana logo
are trademarks of Bloomsbury Publishing Plc

First published in Great Britain 2025

A catalogue record for this book is available from the British Library

ISBN: HB: 978-1-5266-8520-9; TPB: 978-1-5266-8653-4;
EBOOK: 978-1-5266-8658-9; EPDF:978-1-5266-8655-8

2 4 6 8 10 9 7 5 3 1

Typeset by Integra Software Services Pvt Ltd.
Printed and bound in Great Britain by CPI Group (UK) Ltd, Croydon CR0 4YY

To find out more about our authors and books visit www.bloomsbury.com
and sign up for our newsletters
For product safety related questions contact productsafety@bloomsbury.com

For my honorary sister, Georgia Shearman

'We think back through our mothers if we are women.'

Virginia Woolf

The Start

We lay on the floor, clothes covering every surface, talking –
as we were compelled to do – about Mum.

'Have you spoken to her … recently, I mean … about …'
I was careful as I chose the words '… the past?'

Bea looked at me, her eyes were wary. 'I did try.' There
was a pause. 'She said I'd got it wrong. It wasn't sunny, not
that morning, and anyway the curtains round the bed were
blue.'

I reached across and squeezed my sister's hand.

'We saw a therapist, did I tell you? Me and Mum. One
question and we turned. Savage. We were screaming. I ran
out. Or she did. Then there we were again, waiting for the
bus. The next day Mum called: "Sorry that you feel this
way." I told her to fuck off. Twenty minutes later I called
back: "If you can't tell your mother to fuck off," she said,
"who can you tell?" We laughed.'

Bea laughed now and so did I, but I could see our
mother as she would have been, her hair sticking to her
face, her fingers clutching the receiver. Doing her best.
Doing everything she could.

On Bea's advice I'd seen a therapist myself. A woman who said almost nothing, even when a scream came piercing through the wall; even then she kept the same beatific smile on her face. My throat – I'd said – is closing. My chest – it aches. Her smile twitched and settled and we sat in silence as the hour ticked round. I saw a man who repeated one long anecdote. I wanted to believe in him, to excavate the wisdom of his words, and I may have stayed there, slipping and sliding on a plastic couch, if a cushion hadn't sprung loose and hit me on the chin. Would he mind – I'd interrupted – if I sat on the floor? He paused, removed his glasses, and declared me cured. I even tried Bea's therapist, who, despite insisting her role was to remain impartial, to erase from her thoughts anything she'd heard, softened, indulgent, at the mention of my sister; leant forward, suspicious, when I touched upon our mother.

I did my best to reel her in. Mum's resourcefulness, her courage. The adventures of our childhood, roaming through the streets of Marrakech. I described the people we'd befriended, the hotel where we lived in the Medina, the beggar girls we played with in the square. There were camels, mules, a pet hen we named Snowy. An earthquake that I'd slept through. A lake in which we'd swum. She'd frowned and raised a hand. Fez, Essaouira, Agadir. I hurried on. Hitch-hiking through the Atlas Mountains, searching for amethyst in the seams of rock while for two days no car passed.

'How was that, really?' she broke in.

'Nightmare.' Bea was rummaging through the chaos of the clothes. 'I'll be going to the screening naked.' She flung away the dress I'd suggested. A camisole landed in the bin.

'Bea,' I had to say it. 'I know Mum can't see the film before the screening, but maybe she could read the script at least?'

'Too late.' Bea was standing at the mirror. Her hair was long, her body spartan. I tracked the scars, silvered as they were across her arms. Each scar had its own story – razor blades, a compass, the needles that she'd used to puncture veins.

'Lucy,' she threw me a shirt, 'any chance this can be mended?'

'I can't help worrying …' I examined the ruffle and its rip '… how Mum will be, how she'll react …' I caught her eye. She was tying a length of silk around her neck, arranging it into a loose bow.

'Hideous?' she asked.

What else was there to say? 'Kinky,' I assured her, and I imagined the credits rolling, my sister stepping out on to the stage, and I wondered, if it was my story I was telling, where I'd be likely to begin.

PART ONE

1

'The three of you are sisters, surely?' A man waylaid us as we fought through to the lounge. Our mother smiled, eyes fixed on an empty row of seats, while Bea and I stepped sideways to avoid the steam cloud of his breath.

'Quick.' A couple were making their way towards our chairs, and lifting my brother, Mum rushed to intercept them. The boat was cheaper than the plane, the night boat cheaper still, and it was possible, if you were fast, to find enough seats to lie down. Flailing, the man lost his footing, catching Bea around the waist. 'Fuck off.' She yanked herself away.

'Remember, not a word about the move,' Mum said as we sank down.

I glanced at the dark curtain of her hair, her fine-drawn skin and worried eyes. 'Of course.' I took her hand.

Bea twisted round to check the doors, slapping back and forth into the bar. 'Sure,' she said – the word a whip – and Max, who'd recently turned three, ran a train along her arm.

We hadn't been to Ireland since Nana and Grandpa had given up the farm. They were living in a bungalow on the other side of Youghal, and although there'd been invitations in Nana's sloping hand, we'd let the opportunities pass by. Now, with nowhere else to go, we heaved across the sea towards them, the churn of engine oil, the dry salt smell of chips. 'Not a word, remember.' Our mother was determined her parents shouldn't know she'd left The Laurels. Should never guess she'd separated from Max's father, disappearing with no warning to her friend Cathleen in Bath, leaving Bea and me in Sussex till the end of term, where we slept in a series of spare rooms, our hosts watchful and polite, while our old beds, in our old bedrooms, lay empty. Where we would live when we returned I didn't know, and I imagined my sister beginning a new life in London – she'd been willing herself to turn sixteen so she could get away – as I went back to the same school, in the same village, to where our stepfather would still be teaching drama, even if he wasn't to be our stepfather any more.

Nana and Grandpa met us at the dock. 'Look at the lot of you.' Nana had a silk scarf wrapped around her hair and her lipstick made a bright red bow. 'Haven't you got big.' There was the familiar grip of her fingers and the rustle of her mac as she drew close. Grandpa was dressed as I'd only seen him dress for Mass. His farm jacket and wellingtons discarded, he wore pressed trousers and a short beige coat. His beard was trimmed, his bald head shiny. He looked small without his work.

'How are you all, my pets?'

All I could think of was what I mustn't say.

'We're fine,' Mum insisted, and once we'd squeezed into the car she told them about Bea's plans, the college she'd be starting in September – Art, Art History, French – while Nana fluttered that Bea always was a clever one, and hadn't she the smart handwriting, she always admired it, when she wrote. It was quiet as we looked guiltily through the windows, how long the spaces were when her letters lay unanswered, how hard it was to know how to reply.

The bungalow they'd moved to was on a slope above a bay. 'Will you look at the view,' Nana said when we'd taken off our shoes. Dutifully we crossed the carpet and stared out at the rippled mass of grey. Grandpa slumped into an armchair, picking up a magazine – he still read *Farmers Weekly* – and Nana went to put on the kettle.

There were two spare bedrooms in the bungalow. I was in a twin room with Bea. Our mother was to share with Max. 'Fuck.' Bea rolled herself a cigarette, and I thought how often I'd watched her smoke out of a window, had waited for her to come in at night. The first place we'd gone, after arriving home to find Mum's note informing us she'd left, was to the Mitchells'. They had a son, Steve, known for being handsome, and one morning, the night after I'd locked myself in the bathroom for the second time, Mrs Mitchell suggested he escort me to school. She'd given me a fortifying hug, and as I'd clenched my teeth, determined not to dissolve against her bosom, Steve finished his toast. Together we walked under an umbrella, along the edge of the golf course, across the Brighton road and down the cow path, my right arm stiff with the effort of not touching. But even before we reached the school Bea must have been caught climbing in through the open window – I'd told the Mitchells she'd gone in early for an exam – because when I arrived back that afternoon it was only to collect my clothes and my pet rat and move to another family prepared to take us in.

'Fuck,' Bea had said then too, although the place that was found for us was the Todds', whose middle son, Lawrie, had, until that Easter, been my boyfriend. Our room was next to his, and just as we'd done the winter of our going out, we lay on his bed while he flicked through motorcycle magazines, and I breathed in the raw, fresh-air smell of him and wondered how we could find our way back to the time before.

He'll find me more interesting now, I'd thought when I read our mother's note, but if Lawrie did find me more interesting his ways of showing it were subtle. He'd call me on a homemade telephone, two tin cans and a length of string strung between our rooms, and we'd talk, leaning out of our adjoining windows, sometimes for more than an hour. We didn't mention the cause of our break-up (Finola, parallel class, rhododendrons) but neither did he try and kiss me, which left a large, sad stretch of time where kissing once took place.

'I'm going for a walk.' Bea flung away the mashed end of her roll-up, and when I offered to come with her she turned her back. I started into the sitting room, and then, fearful of getting into conversation and finding myself tripped up, I pulled on my coat. Bea had reached the end of the short drive. 'Let's go down,' I called, pointing to the water. She strode uphill.

I followed. The bungalow was new, and above it at regular intervals were other, newer bungalows, all with the same plate glass to frame the view. We kept on, passing fields crossed with low stone walls, rocks stacked so slackly they looked ready to slide. A flock of sheep surged, thick as porridge, round a bend. We climbed on to the ridge to let them pass. 'Afternoon.' The farmer squinted, curious. He whistled and his dog slithered ahead, worrying the sheep into a field.

On we walked through spits of rain, and I thought about the places we might live when we were back in Sussex. There were two rooms in a converted house, a kitchen, sour with damp and gas, shared with the woman who showed us round. 'It's very reasonable,' she'd said, 'although you'll have to keep the little one quiet.' She watched us, hopeful, as we hurried Max away. There was a flat on the road that led out of the village. Its walls were thin, the windows rattled, and the rent, even if we'd wanted it, was twice what we had to spend. The communal house was the one that I'd liked best. Square and solid, it had a swirling, flowery carpet and a dark wood staircase that led up through its centre, changing to a laddered flight of steps, where built into the attic were three rooms around a lightwell. The best room – my room, I'd decided – had a balcony that looked out over fields. The landlord would have to accept my mother's offer of help with the garden – the grounds were large, with formal beds that ran in terraces to a pond – if we were to afford it. 'What about …?' Bea had nodded towards Max. 'Can't his father help?'

'Do you not think I'm exhausted?' Our mother tensed. 'Years of begging money from *your* father, I'm not about to start again.'

'Bea.' I was breathless as I caught her up. It was strange to think she'd not be living with us again, that she'd be leaving home at the same age our mother had left Ireland.

'Should we go on?' We'd reached a plateau and the road had narrowed. I was relieved when she turned back.

Mum was already at the table, Max beside her. Nana, a ladle in her hand, was describing the ailments that afflicted her, the arthritis in her joints, the heart trouble that had forced them to retire. 'Stop the moaning, woman.' Grandpa knocked his pipe against the chair. The stain of its tobacco ran in a yellow stripe across his beard.

'And there's himself, with his bad chest.'

'Enough!'

Nana bit her lip and served the soup. It was a leek soup with potato. Nubs of mutton floated on the top. 'It's only the smallest bit,' she said. 'For the taste.'

Bea put down her spoon. We'd not eaten meat since arriving one summer to find our lambs, bottle-fed at Easter, carted off to market, but today there was nothing else except a buttered triangle of bread, so I ate the potato and left the mutton in a grey pile.

Max gobbled his up. 'He likes that,' Grandpa said. 'Give the child a steak, that'll set him right.' He turned to Nana. 'Get into the kitchen and put one on to grill.'

'No!' Mum's eyes flashed, dark.

Nana hovered above her chair.

'It's what the boy needs.' He stared at Max as if he was defective, and we all looked, at his pale face and straight pudding-bowl hair, and no one said it – how fearfully he looked like his father.

'There's no need.' Mum stayed firm, and she turned to Nana and told her to sit down. Grandpa glared, and Nana, nervous, clattered her spoon against her bowl.

'I hope he dies first and then Nana can have fun,' Bea said that night in bed, and I crossed myself below the covers as I sometimes secretly did.

We stayed for three days before setting off for Bantry.

'Whatever is there in Bantry?' Nana had lipstick on her teeth.

'I have a friend, and the girls can see the country. We'll be back, don't worry. We'll be back before you know.'

It didn't start to rain until they'd dropped us at the bus. I thought then that we might catch the bus, but as soon as their car was out of sight my mother took Max by the hand and walked off along the road.

'Fucking hell.' My sister stared at the flared ends of her trousers, soaking up the wet.

'Smile.' Mum stuck out her thumb, and I did smile – at the men and women peering between wipers, at children turning round to look. A car approached, a man and woman, side by side. I froze, sure it was our grandparents returned, and I lowered my thumb, expecting the screech of brakes, the accusations. *Nothing but tinkers.* It wasn't them, or if it was, shame had turned them blind, and they drove on.

'We'll need a van,' Bea huffed, her trousers stained wet halfway to the knee. 'Who's going to stop for all of us?'

Just then a car pulled over and a man leant across and rolled the window down. 'Where are you off to?'

'Bantry Bay.' My mother pushed back the strands of her black hair.

'That's a way.' He hesitated, but even as he spoke, explaining he was only going as far as Ballincollig, she swung open the door.

'Thanks so much.' She picked Max up and slid him in.

Max sat between Bea and me and played with his trains. In one hand he had Thomas, in the other Gordon, and he ran them up and down the seat muttering to himself: 'Ballincollig Collinballig.' Mum sat in the front and studied the map. 'If we could make it to Clonakilty I know people there.' She looked back at the three of us. 'Martin and Petula?' When we said nothing she gave her full attention to the driver, listening intently, nodding her agreement, flashing her wide smile.

The rain had eased by the time we were set down at the turn. 'Good luck,' the man said, low, and we shook ourselves and Mum stood Max against the verge and we watched as the snail of his willy fattened and unfurled.

'Damn, now I need to go.'

'And me.' I followed Bea towards a scrubby bank behind which we squatted, our pee steaming against the turf.

'Quick!' Mum yelled as we were shaking out the drops.

'For God's sake.' Bea buttoned up her flies and the elastic of my knickers twisted as I tugged them up.

A car was waiting on the road.

'Here they are.' Mum waved, and the driver, a woman in a plastic mac, widened her eyes in alarm. The woman was going to Clonakilty, and although she didn't know Martin and Petula, it was clear she'd heard their names. 'They're up at the farm, with all the dogs, is that it?' Her hands tightened on the wheel.

At the entrance to the farm there was a statue made from rubber gloves, the fingers stuffed and pointing, and as we eased open the gate a pack of hounds came barking out to meet us. I held tight to Max although it was me who was afraid, but the dogs only circled, sniffing, and soon there was a shout and a woman sloshed across the yard.

'Petula!'

Petula looked at our bags with concern. It was clear she didn't recognise our mother, although when prompted – 'I'm a friend of Cathleen, you remember, Appleby?' – they embraced, and we were told to come and see the puppies, seven of them, born the day before. The mother, Sorrel, was a lurcher. She lay in a heap of straw in the corner of the barn. 'Aren't they adorable?' The puppies were bald and blind, and Petula was so delighted by them, their snuffling noses, the greedy way they sucked, that we knelt down to pay homage as each one was unplugged from its teat and passed around. Sorrel looked up with proud and weary eyes and I was reminded of Mum the day she came home from the hospital, how we'd crowded round to examine our new brother.

Martin was in the kitchen hacking up a rabbit. He grunted and said welcome, and slowly over that slow afternoon, the rabbit bubbling into a stew, men and women drifted in and sat at the table, playing music, dealing cards. The stew, when it was ready, was served with potato, mashed with skin and eyes, and too hungry to object to it, we ate. Afterwards we were shown to two sofas in a dark-beamed sitting room, so damp we made a fire with paper to cheer us while we undressed.

We were woken by shrieking in the yard. Mum threw off the covers and ran from the room. Max sat up and whimpered, and I crawled across to him and climbed into the warm space where our mother's body had been. He curved his knotty back against me, and we listened as voices rose, anguished, angry, interspersed with wails.

'Hell.' Bea pulled on her boots, and with a quilt around her, she went out. Minutes later she was back. 'The puppies are dead.'

Max went rigid in my arms.

'It's a blood bath.'

I put my hands over his ears.

'They think it's a local, came in and killed them.'

We waited in silence until our mother returned. 'We should probably get out on the road. Make an early start.'

'What if they think it's us?' My teeth were chattering.

'It was Sorrel,' she said. 'And they know it.'

'Sorrel?'

'It happens sometimes if the mother is too young.'

I thought of our mice and how the father, Cassius Clay, had eaten the entire litter. We hadn't known then that parents should be kept apart.

'They're doing it for their own good,' our mother had said then. She said it again now as she gathered up our things.

There was very little traffic going out of Clonakilty. A van passed, a trailer attached, and when the farmer stopped it was to tell us he was collecting sheep from the field beyond. He'd be happy to take us, but it might be quicker to walk. We did walk. It was warm and thick with the smell of manure, and soon the trees in the lane stretched above our heads and made a hollow leaf-green cave. Mum handed out raisins from a packet in her bag.

'Are we going to the dog farm again, later?' Max asked, and when we said no he stamped in one of yesterday's puddles and shouted 'Hurrah' and we all laughed. Even Bea was cheerful.

Bantry, when we arrived, was quiet. It was lunchtime, and the sky had clouded over. Xavier had been our stepfather's friend, he'd visited us in Sussex, all bone and Adam's apple, and now for no other reason than convenience, we were to stay with him for a few days. 'He said to find him at the Bantry Inn.'

'What, whenever?' Bea despised our mother's attitude to time, the hours we'd spent waiting outside school, even though increasingly Bea made a point of being late herself.

The pub was small and plain with two men at the bar. Neither of them was Xavier.

The landlord hadn't seen him. Not for days.

Tears sprang into our mother's eyes. *Don't cry!* I willed her. 'Last week he was here, and most likely next week he'll be sitting on that stool, but just now he's gone away to Galway to bring back his wife, God help him.'

'The thing is,' Mum was blinking, 'we've come from England. He said we'd find him if we ...'

'Ah. It was you he was expecting, so.' He rummaged through a drawer, and not finding anything he disappeared to a back room. 'It's a bit of a walk,' he called, 'down to the harbour, keep to the right and up the hill, and you'll not miss it, it's the last house.' He laid a key on the bar.

We were so relieved we stopped and shared a plate of chips, and while we were waiting, a packet of crisps. Restored, we set off, climbing, carrying and cajoling,

—leaving the town behind. The sky was grey by the time we reached the house. A stone house built up from the cliff, and if you peered down from the back windows there were the waves churning against rocks.

Welcome. Xavier had left a note and a large raw salmon on a plate.

My mother switched the oven on while we explored. The bedrooms were downstairs: the largest, Xavier's, a mattress on the floor; the smallest, a child's, dusty and shut up. Max rushed in and examined the toys. Two teddies tucked into the bed, and a mobile swaying in the draught. There was a shelf of books, none of which featured trains. Upstairs below a row of windows was one long daybed, its foam seating wrapped in Indian prints.

I read Max a story – one of three that we'd brought with us – about an engine, banished to a siding, who learnt to be good and was grateful for it, and when it was finished I looked down at the beach and there was Bea climbing over rocks. As I watched she stopped and stared out at the sea and I looked too, at the stretch of water, the lowering sky.

'Bea!' I called when I'd run down to her, but my voice was thrown back by the wind. I pulled off my shoes. 'Bea!' I was panting by the time I'd scrambled close.

'What?' Her nose was swollen, her eyes two slits of red, and alongside my pity was a small mean streak of curiosity to see how her beauty had dissolved.

'Nothing.' Beyond her was a white-sand crescent, washed smooth by the tide. 'Just bored, that's all.' What I wanted to ask was, would she miss us? Would she come home? Would it just be me now? Navigating the next foothold, I began to scale the sharp black stones.

———

There was the smell of baking salmon, and *Desire* boomed from two tall speakers. 'Saaaara,' Dylan pleaded, 'Saaaaira,' while Mum whisked oil for mayonnaise.

'What are we going to do here?' Bea scowled. She'd flicked through Xavier's records. No Sex Pistols, no Clash. She slumped down at the table, and I wondered how it would feel, to be loved as much as Sara.

'I don't know.' Mum smiled, sad. She beat the egg.

I sat with Bea on the daybed and we listened, over and over, to *Desire*, startling when the wind rattled the house, grateful to find it wasn't Xavier, returned. When the first side of the record ended we let the hiss and crackle of it play on, the small regular bump as it rotated, until one of us got up and flipped it round. We ate the salmon with potatoes and afterwards, by candlelight, lay down on what were now our beds to mourn the lost hopes of the boxer, Hurricane, languishing in jail, and the death of the gangster Joey, gunned down in a clam bar in New York. Bea and I mouthed 'Oh, Sister' to each other, and sang along to 'One More Cup of Coffee', howling like hyenas, rising above the wind, the chorus coming round so often that Max's thin voice wound its way from below where he'd been tucked into Xavier's daughter's bed.

The next morning the sky was clear. Small breezes shuddered the windows, and gulls called as they swept by. I stood up and stretched, and before I'd had a chance to turn, Bea clicked the record player on and let the needle drop. 'Hurricane' began again, his story so familiar by now I could have testified on his behalf in court – and to avoid the painful unwinding of his fate I pulled my clothes on and walked up on to the hill. The grass was short and scattered with droppings and as I stood, eyes closed, the sun on my face, I wondered if The Hurricane was still in prison, and hoped to God he was not.

'Luu … cy, Luuu … cy,' Bea warbled as she ran towards me, and picking up speed she raced across the field, her hair streaming, pinching me as she passed. I followed, my own hair streaming – bursting, as I'd always been, to catch her up – and when she stopped I rasped out our own song, mangled as it was from the original: 'I don't know how to … hate her. What to do, how to beat her.'

'She's a girl.' Bea faced me. 'She's just a girl.'

We raised our faces to the sky and roared, asking, should we rage and shout? Let our hatred out? Declaring that we never thought it would come to this! Why's she such a lout? We were back in our old bedroom. Stamping, growling. 'And I've had so many sisters before, but she … is … just … the … worst …' Here we fell upon each other in a re-enactment of all the other wild and necessary fights, rolling and laughing and showing our clawed nails.

The salmon lasted for three days and then we were forced to walk down the hill to Bantry. It was warm and the grass blazed green, and the bay from above was turquoise. Gulls floated in flocks, and boats with their furled sails were anchored in fleets. We were crossing the square when a young man in saffron robes rushed towards us. 'Have you heard of the Beatles?'

We stared at him, affronted.

'George Harrison has a solo album.' He slid a record from his bag. 'He'd like you to have a copy.' He thrust it at Bea. 'For a small donation to the monks of Skibbereen …'

and he went on, talking so fast and so determinedly that our mother opened the drawstring knot of her purse and paid him to stop. He bowed, his hands pressed together at his heart.

'Now what am I meant to do with this?' Bea said when he was gone.

'I don't know.' Mum was counting our diminished funds. 'Leave it by the side of the road?'

But we couldn't leave it. It had cost more than tickets for the bus, and what if the monk found it, or worse, George Harrison himself who might happen to pass by.

'Damn,' Bea muttered, walking on.

We bought bread, and cheese, and a bag of tomatoes and we were looking for a bench where we could sit and make a sandwich, when we passed the Bantry Inn. Music drifted out. A lone voice, singing. We stood and listened, and then our mother pushed open the door and, finding the place full, we squeezed in.

A man was sitting at a table near the back, a young boy on his lap. When he reached the chorus – 'Bobbing up and down like this, bobbing up and down' – the whole pub bobbed. We bobbed too; there was no resisting it. We bobbed again, and then again, until even we were laughing. When the song came to an end, there was a cheer, and another man began. His voice was clear and carrying, it was the story of how his village came to have a bus, and while he sang there was a deep, attentive silence. Verse after verse, the song unspooled, his eyes fixed on the distance, every breath in the room his. He finished, and his neighbour pressed a glass of drink into his hand.

'Come all you roving blades that ramble through the city.' The words were slurred, and had a tang of English. 'Kissing pretty maids.' I turned, and there at the bar was Xavier.

'What'll it be?' he asked when we'd pushed our way towards him. 'Pretty maids indeed.' His eyes were wet, his mouth too, and although we declined he ordered us Guinness, and a lemonade for Max.

That night Xavier made a seafood stew, and as it cooked he talked, his words rising above the waves, about his wife who wasn't coming home. 'The bitch.' He poured more wine, detailing her faults, her jealousies, the demands she made. When I thought at last he'd stopped, he lowered his voice to tell us how he'd caught her on the strand, her skirts hitched up, masturbating.

I looked quick at my mother. Had she not heard? Her eyes were flat and far away and she was twining a strand of hair into a curl. Xavier bent low over Bea's chair. 'Is that what you're up to yourself down on the beach?' He licked his lips and sloshed a spoon of stew into her bowl. 'I thought maybe I'd seen you there when I was peeling prawns?'

It was dark on the hill and there was nowhere else to go, and I thought of my stepfather and his babyish words when I'd gone back to collect my rat. 'I loved your mummy,' he'd said, although I knew by then he'd spent the half-term holiday with a girl he'd cast in the upper-school production of *Medea*. I'd looked at him, his hair mussed, his trousers shrunk to reveal his crotch, and I'd been clear, although I couldn't say it: *You did not.*

———

The return journey was long. We carried our album under our arms, on our heads; Max even used it as a branch line for his engines when for more than an hour no car passed. 'Leave it,' Bea sighed as we were dropped, finally, on the road that led up to the bungalow.

'You leave it.' But we didn't let it go.

'There you are.' Nana threw open the door. 'You've only now this minute missed him.'

We looked at her, blank.

'Your man, he rang about the … commune, is it? He says you can have the rooms, in exchange for gardening, at a nice low rent.'

Our mother paled.

'So you've left him.' It was Grandpa.

'Sit down if you're sitting down.' Nana's voice was high, and she ushered us towards the table which she'd laid with a cold tea – sliced bread, egg mayonnaise, coleslaw – while we waited for the row. 'I never thought, for sure, he was the right one for you.' She looked sternly at Grandpa. 'It may be for the best to make a break for it. While you're still young.'

'Is that so?' Grandpa blew a plume of smoke into the air, and he leant back in his chair.

We ate in silence until, unable to bear the strain of it, I described our new home. The flowered carpet in the hall, the staircase, the flight of wooden steps that led to our front door, and all the while I was thinking how when Bea and I were babies, Mum had been too afraid to tell her parents we'd been born. Too terrified to return to Ireland with the two of us, sure she'd be locked up in a home for wayward girls and women.

'And where will you be staying when you start your studies?' Nana turned to Bea, and Bea told them how our father had found a place for her to live, not far from college.

'Now isn't that something,' she exclaimed.

'Don't be ridiculous!' Grandpa snapped. 'It's only his duty that he's doing.' He looked at Max and shook his head as if they'd all be fools to expect any decency to come his way.

Late that night, as I slipped out to fetch a glass of water, I saw my grandparents through an open slice of door, wrestling in the gap between their beds. 'Will you calm down, woman.' Grandpa held Nana by both arms.

'I will not.' Tears blurred her face.

'You'll wear yourself out.' His voice was pained.

She laid her head against his shoulder. There was a silence as they rocked from side to side. 'How is she to manage?'

'Stop fretting.' It was his familiar, cross voice, but as I readied myself to tiptoe past I heard the crack in it.

The next day they drove us to the ferry. We stood on the deck while all around rose up the wrench of chains, the bellow of the funnel, the shrieks and squalls of parting. 'Bye,' we shouted and we watched their open mouths, their open palms, and when we'd waved enough we went inside to find our bags which we'd thrown on to a row of seats.

The crossing was calm, and as I lay sleepless I saw us travelling through London, boarding our train south to Sussex, the bus we'd catch, swaying through country roads, turning at the church where in our old life we'd leap off. We'd stay on now until we reached the next village, pull open the door of the communal house, trail past strangers to the flat on the top floor where we'd make a new triangular family, with me at the furthest point, while Bea, escaped, would spin off into her new life.

'Bea,' I hissed, 'are you awake?' I nudged George Harrison on which her coat was heaped to make a pillow.

'No,' she said, and together we listened to the great steel ship pounding through the waves.

That August I took the train to Scotland alone.

'Elvis,' Ted called as I carried my bag into the hall. 'We're in the TV room, watching.' He squinted beyond me at the spitting rain. 'Where's Bea?'

'Not coming.'

His face fell.

Janey was sitting on the floor, her arms slipped from the sleeves of her jersey. 'Just you?' She rose to say hello.

Ted slumped on to the sofa, his long legs bent, his feet in brothel creepers, his fingers drumming on the bones of his knees. 'Sorry.' I looked behind me, as if Bea might appear.

All afternoon we watched Elvis's films. Elvis as a cowboy, a soldier, a surfer in nothing but his shorts. By the time we reached the news I was a wreck. How had I come to him too late? And when the headlines reannounced his death, showing him – The King – aged and bloated, sweat in runnels down his face, Janey protested 'No!' and to preserve his dignity we switched off the TV.

There was a fire lit in the nursery, and the table was laid with three choices of cake. Val, the governess, sat between Timothy and Maud, the youngest Colquhoun children, ensuring that they start with something savoury, and although we were beyond her jurisdiction, we lined up, pressing sliced bread into the toaster, slathering on sandwich spread before piling our plates with sponge. 'Hello,' I said, as I sat down. Val blinked, curious, and I wondered as I often did at Craigmont if any of the adults had realised I was there.

Once I'd gone with Janey in search of her mother. 'What is it, darling?' She was writing letters in the floral study, her hair pinned softly around her head, her grey eyes sloped like Ted's. When Janey didn't answer she suggested we pick raspberries. 'Mrs H is making a pavlova, she'll be awfully glad of the help.'

I nodded, eager. I had a great desire to do as she asked, and as I reached the door I felt her gaze, and not for the first time I caught her puzzled frown. Janey and I were silent as we moved between the fruit canes. She'd wanted to ask if we could take a trip to Edinburgh, but to get the Edinburgh train we'd need a lift to Berwick, and there'd be no one spare to drive us, not with the Americans, who'd arrived the day before. Then there was the money for our tickets, or lack of it, which was why there *were* Americans, whose fortnightly stays, during which they'd be given the full Scottish Country House experience, were to go towards the scheme for saving Craigmont. Shooting and stalking, a formal dinner hosted by Sir Hew and Lady Colquhoun, and in the mornings, scrambled egg and haggis served in heavy, silver-lidded tureens.

That summer all the children except Timothy and Maud were banished to the east wing, to a flat with kitchen cupboards stocked with tins. Tomato soup, baked beans, and our favourite, ravioli. We catered for ourselves, every meal except for tea. Soon the table was so heaped with unwashed dishes that we ate breakfast on the floor. On earlier visits Bea had slept in with Daphne – the second-oldest girl – while I'd shared Janey's bedroom. To get from there to the bathroom you had to pass the Egg, a dome that filtered light into the hall, where, even in the daytime, there were ghosts. No one ever went alone. To ask for company was allowed, and clasping hands we'd run together, fast. 'Wait for me!' I'd call as I pissed, and Ted, who'd taken to playing drums in the attic and swearing he'd not been up there for years, even Ted would wait.

After tea we watched another film. 'The first Elvis movie that isn't in black and white,' Ted told us at the start of *Loving You.*

'Shhh.' Janey held a knuckle to her mouth. The television was ancient and had to be thumped to get it started and we could only wonder how much more beautiful Elvis might have been in colour. By the time the credits rolled my heart was ragged. The melt of his eyes, the swivel of his hip. I wanted him to live again. I'd dress in jeans and gingham. I'd catch him as he fell.

I'd inherited the Colquhouns as they'd inherited me. Bea had befriended Daphne on a visit to London, and they'd begun writing to each other. Daphne, miserable at boarding school; Bea, unhappy at home. That next summer Bea had begged our father to drive us to Scotland, and, surprisingly, enthusiastically, he'd agreed. I'd sat in the back of his car eyeing myself in the side slice of mirror while he drove so fast towards the border we were in Wales before we found we'd taken a wrong turn. 'There'll be friends at

Craigmont for you too,' Bea promised. I was nine, and I'd wanted to stay with our mother.

Janey was ten then, fair and watchful; Ted, eleven, dark hair curling to his collar. I'd trailed after, across the lawns, through the walled gardens and out around the front of the house. Ted had a pot-bellied pig, Janey a horse once owned by the eldest, Marina, who'd long since lost interest, choosing instead to drive into the Highlands with my father. It was the year Ted was starting school. 'What's school like?' he'd asked me and I'd shrugged. I didn't know. It was a bit like school.

There was a chapel at Craigmont, built into the east wing of the house, and there'd been a christening for Timothy who was six months old. Marina was to be a godmother and when, an hour before the service, neither she nor my father had returned, I caught Lady Frances looking at me with that soft crease of a frown.

Janey was nudging me. The television had faded to a speck and Ted took my other hand and the three of us snaked from the room. We edged past the nursery, and the closed doors where the Americans now slept, hurrying when we reached the Egg, running down the staircase where Colquhoun ancestors in hunting dress and white frilled shirts peeled down from the walls. The scent of rose dust floated up, and as we passed the hall table I trailed my fingers through the dried husks of the flowers. From here we skidded across flagstones, past the boot room where once, searching for gloves, I'd found Sir Hew camouflaged by coats. 'Sorry.' I'd backed away, and in my confusion found myself in the gun room where rifles were displayed in long locked cabinets, ammunition in shallow drawers below.

'Don't be cruel,' Ted crooned and then he stopped. 'Did you hear that?' Lowering his head he whispered, 'Maybe it was him?'

'Shut up!' Janey shivered.

Ted raced ahead along the corridor and pushed through the door that led into the kitchen. The kitchen was industrial. An eight-ring range built against the wall; two sinks, side by side. Pans, scoured, hung from hooks; knives glinted in ascending size. We'd made toffee here one winter, melting sugar, butter and vanilla extract, turning the heat so high it boiled, and when the ruined pan had been discovered we'd faced Mrs H's fury and Lady Colquhoun's disappointment. Even now I could feel the molten mixture sticking to my teeth as we stood and hung our heads.

Ted lifted down a tray of eggs and, pouring a sloop of oil into a pan, cracked one against the edge. The white frayed, turning lacy as he added another and a third. 'Let's light a candle for him,' Janey said when we'd heaped our plates and left them in a sink, and collecting bikes, thrown down, we screeched along the hall. The chapel lay behind a heavy door. It smelt of damp and incense, and we hushed our voices as we stepped inside. Ted struck a match which died, and then fumbling in his pocket he brought out a lighter – Zippo – and spun it till it caught. The flame illuminated his face, the black length of his lashes, the twist of his wide mouth, and when he held the lighter out our fingers brushed. Another, tighter flame flared up inside me. '*In nomine Patris* ...' Ted intoned as I lit the taper. We sat in the back pew and watched the flicker of our candles while Janey sang 'Love Me Tender' as softly as a hymn.

The next day Marina arrived. She hugged her siblings, and even though the last time I'd seen her in London she'd kicked my father in the shins, she held me warmly in her gaunt embrace. 'Are the Yanks still here?' She stepped over the dishes on the floor. When Janey said they were, she swivelled round. 'Let's have some fun, we'll need the little ones. Where's Daphne?'

Ted and Janey shrugged.

That night we filed into the dining room as Sir Hew was raising a toast. 'Hungry.' Marina had rehearsed us. 'No food. So long.' We stood mournful by the fire.

The Americans froze. The women's mouths dropped open. One pointed at Timothy in pyjamas, a smear of ash across his cheek.

'Most amusing.' Lady Frances stood. 'Did I fail to mention there'd be entertainments?'

'Off with you.' Sir Hew's usually flushed face was brick, and he staggered up and ushered us from the room, lingering on the landing to hug Marina – 'Darling girl'– and hang Timothy, briefly, upside down.

'Papa?' Maud held out her arms.

'Bed.' He ruffled the tangle of her hair.

He turned away then, and we turned away too, shepherding the small ones to their room where they cried so wretchedly Val appeared and asked what did we think we were doing making trouble when there was trouble enough at hand? We wandered out into the gardens where we sat on the stone wall that divided the lawn from fields. It was a clear night, the stars cracking through the black, and when Marina offered up a pack of Camels, Ted pulled out a bottle. Tonic, the label said, although its contents were a mix of browns. 'I topped it up, an inch a day.'

'That's the way,' Marina laughed, and the drink was passed round.

My first gulp scorched, I spluttered, but the next I swallowed and kept down. I lay back on the nibbled lawn and looked up at the sky. There was the Milky Way, and the Plough, Venus the brightest planet of them all.

'The planet of lurve,' Ted said when I pointed it out, and I held my breath, our shadows overlapping, as he nudged his foot against mine.

That winter, after Christmas – our first Christmas without Bea – I arrived once more at Craigmont, alone. The trees along the drive were bare. Snow laced the fields, and the lake had thickened into ice. Ted and Janey had their old rooms back, and we spent long hours in Janey's bed, too cold to venture out. Only the nursery was warm, and one small kitchen where Val prepared meals. On Val's night off Lady Frances made a macaroni cheese and we all sat round, with extra chairs squeezed in, and she asked what did everybody think, should she have another baby?

Marina was at home, and so, unusually, was Daphne. 'Oh do!' Voices rose. 'Have one more!'

Only Daphne was silent.

On New Year's Eve we planned to have a party but there was no one who lived near enough to come. 'Call Bea,' Ted insisted, 'she'll know what to do for fun,' but there was no answer when I rang.

We trudged around the grounds, sipping from tonic bottles, roaming across the muddied snow, searching out fresh drifts between the lanes of box, falling against branches, showering ourselves with flakes. Vinska, we named the brew we'd made – whisky, vodka, gin – (we'd been topping up our bottles from the drinks tray) and as we drank we concocted a moneymaking scheme of vast potential. Vinska, we decided, could make more for Craigmont than the hosting of Americans who, according to Sir Hew, cost more than they were worth. 'When you inherit,' Janey nudged her brother, 'you'll be rich enough to instal central heating.'

'I'll have rock festivals in the grounds, with Vinska as the sponsor.' Ted spun around. We agreed this was an exceptionally good plan.

There were three hedges that led into an ornamental garden, and as it neared midnight we climbed on to their boxy tops and bounced as if on beds. 'Ten, nine, eight …' Ted lost his footing, and although he yelled as he was falling, once landed, he lay on the ground and smiled. 'Coming down!' Janey threw herself off, and closing my eyes, I followed. The snow was thinner than it looked and I was too winded to speak.

My Vinska was half-gone when we headed for the lake. 'If only we had skates,' Janey said, but as we stepped on to the ice our legs flew out from under us and we lay there on its glassy surface, snorting and choking, our laughter booming through the dark. Up we got, blind with tears. Down we crashed. My spine was jelly, my insides ached. My ears burned so hotly that they itched. A great white crack appeared, and we ignored it. I hit my head and struggled up, but the next time I fell I crawled to where the others lay and Ted dribbled the last of his drink into my mouth.

The following day I couldn't move. There were black bruises on my arms and legs. I looked across at Janey. Her face was pale, her hair tangled with leaves. I had no memory of how we'd got here from the ice. Only of Ted, stretched out in the middle of the lake. I sat bolt upright, and when the razor pain that raked my skull had dulled, I hobbled from the bed. Ted's door was closed. I knocked, and when there was no answer I stepped in. The room was cold. There was frost on the inside of the windows, clothes stiff on the floor. Ted lay on the bed. One shoe was off, the sock dark with wet. I crept closer, put a finger to his cheek. 'Ted?'

His hand sprang up and gripped me. I screamed, and he yanked me in against him. 'Warm me up,' he ordered, breathing out hot fumes, and I pulled the quilt around us both, feathers spiking through the paisley silk. 'That's better.' He hooked a foot around my own. I could feel the long bones of his leg pressing against mine. 'Don't move.' He drifted back to sleep.

Janey was cool with me that day. She filled a bath and lay in it and didn't invite me in. Later she wrote a letter to her friend Christel, a girl from school she'd told me had the surname Chanda-Lear, but I saw the envelope when she'd addressed it: Brookes. And I'd believed her.

Ted was cool with me too. I *had* moved, after an hour, when he'd shown no sign of waking, and I'd crept numbly back to Janey's room where she surveyed me with hard eyes. Ted looked ashen when he sidled in, and he'd sat, wrapped in a blanket, groaning, suggesting hangover cures, each one more disgusting than the last, until Janey told him to get lost. But after tea, when I asked if anyone was thinking of making a trip to the loo, Ted stood and ambled out into the hall. We didn't hold hands, not even as we passed the Egg, but once we were safely on the other side, he stumbled as if by chance into an alcove and, stooping down, pushed the hair from my face. 'You all right?' His breath smelt new again, of cake.

'You?' I waited, and to encourage him I closed my eyes.

It worked. There was the touch of his lips. Then harder, knocking out my breath as our teeth clashed. He pulled away, and we ran on.

'Don't leave,' I called as I locked the door, and although he said he wouldn't, when I came out he'd gone.

The following summer the Americans were there again. 'Damned nuisance,' Sir Hew cursed as he slid a flask against his hip. There were worn patches on the sleeves of his jacket and his trousers flapped against his legs.

'Do be careful.' Lady Frances waved him off.

'I'm always careful.' He kissed her powdered cheek.

The three of us ranged through the guest bedrooms placing scribbled spells between the pillows, a brewed black potion on a nightstand, a lollipop that said *Fuck Off*. From out on the estate the sound of gunshot echoed.

We'd written to each other, Ted and I, our letters not so different from the ones exchanged with Janey. Complaints about parents. Complaints about school. Sketches of guitars. Song lyrics copied out. *My love to Bea*, Ted always ended, although I hardly saw her. Did that mean they weren't in touch?

Now I was here, we were shy. 'One more year,' Ted said as we made pancakes in the kitchen, and he took an egg and threw it so high it broke against the ceiling, and slowly, stickily dripped down. 'Then what will I do?'

'I thought you were going to be a drummer?'

Ted whisked the batter. 'I can't be a drummer. One: I'm rubbish. Two: I'll have to take over this place.'

'Not for years,' Janey tried. 'Papa, he's ...' They looked away from each other.

Sir Hew had formed a society for the protection of the Loch Ness Monster. If anyone dared mention that the monster may not, in fact, be real they were shot down with a stream of invective as fierce as it was funny. Now, instead of stalking, he suggested he drive the Americans to Loch Ness. Lady Frances surveyed him, calmly, asking where would their guests stay when they arrived? Were they planning to camp?

'Then I'll take the children.' We were in the small kitchen eating macaroni cheese, and he cast his eyes around the enthusiastic crowd, squinting a little when he encountered me.

'Yes!' Fists thumped against the table.

In a break between Americans we set off, streaming out of the house and into a white and rusting van. Timothy and Maud sat with Marina in the front. Ted, Janey and I lolled on an old carpet in the back. 'Where *is* Daphne?' Lady Frances looked in at her husband, but he hooted his horn and we drove off.

The drive to Loch Ness was long. We stopped to eat sandwiches by the side of the road, and then again several hours later when Ted dropped his cigarette between the hollow panels of the doors and Sir Hew pulled over to douse the flames with Irn Bru.

It was late afternoon when we arrived, and the loch was bathed in light. Small ripples lapped against the shore and we sat on a pebbled beach and looked out across the water. 'Where's Nessie?' Maud wanted to know.

'Loch Ness is one hundred and twenty-six fathoms deep.' Sir Hew raised his binoculars.

'What's a fathom?' Timothy asked.

His father scanned the surface. 'Full fathom five thy father lies; of his bones are coral made. Those are pearls that were his eyes.'

'Papa.' Maud's lip trembled. 'Say a different one.'

'About as long as …' he looked around, and finding his tall son '… as Ted.'

When we'd sat there for an hour Marina kicked off her shoes. She unbuttoned her shirt and tossed it on to the stones, and like a stork, she hopped out of her trousers. She was tall, her hair cut short. Green veins ran below her skin. 'I'll find your monster, Papa.' Wearing nothing but knickers, white, with the elastic loose, she waded in. We watched as she sliced through the loch. We watched until she was out of sight.

'It's bloody freezing.' Ted stuck in his hand, and we waited, craning out across the water: at the mountains, distant on the other side; at the shadow of firs where the loch turned.

'Where is she?' Janey's voice was high. The lowered sun was in our eyes, catching at dark patches that might be her, that might be gulls.

Timothy threw a stone. It disappeared with a gulp. Sir Hew roamed with his binoculars. 'Patience,' he said, unsteady.

Then Maud began to squeal. Marina was rising from the shallows. Her lips were blue, her arms and legs chafed red. Janey ran to the van and, finding no towel, dragged out a blanket, shaking off the crumbs.

'Nessie would like to thank you.' Marina turned to her father and saluted. 'For keeping the faith.'

Sir Hew bowed his head.

'These all yours?' the barman asked when we found a pub still serving food.

'Hope so,' Sir Hew replied.

I pressed myself against the flocked wall of the dining room and did my best to fit in while Sir Hew ordered the drinks. Whiskies and lagers, and Irn Bru to make up for the bottle that was lost. We ate scampi and chips doused with tartar sauce, and when it was dark and the pub was closing, we went back to the van and lay down.

I woke in the dark, the jut of Ted's knee against my back. Above the engine's roar I heard Marina. 'You need to rest.' The van shuddered, shifted gear. 'Papa?' The road rushed away beneath us.

When I next woke it was light, and again we were parked by Loch Ness. Sir Hew was crouched on the shingle. He had the binoculars raised to his eyes. 'We're hungry,' Timothy complained.

Ted was asleep beside me. Marina crawled in and shook his shoulder.

'Ted?'

He sat up, bleary.

'Can you drive us?' We'd all seen him rattle the trailer across fields. 'Papa's not ...'

Sir Hew was wading into the lake. 'Come back!' We splashed out after him, seizing his shirt tails and his sleeves. Timothy and Maud held tight to his jacket and tugged. Slowly, reluctantly, he wheeled around, a great, shaggy cormorant, his wingspan wide. Marina led him into the van where he sat and shivered, the blanket draped over his head.

Ted gripped the wheel with both hands. 'Where to?'

'Home,' we chorused and he revved the engine and pulled on to the road. We sang to encourage him. 'One man went to mow'. 'Twelve green bottles'. 'Speed, bonnie boat'.

'Let's go to Skye!' Ted swerved past a sign, but when no one answered he kept on towards Craigmont.

III

A week after we moved into the communal house, Max's father arrived with a dinner service for my mother. It was her birthday and maybe he'd asked her what she needed, because although she laughed, grim, over the design – a couple, hands clasped, encircled with hearts – she continued to use the bowls, the plates and cups for years, decades, until only one cracked saucer remained. I thought of the plate people as Dutch. They wore clogs and cross-stitched clothes; the man had a thatched haircut, the woman a straw bun. I examined them below the crumbs of cake while my stepfather talked, wedged as he was under the slope of the ceiling, and when he'd run out of conversation he got up, too fast, and bashed his head. He hopped, undignified, from foot to foot while my mother, who'd developed a habit of laughing whenever anything went wrong, stood with her hand over her mouth.

On Mondays, Wednesdays and Thursdays we took these dishes and filed downstairs to collect our communal food. The McNamaras, whose rooms were on the ground floor, served soup, while the Jacobsons, who monopolised the landing, produced a series of root vegetable pies with side dishes of kale. Samira, who shared the Jacobsons' kitchen, sleeping with her small daughter in what was once the lounge, cooked delicately flavoured rice, exquisitely presented. Tuesday was my mother's night to cook, and anxious, and invariably hurried, she made spaghetti with a watery tomato sauce, never quite enough. Liz, in the basement, refused to be involved. Recently separated, she had four children under six, and it was easier, she said, to feed them early and get them into bed. Polly also opted out of these communal meals. She lived in the front section of the basement, in a series of cave-like rooms. I knew Polly, or knew of her, because her twin, Pete, had been a boyfriend of Bea's, and sometimes when I was lonely I'd wind down the stairs, step out on to the drive and tap at her side door. Pete was unusually good-looking – raven-haired and angular – while Polly was plump and pale. She'd welcome me in, her eyes protruding, and I'd follow, indignant on her behalf – the egg split so unfairly! – as she moved through the half-dark. But rather than self-pity, Polly emanated a mysterious, milky glow. Her feet were bare, her body swathed in cotton, and she'd invite me to sit on cushions piled against the walls.

'Can you keep a secret?' she asked me once, and when I said I could, I was known for keeping secrets, tears slipped down her face. 'One day,' she promised, and she poured more tea.

It soothed me to sit with her, the only one who knew me, who knew Bea.

That was before I met Zara. I hadn't noticed her at first – a new girl in the parallel class at school – but there she was at the Jacobsons' party, black crinkled hair, a wide

American chapsticked mouth. She had an older sister who'd stayed behind with their father in New York, embarking, like mine, on her own life.

'What do you do in this place?' she asked, her accent twangy and despairing, and I knew that we'd be friends.

Every lunch hour she'd come into my classroom and we'd sit on the window ledge and eat our sandwiches; or I'd eat her sandwiches – I'd finished mine and she seemed never to be hungry. Tuna. The luxury of it. With mayonnaise. Afterwards we'd walk into the playground and down to the valley field where we'd climb in among the rhododendrons and share a cigarette.

At night we talked on the phone. There was a payphone in the stairwell and I'd hear it ringing from the attic. 'I'll get it!' I'd shout as I came hurtling down, and there she'd be, scattering questions and exclamations, interspersed by the gurgle of her laugh. 'Love you,' she'd say as our conversation ended, and much as I liked her, was grateful, would have thanked God if I'd had one, for the life-saving miracle of her arrival in this dreary corner of East Sussex, I couldn't bring myself to use those previously unspoken words. 'See you,' I'd say instead, and I'd uncoil myself from where I sat on the swirl of the hall carpet.

'You have got to get yourself over here,' Zara said one evening. It was a McNamara night and I could hear Danny clattering about in his kitchen.

'I can't.' There was a bus, but the last one left at seven.

'Your mum?'

'She won't.'

Zara didn't persevere. Her mother never drove her anywhere either.

'I'd hitch … but …' It was November, dark and squally, and how would I get home?

'There's something you just have to hear. Soooo gooooo. You are not going to believe it!' Zara was forever telling me I was Not Going to Believe It, even though usually I did, and I imagined my night unspooling, an essay I should finish, my rat's cage that needed cleaning out.

'If only there was someone who could drive me.'

'I'll drive you.' It was Danny McNamara, an apron loose, his sleeves rolled to the elbow.

'Oh my God,' I said, muffled. 'Danny. He's offered!' Zara knew about Danny. Shy and lanky, he'd once asked, so quietly I'd had to lean close in to hear: was it really true I was fourteen? 'You are not going to believe it,' I muttered to myself as I rushed up the three flights of stairs, brushed my hair, blackened my eyes, tugged on a jacket, called to my mother that I'd be back later. Zara. Yes. I had a lift.

I'd been in Danny's car before. He drove his daughter to nursery three days a week, packed into the back with Samira's girl and Liz's eldest boys, while I sat in the front. We'd talk about books, and music, his time in India. He and his wife – a tall woman with crooked teeth – had been disciples of Rajneesh, and although mostly now he wore a waistcoat, unbuttoned, over a collarless shirt, until recently they'd both dressed only in orange.

'Thanks so much.' I slid in, and without speaking he nosed the car on to the road. It was dark and the wipers slashed and smoothed. I searched round for anything to say and finding nothing I stared out at the hedgerows, directing him up past the school and on towards Wych Cross. What was it that I had to hear? I thought of Zara as she leant over her guitar, her voice deepening to blast out Meatloaf, or Meat, as she called him – she'd once been to a concert – singing me 'Bat Out of Hell' so often that without ever having heard the record I knew the lyrics by heart.

Zara ushered us into her kitchen. An album was propped against the sideboard. Fleetwood Mac. She slid it from its sleeve. Its newness crackled static, the black of the vinyl slick as oil. *Rumours*. No one spoke as the first notes rose. We sat at the table, a vase of flowers pushed to one side, our heads bowed.

'If I had to pick a favourite …' Zara said when there was nothing but the bump of the needle '… it'd be "Don't Stop".'

'"Dreams".' I was still reeling from the raspy heartbreak, the siren call of the refrain.

We looked at Danny. He'd rolled himself a cigarette. '"Never Going Back Again".' He struck a match and leant into the flame.

When the second side was finished Zara turned it over. Now we were swaying, singing, getting up to dance. I caught Danny's eye. He gave me his slow smile.

We were playing *Rumours* for a fourth time when Zara's mother returned from her night out. She stood in the doorway, black hair, red lips, and slipping off her coat she threw herself into the dance. 'Mom!' Zara protested, and when she continued, sashaying her hips, pirouetting before Danny, Zara flipped the music off: 'Miriam!'

'Well, hell.' Miriam beamed. 'What fun you're all having.' Lowering her voice, she hissed, 'What's with you?' Bickering and scrapping, they moved into the hall.

I turned to Danny. He lifted a flower from the vase and held it out. It was a daisy, the undersides striped pink. 'Shall we?'

Our fingers brushed.

A fog had descended, and we drove in silence, following the headlights' thickened beam, crawling, alert for deer, down the hill and through the village, past the shrouded playground, the plaited iron of the swings. Danny's foot pressed down on the pedal. 'Never going back again …' he said, quiet, and I felt him glance my way. My eyes stayed fixed on the road. What was there, I wondered, ahead? Danny gathered speed as we climbed out of the valley, leaning towards me as he rounded each bend, passing lanes that led to tracks, that led to homes, that led to The Laurels where Max's father still lived with his daughter, Cora, who I sometimes saw at school. We sped down the last hill, took the final turn. Squat and square, the communal house came into view. Would we stop? The car raced on and I gripped the flower, warm and wilting in my hand, crushing it as Danny braked and swung into the drive. He pulled up between my mother's rusted van, and Jonas Jacobson's coffee-coloured Citroën – so precious, he was the only one allowed behind the wheel.

All was silent as we stepped into the house. The door to the room where the McNamaras slept was closed. A pillow and a blanket had been left outside. 'Night.' I looked away, but halfway up the stairs I craned between the banisters to see him retreat into the room where earlier he and his wife had served us soup.

My mother was still up. She'd been washing clothes in the bath and she was twisting them through a mangle, an antiquated and oddly useful contraption, already here when we arrived. 'How was it?' she asked, and I told her I knew what I wanted for Christmas. *Rumours*. Nothing else.

She forced her dungarees – the ones she wore for gardening – through the mangle's narrow mouth. 'So Danny drove you?'

I shrugged as if it meant nothing.

'That's kind.' With a scraping the buckles caught in the machine.

From then on I thought of little else but Danny. I played his words over in my head, pictured the melt of his smile. In the mornings on our drive to school I willed his foot to press down on the pedal, but there were children in the back, snuffling, repeating rhymes, and we drove, sedate, in silence. When I wasn't with him, I saw the long white bonnet of his car. Sliding past the bus stop. Creeping round corners as Zara and I trudged from one village to the next, singing at the tops of our voices: 'Two out of three ain't bad.'

'You all right?' my mother asked as she caught me staring through the banisters. Her dungarees were dry and pressed and she was on her way to the garden.

'Sure,' I told her, and there below us, a pair of secateurs ready in his hand, was Danny.

'You coming?' He looked up, and she skipped towards him down the stairs.

I didn't mention Danny when I visited Bea. She was sharing a flat with Daphne Colquhoun: two floors of a crumbling terrace; wrought-iron balconies; ferns, half-dead, in pots.

'Quick, get changed,' Bea said. She'd cut her hair. The whole length, lopped. 'We're meeting Dad for supper.'

I'd already changed, but I rifled through my bag. I had a shirt I'd made on Mum's old Singer. Liberty-print silk, the flowers incongruous beside Bea's black-clad form.

'Nice hair.' Our father's eyes widened. Bea ran her fingers through its bristled ends. 'Although I'm already missing the old tresses.'

Bea grinned. Nothing our father said could offend her. 'Daphne cut it.'

Daphne's own hair clung fine and mouse to the pale nape of her neck.

'Enjoying London?' he enquired of us all and Bea said she was looking for a job. He paused. 'Will you have time, with college?'

'I'll squeeze it in,' she said.

Daphne, whose Colquhoun skin was thin, flushed pink.

The restaurant was low-lit, the tables hushed by the thickness of the linen, and while we waited for our food Bea rearranged her cutlery, testing the sharpness of each knife against her thumb. 'Do say,' our father offered, 'if you need money.'

'Oh no,' she winced, 'I'm fine.'

I took a sip of wine, so cold I was able to ignore the sharpness, and listened while they discussed our father's latest invention: illuminated gloves. I bit down on an olive, reached for my glass which seemed always to be full, lowered my voice, as they did, in case anyone listening might steal the idea before the patent was secured. Then I must have drifted off. The conversation had moved on to a Colquhoun cousin's marriage. 'He'll make a perfectly fine first husband,' my father was saying, and Daphne choked on her drink. It was only when I went in search of the ladies, I found that I was drunk. 'For God's sake.' I fell against the door, and I imagined myself, falling, falling, into Danny McNamara's arms.

After we'd eaten – smoked salmon, fish pie, a lemon tart I'd been unable to finish – we filed into the street. 'Treat yourselves to a taxi.' Dad slipped Bea a note, and anointing our foreheads with a kiss, a peck for Daphne and a muffled enquiry about the whereabouts of Marina to which she said she didn't know, he hailed a taxi of his own.

Daphne walked between us, linking arms. 'How's life back home?' she asked, and leaning forward so Bea might hear, I told her about the communal meals, our mother cooking the same spaghetti every week; how, rather than sit down together, each family collected their food and hurried back to their own rooms.

'No second helpings.' My sister's voice was gloomy.

'Sometimes there's pudding.' Danny's wife had made a blackberry and apple pie. She'd served me an especially large slice.

'Damn.' Daphne stopped. 'I'm heading the wrong way. I promised to pay a visit to …' she released our arms '… a friend.'

'Say hello from me.' Bea palmed her the money Dad had handed over.

'I will.' She sloped away into the night.

Cold, and diminished somehow, we hurried into the underpass below Park Lane. 'Have you met anyone since … anyone … new?'

'A few.' Bea began to run. 'Mostly I see Daphne. And sometimes if Marina's with Dad …'

'And … do … how's …' My chest was tightening. There was only one question I'd been charged with. 'How's college?'

We raced up the far steps and walked towards the round-about at Marble Arch. 'Boring.' A bus slowed. It wasn't ours. A taxi passed, the lozenge of its light lit up. 'I tried it. Once.'

When our bus drew in we clattered up the stairs. The clack of heels, the heady jangle of the bell. We sat at the front, the city stretching out before us. 'Who's Daphne's friend?'

Bea scowled. 'What friend?'

'Oh. I don't know.' I waited for her to ask for news. Our school. Our mother. Max, whose existence she seemed to have forgotten. 'Mum would love to see you,' I tried.

'Maybe.' She turned and gathering up my hair she held it bunched against my neck. 'You should try something different.'

'Really?' I craned to catch my reflection in the window.

'Daphne would do it, just buy her a drink.'

The next night we went to a club. 'Say you're eighteen. If they ask.' No one asked, disguised as I was by make-up, and my hair, sprung into curls by the shock of being cut. We paid our money and bundled down a flight of steep straight stairs, through a door, and into a dark pit. Daphne tunnelled ahead to the bar. 'What do you want?' Bea yelled.

'Should I?' I began to count my change. Bea rolled her eyes. 'Vodka,' she decided, and Daphne ordered vodka for us all.

It was like being in a soup. Too close to move, too loud to talk. I pressed the glass against my face. Daphne was on the dance floor, head bent, her white neck cool, while Bea flitted through the crowd. I glimpsed her among a knot of people, men, their dreadlocked hair in hats, girls with safety pins hanging from their ears.

'Not seen you here before?' A man pressed in beside me. He smelt so strongly of aftershave I could barely breathe, and to avoid him I stepped on to the dance floor, no sign of Daphne now, and closing my eyes I did my best to lose myself in the beat. But the scent of aftershave followed, and a body moved behind me. I edged away. A knee knocked mine. I flipped open my eyes. 'Hi again.'

'Hi.' I shuffled from the floor.

Bea was nowhere. I searched the length of the bar. For one hopeful minute I thought I saw Daphne, but when she turned, it was a boy.

There was a roped-off doorway at the back of the club. Two girls swayed through, their arms around each other's waists. I squeezed in after, and peered into the room beyond. Small tables. A low banquette. 'Bea!' I'd found her.

'Lucy.' Her smile dazzled. Had she just remembered I was here?

'I think I'm ready to go.'

'OK.' She made no move. 'You know where to find the key?' She cupped my ear.

Out on the street the air was sweet. A wash of rain glinted off the pavements. The Tube was locked, a grille pulled down. The bus stop was deserted. I scrutinised the time-table, a myriad of destinations, none familiar. I began to

walk, and found myself on Regent Street. Without knowing which direction I was headed, I put out my thumb.

'Where are you heading?' Two men were looking up,
and when I gave them the address, the man in the passenger
seat, too large for the small car, squeezed out, and tipping
his seat forward, held it so I could climb into the back. The
door slammed, and we accelerated down a one-way street.
No one spoke, not even when we turned at a junction
and found ourselves in traffic. Traffic in the middle of the
night! I let out a breath. Nothing too bad could happen in
a crowd, but before long the traffic eased and we slipped on
to a bypass. I swallowed as we picked up speed. We were on
a bridge, lifting; a web of tracks, jewelled carriages, below. At
the next junction we swerved. I reached for the door, but
there was no door. The seat in front bulged against my legs.

'What number?'

'Sorry?'

'This is your street?'

I looked. There was the pub, the shop, familiar, its awning
rolled. 'Yes.' I sat up, but the car jumped forward, gathering
speed, taking the corner so fast I was thrown back in my
seat. We roared along a wide straight road, the trees a blur,
and I thought of my stepfather and how he'd reported me
for hitching after school. Why hadn't he stopped if he was
so concerned? We turned sharp right and skidded up a side
street. I closed my eyes. My ears whirred. We braked. This
time I didn't move.

'Only joking.' There was a click and the large man was
opening his door.

Unsteady, I uncurled into the night. 'Thank you.' I didn't
meet either of their eyes.

The engine was still idling as I drew the key up on its length of string. My fingers trembled as I turned the lock. I was in. I ran up the stairs. The flat was shadowy, the kitchen scattered with snippets of my hair. I looked into the mirror. My face was pale, my eyes stretched round. Was this who I was going to be? I kicked my shoes off, lay down on the sofa, sprang up and searched through Bea's records for the Clash. 'London's Burning' burst through the speaker. I pressed my face into the cushion, imagined telling Zara. *You're not going to believe it. An actual nightclub. You are not going ...* I repeated as the music blasted out.

I woke to the sound of the front door. 'Home!' Bea called, cheery. She'd bought pastries, and a bottle of milk. 'Great night.' She was glamorous in last night's clothes, socks over fishnets, a T-shirt that zipped from cuff to cuff.

'I love that top,' I said, and she stopped in the middle of the room, and sliding a zip down from each shoulder, let it drop. Her bra was see-through, her stomach flat. She held it out and I unbuttoned my own shirt.

'Hey,' she encouraged. 'That looks great.'

Studying my reflection, unconvinced, I saw her arms, the veins punctured and bruised. She caught me looking. 'I think I'll get a bath.' She must have forgotten Daphne's clothes left soaking, because there was cursing, and her voice complaining from the landing. 'Fuck.' Before her footsteps trailed upstairs.

I ate a croissant, and then another, and afterwards I pinched the flesh around my waist, and swore I'd never eat anything fattening again.

'How was Bea?' my mother asked.

'Fine,' I said.

'And college?'

I tilted my head, thoughtful, as if there'd not been time to find out.

It was our first Christmas alone. I woke early and listened to the sounds of the house. Running, hushing, the squealing of children, and through the stairwell, the strains of Fleetwood Mac. I leapt from my bed and stood on the landing waiting for our track until the whine of Max, agitating for stockings, forced me up the ladder to the platform where my mother slept.

'Happy Christmas.' I slid in beside her.

Max received three engines and a packet of gold coins. I had a hairbrush, and a strawberry lip gloss, and Mum, who'd been expecting nothing, was tearful when she found an egg I'd made in woodwork in the toe of her sock.

Bea hadn't sent a card. Instead she'd given me two pills, nestled in a matchbox. 'Wash them down with beer,' she'd said, but before I'd had a chance, Mum had come upon them, looking for a light, shouting so loudly a vein swelled in her neck. 'Why is she like this!'

I didn't know.

By the time I unwrapped *Rumours*, I'd already heard it twice.

'Familiar.' Mum raised an eyebrow as I set the needle to 'Never Going Back Again', and I stood by the lightwell, listening, imagining Danny, listening, below.

———

'We have to meet new people,' Zara said when she returned from New York. She didn't want to go back to Manhattan, a virgin, in the summer. I kept Ted and my New Year to myself. Instead I told her about the nightclub.

'Let's get there!'

I suggested we try the pub.

There were three pubs in the village, unknowable behind glazed doors. We chose the least popular, for practice. It was modern while the others were ostentatiously old. On the outside of the building was a smart white sign: *The Wartlington Hotel.*

'I'll have a Tom Collins.' In an attempt to stand taller, Zara propelled her chest towards the barman.

He looked at her, aggrieved. 'Tom Collins? What in God's name is that?'

'It's ... You don't serve Tom Collins?' Gaining confidence from the realisation that *what* they were going to serve us seemed to be the issue rather than *if*, Zara swapped her order for a rum and Coke. 'And my friend ...' I smiled, adrift behind a lacquer of lipstick, 'will have a Pernod and black.'

I said nothing, even when Zara gathered up the drinks, only followed, clip-clopping in my new high heels, to the dimmest part of the pub. Here tables were arranged around what seemed to be a dance floor, a rectangle of parquet, studded with lights. 'Cheers,' Zara grinned once we were seated. Our glasses clinked and I woke out of my disbelief to find we'd swum down through an underwater tunnel, ascending into a new and glittery land. I took a fizzing sip.

That's when I saw them, on the far side of the room. Three boys, in donkey jackets; one, a scar across his lip, his black hair and white face an echo of his Guinness.

'Let's go over.'

'No!' I put out my arm, but Zara, who considered herself in exile, was prepared to do anything to pass the time.

'Mind if we join you?' She strode across.

Another minute and she was beckoning, impatient, and there was nothing for it but to pick up my drink. 'Move over,' Zara instructed and a curly-haired boy, Moon, made space for us both.

That was when Malcolm spoke. He addressed us with formality. 'It's good of you to introduce yourselves. Gregory here …' Gregory was small with a lank side parting '… was bemoaning the lack of company, and as for Moon, he was threatening to leave and go up to the Hart.'

'Just as well we didn't wait.' Zara shot me a look.

Malcolm turned his eyes on me and I could feel it, even then, the loosening of Danny McNamara's hold.

Soon Gregory was telling us about their lives. He and Malcolm were at an art college in Eastbourne, home for the weekend because it was a dump, a retirement town of pensioners staring out to sea. Art college, Malcolm leant forward, was supposed to be a breeding ground for revolutionaries. It was where he'd hoped to meet his people, but not a single one had heard of Che Guevara, and when the Baader–Meinhof were assassinated, gunned down in their cells at Stammheim Prison, no one questioned the lie that it was suicide.

Zara pinched my thigh under the table. 'Is that where you met Moon?'

Moon, discomfited, explained he worked at an electrical shop in Tunbridge Wells, that his name was in fact Jeremy.

They didn't ask about us. And we didn't tell them. Zara went to put money in the jukebox, and as if I'd been ordering at bars all my life, I bought a packet of crisps. The boys, who at first resisted, tore into them as if they were starved. With the shared food our spirits lifted, chasing each last salty crumb, licking our fingers, members of a tribe.

'Does anyone dance?' Zara called from the lit-up square of parquet.

Gregory shuffled fearful and Malcolm took a long swallow of his pint.

Don't. I held Zara's gaze as 'Go Your Own Way' burst out, and in an agony in case she forced me up, I asked if there wasn't somewhere else to go?

Malcolm looked at me, revealing nothing. 'Moon's the one with the car.'

'It's my father's car,' Moon said, miserable. 'I'm not meant to have it.'

'I heard there was a party,' Gregory volunteered. 'Tim Bosun's sister. They live in Ashurst Wood.'

'Might that be fun?' Zara was already pulling on her coat, and as if it was agreed, we all stood up.

The party was in a house on the outskirts of East Grinstead. Every light was blazing and guests wandered, aimless, through the rooms. The table was dense with bottles and cans. We found a stack of plastic cups and dripped in wine from a box. Music was playing in the sitting room, people dancing, negotiating the armchairs and the sofa. Zara and I joined them. It was easier than making conversation, and the house was cold, with the front and back doors open. I could see Malcolm talking to our host, a jug-eared boy, Tim Bosun. Zara shimmied across the carpet to Moon.

I walked into the kitchen to top up my wine, and there in the doorway was a horse. 'This way!' A girl dipped her head against its mane, and she turned the animal around.

'What the hell.' Malcolm was beside me; I could smell the musty scent of him, tobacco and damp.

'Happy birthday Tizzy,' the guests chanted as they chased after the horse, 'sweet sixteen,' and we ran too, across the gravel drive and over the lawn. We passed outhouses and stables – the garden was a park – and by the time we'd arced back to the house I was shivering.

'You OK?' I'd lain my coat upstairs on a bed, and Malcolm looked as if he might slip off his jacket and drape it over my bare arms. Too quickly I told him I was fine.

His hands dropped to his sides.

Tizzy urged her horse up the steps and in through the front door. We swarmed after, through the dining room, across the kitchen and into the sitting room where the horse lifted its tail and expelled a steaming mountain of manure. Girls screamed and boys backed away, and I thought of my nana telling me how during the war, when she and Grandpa lived in London, people would dash into the street with a shovel if they heard a passing horse, so desperate were they to fertilise their gardens.

'Where's your helmet?' Tim shouted as the horse skittered, and he added, indulgent, 'My little sis always did like to show off. Hey,' he fixed on me as the others dispersed, 'guard this, will you?'

By the time he returned with a bucket and a spade, Malcolm had disappeared. I wandered through the emptied rooms and found Gregory, rolling a joint. 'Where's Zara?' I asked. He didn't know.

Upstairs there was no one, and on the bed the only coat was mine. I pulled it round me and lay down, and as I closed my eyes I saw myself, my thumb out, standing on the road.

When I woke Tim Bosun was in the bed beside me.

I shifted and he opened his eyes. 'Hello.'

'Hello.' I looked at him.

'Would you like a cup of tea?'

'All right.' Was this how people started drinking tea? I watched as he swung his legs from the bed in nothing but a T-shirt and the same red underpants as the ones Max sometimes wore.

I ran to the bathroom. A cigarette was floating in the basin. I looked into the mirror and saw my eyeshadow collected in creases, the lipstick gone.

When I returned Tim was back in bed. 'Get in.' He smiled his jug-faced smile.

I hovered. 'I should probably go home.'

'Where's home?'

I told him.

'Help me tidy, and I'll drive you.'

Downstairs three black bin bags sat knotted by the door. The stain on the carpet was scrubbed raw. 'I thought, I might as well ...' Tim flushed as if accused.

I found a cloth and wiped the table, swept the floor, squirted Fairy liquid into the mop bucket, too vigorously, so that it frothed.

'Good job.' Tim put on a record, something pounding that I'd been encouraged to despise, and when he'd hoovered the stairs and I'd shaken out the doormat, he made us breakfast, fried eggs, bacon and tomatoes, grilled. 'If it's too clean ...' he left the dishes on the side '... the parents will suspect.'

Where's Tizzy anyway? I thought.

Tim's car was red. Three furry dice hung from the mirror. 'Ironic,' he assured me, and as he edged on to the road I thought I saw Danny McNamara speeding by, his worried face above the wheel. We turned the other way, through the outskirts of town, into the village, past the Wartlington Hotel and up over the hill.

Danny's white car was parked in the drive. Tim pulled in beside it. He twisted round towards me. 'When will I see you?'

'Next weekend, at the Wart?' That's what Malcolm had called it.

He leant forward, his lips pursed, and although my instinct was to draw away, it didn't seem polite. For five seconds his mouth mashed against mine. I thought of Ted and the taste of cake when we'd kissed. I'd write to him, even if it wasn't my turn. I'd write to him tonight.

The house was quiet. Even the middle floor was silent, no toddlers whining, no Jonas Jacobson proclaiming how this or that should be done. Our flat was empty too. Only my rat, Reggae, came squeaking towards me as I threw open the door. I scooped him up and found him a carrot. Where was everyone? There were breakfast bowls on the table, the congealed remains of porridge, and it occurred to me that they'd gone searching – the entire

household – my mother tracking through the under-
growth, Samira scouring the abandoned railway, Liz and
Polly raking the paths that led on to the forest.

I ran down to the payphone, and remembering I needed
change, I charged back up. By the time I dialled Zara's
number I was breathing hard. *Where the hell were you?* I
practised, but no one answered, and I slunk away upstairs.

I ran myself a bath and lay in it. When we first moved here
I'd heard music drifting through the window. Hopeful, I'd
stretched out as far as I could squeeze, but there'd been no
one except a man mending a motorbike, bearded, older; a
radio, tinny, on the ground. Now I heard it again. 'Uptown
Top Ranking'. The voices of two teenage girls. If only I
could get to them. Get anywhere. Make a start.

I was still in the bath when Max came barrelling in. He
was red-cheeked, wriggling, and as he peed into the bowl
behind my head, he told me they were making a ginor-
mous bonfire. If I wanted I could help.

'Maybe.' I sank under the water and let my hair trail out,
and alone again, I ran my hands over my stomach, the jut
of my hips, the circles of my breasts, and imagined myself,
drowned.

Dear Ted, I wrote. *It's boring in the country. Everyone in this
house is either old or young.* I told him about the party and the
horse, in the hope he'd be impressed, and when I finished
I drew a Stones tongue, lolling. *Send my love to Janey when
you see her.* Was it safe to add a kiss? I found a book of
one-pence stamps and pasted them across the envelope,
leaving a window for his boarding-school address.

'Where were you?' Zara asked the next day at lunch.

'Where were you?'

We glared at each other on our window ledge, the heat from the radiator scalding.

'You vanished,' Zara said. 'And Moon was leaving.'

'I was chasing a horse.'

'All night?'

'Tim Bosun drove me. The next morning.'

'I Don't Believe It!'

I took a bite of her tuna sandwich. 'Friday. I said we'd be at the Wart.'

Everyone was at the Wartlington Hotel when we arrived. We'd spent so long doing our make-up it was after nine. Tim leapt up and offered to buy drinks, and I looked across at Malcolm, but he turned away. We talked, ate crisps, played music on the jukebox, and later, when there was no suggestion of a plan, I said, if anyone wanted, they could come back to mine.

Silently we traipsed through the house, past each landing of closed doors. 'Mum?' She'd left a lamp on for me. 'I've got friends, is that OK?'

I heard her stir, above me, on her platform bed. She'd lost Bea when she'd attempted rules. 'As long as you're quiet.' She was trying a new way.

I led them into my room where my rat, his eyes like pips, watched us from his cage. Everyone sat on the floor. 'Tea?' I offered, and when they looked eager, I crept into the galley kitchen, and put the kettle on the hob, waiting for what seemed like hours for it to boil. When I came in with the tray Tim had rolled a joint and Malcolm was talking about how every house should be like this. Communal. The rich had monopolised for long enough. It was time for the people to join forces, share resources. We nodded. We all did. And I didn't say how my mother had collapsed when, after returning from a trip to London to see Bea – she'd been late, or Bea had, either way we'd missed her – we'd found our gas canister emptied, leaving no fuel, not even enough for a cup of instant coffee. I released Reggae from his cage, and unused to so much company, he ran up my arm to nestle in my hair, his tail like braid across my shoulder.

The next weekend Malcolm wasn't at the Wart, and he wasn't there the weekend after. No one mentioned him, and I didn't trust myself to ask, but one Sunday, Marie Jacobson, pregnant again, and too tired to walk up the stairs, hollered that I had a visitor. There he was at the front door.

He sat at our table, folded in against the wall, and I was thinking I should warn him to watch out for the slope of the ceiling when he leant forward and fixed me with his eyes. 'Can I trust you?'

I glanced round for my mother, who I knew was out. 'You can.'

'I'm planning some ... activity. I may need your assistance.'

'What kind of ... When?' My heart swelled.

He drew out a square of paper and wrote my name. *Lucy*.

'But when will I ...'

'No questions.'

We sat in silence, and then, worried he might leave, I asked how he knew Tim.

'Your boyfriend?'

'Not really.' Although maybe he was? Last weekend he'd put a hand under my shirt and I'd been curious to find that I felt nothing, only the coldness of his touch.

'Have you done it yet?' Zara had asked, and I'd insisted: 'No!'

'You'll tell me when you have?'

'I will.' I might. Most probably I wouldn't.

'Malc ...' I watched as he folded my name into a square. 'How will I know when—' There were steps and the door burst open. Malcolm stood up and smacked his head.

'I'm sorry.' I'd inherited my mother's habit of inappropriately laughing. 'This is Malcolm,' I managed, and mortified, her hands over her mouth, she asked if he would stay for supper.

While she cooked I showed Malcolm into my room, and on to the balcony that overlooked the garden. Trees studded the bare fields and in the dip of hills there was a haze of red, still visible where the sun had set. The balcony was lined with lead. Names and messages had been scrawled there. Malcolm pulled a penknife from his pocket. Would he carve his initials, would he carve mine? 'When Andreas Baader met Ulrike Meinhof,' he said, 'it was only twenty years since the end of war, and those in charge of Germany – the police, the schools, the government – they were the same people who'd been Nazis.' He'd drawn a rifle, now he formed a star. 'No one was discussing it. No one was asking their parents: what did you do in the war?' Malcolm glanced at me, the scar on his lip livid, and I nodded as if this was my usual conversational topic. 'You may be the type to disapprove of violence, but if you compare your country to a fascist

63

state then surely that gives you permission to oppose it? Think of your action as resistance. The resistance your parents failed to put up.'

I wanted to say my mother was a teenager when she'd thrown off the trappings of an easy life. That my father had been a refugee himself, arriving in Britain from Berlin.

'Supper time,' Mum's voice rang out, and when Malcolm took a seat below the skylight she implored him to be careful when he next stood up.

Malcolm ate hungrily, answering questions, while Max, unused to competition, kicked the table with his feet. To quieten him I set out a row of dominoes and as they tipped, one against another, Malcolm described the dreary constraints of Eastbourne, the students and the lecturers, so passive and polite. My mother brought out baked apples, the cores stuffed with sultanas and butter, and when every last scoop was eaten, he stood up and cracked his head.

All three of us laughed, we couldn't help it, our shoulders shaking, our hands clamped across our mouths. Malcolm hopped, as my stepfather had done, from foot to foot, while a seep of blood trickled past his ear. Mum rushed to fetch a tissue. 'Can't he stay?' I followed.

'No.' She was firm.

'He could sleep on cushions, on my floor.' I looked at her wide-eyed, to remind her I was guileless, a child, but even then I was creeping across the carpet, slipping in beside him, holding his injured body in my arms. 'Please.'

Hope sprang. She was wavering. A frown descended, and pushing past, she handed him the tissue and waited while he dabbed the blood. *No.* She shook her head.

I walked Malcolm downstairs. 'Await instruction, and remember …'

I opened the front door. Danny was splitting logs in the half-dark. 'Not a word,' I promised and I watched as he loped into the night.

Now, instead of waiting for Ted's letters, for Danny – to whisper to me, to play our song – I waited for Malcolm. Weeks passed, a month, and then one night, after pub closing, I saw him by the bus stop. 'Do you need a lift?' I dashed across, leaving Tim, patient by his car, but Malcolm said he'd prefer to walk; he liked walking, alone.

I was still waiting when Marie Jacobson gave birth. All day we listened to her labouring, gathering on the landing, breathing through her moans and calls, until, as it neared evening, they rose up on a roar, and there it was, the cry of a new voice. We clapped, and hugged, and Jonas came out with the baby in his arms. I jostled to get a glimpse and found myself pressed in against Danny. There were tears in his eyes. 'She's beautiful.' She was wrinkled as a prune.

Samira had wound jasmine in her hair. She opened a bottle of elderflower champagne, and a glass in my hand, I ran round to the side door. 'Come and see the baby.' Surely Polly had heard the commotion? I took hold of her hand. 'No,' and as she pulled away, her gown fell open, and there it was, the mound of her own stomach. She put a finger to her lips. I was good at keeping secrets. I'd been keeping Bea's this whole last year. *Why does she never visit?* Had no one seen the track marks on her arms?

It was high summer when the police arrived. Someone must have let them in, and shown them up the stairs. They stood, a man and a woman, awkward in shirtsleeves, at the door. 'What's this about?' my mother asked. Max clung to her skirt.

'We have reason to believe your daughter may be implicated in a crime.'

I blanked my face. I'd seen it: *Free Astrid Proll* in red letters on the bus shelter. *Baader–Meinhof* scrawled across the Wartlington Hotel.

'No.' I shook my head.

'We have information relating to a terrorist cell.'

'Here, in East Sussex?' My mother laughed.

I laughed too and they turned to look at me, in my school uniform, ink from a pen I'd used to do my homework staining my thumb.

'We have the name Lucy on a list.'

'Wrong Lucy.' My mother crossed her arms.

They retreated, clattering down the stairs, wading through the debris of the Jacobson children, the wailing of the baby, and spiralling from the basement, the sharp cries of an even newer baby – Polly's – whose father's name hadn't been revealed.

'Honestly,' my mother said. 'Whatever next.' It was our night for cooking, and together at the sink we washed our hands and made a start on the spaghetti sauce.

'You are not going to believe it,' I hissed to Zara when she called, and I told her about the police, and the graffiti, and how valiantly my mother had defended me. I didn't tell her about the letter I'd received, indecipherable, possibly in code, a list enclosed: petrol, fertiliser, matches, manure.

———

The following summer, not long before we set off for London, I'd still told no one when I slipped the list into the grave I dug for Reggae, sprinkling petals over his stiff body and placing the Rolling Stones tongue Ted had sent me across him like a quilt. Only Max was there to observe the ceremony. Tim Bosun had given up on me, or I on him, and Danny had moved with his wife and daughter to a home of their own.

On my last day, after hugging Zara, promising to stay in touch, forever, I walked down to the village and on through the maze of houses that backed on to the golf course. 'Danny?' I called, and when there was no answer, I stepped inside. All was familiar. The same spider plants, the same carroty smell of soup.

'Hello?' I tried again, and from a room beyond the kitchen I heard his wife. 'Come through.'

I pushed open a door. 'I just wanted …' I stopped, appalled to find her rising, naked, from the bath.

'It's you!'

'… to say goodbye.'

Reddened, gleaming, she reached for a towel. 'Danny will be sorry to have missed you.' Her shoulders lifted as she pushed back her hair.

'Bye, then.' It was as if I'd never seen her. Hips and breasts. A woman. Invisible till now. She held me in her warm wet arms. 'Take care, won't you?'

'I will.' I turned and ran.

I waited at the bus stop. I was desperate to start packing, in a hurry to be gone. Grateful too that Mum and Max were moving with me, that I wouldn't be in the city fending for myself alone. I stepped into the road. I'll hitch,

I decided, and speeding towards me was a familiar car, not Danny's, but Jonas Jacobson's low-slung Citroën, and in the seat beside him, leant over as if to catch his every word, was Polly, the baby in her arms.

IV

It took more than an hour to travel across London. Once home I climbed into bed. The house was quiet; even Cat, owned by the woman who lived on the top floor, refrained from scratching to come in. My room was downstairs, with a window that looked on to the street, so that I heard them, my mother and Max, as they rounded the corner, arguing familiarly – an old married couple – although Max was only seven.

'Mum?' I called as they rattled in, but my voice was drowned by the slam of the front door.

The smell of frying onions drifted from the kitchen. Max was skipping up and down the stairs. The phone rang. 'I'll see.' My mother's cool tones floated from the hall, and she was looking in, surprised at the hump of me below the covers, still wearing my coat. 'Nathan?'

I shook my head.

'Sorry,' she told him lightly. 'She can't talk.' There was a pause, some remonstration, the chime of the receiver as she set it down.

'What's wrong?' She was sitting on my bed.

The finality of what was wrong dissolved me. Tears slid across my cheek. I shook my head again.

My mother rested her back against the wall. I waited, but she didn't speak. If I told her would she say she too had had a baby at eighteen? That she'd been happy? That she'd kept the news from her own mother, who might never have known if she hadn't been spotted, wandering through London with two girls? She was staring at the cracked glass of the window, a crescent that arced the length of one large pane. Would she imagine she'd have to raise the child herself?

'I'm pregnant.' I closed my eyes. 'I don't ... I can't ...' When she still said nothing, I pulled the bedclothes round my ears and listened as she stepped out of the room.

Nathan rang again while she and Max were eating supper, and then, when I refused to leave my bed, there he was, tapping at the window. I let him in. If I didn't, he was liable to crack another pane, or shout and wake Teri, asleep on the top floor.

'Why are you avoiding me?' He wasn't angry. I knew his anger, and the range of it – sulking, spiteful, dangerous as knives. 'Christ.' He paled when I told him. 'And me the father!' He'd lost his own father in an accident. His mother was a shadow, shuffling in slippers, her pinny loose over her clothes. The one time we'd visited, Nathan had nudged me into his old bedroom and down on to the bed where we had sex, so quickly that she was still in the kitchen, stirring tea, when we returned.

Now he unbuttoned my coat, helped me out of my clothes, holding up a nightdress he'd found mashed under the pillow. My breasts were sore, the nipples tender, catching on the cotton as I pulled it on. We didn't talk. What was there to say? But sex at least was safe, and tonight there'd be no need to scrabble for my cap, squirt in gel, grapple the disc into a tight, sprung line.

Next morning, hand in hand, we walked into college. We were rehearsing a play in which almost every character was killed – poisonings, strangulation, stabbings in the back. Soon I lay lifeless beside Nisha, our limbs splayed in a prearranged design. 'Nathan?' she mouthed, impressed, appalled.

I shrugged to let her know that it was casual, which it had been, until now.

A week passed while I waited for a letter. And then another week. Dr Monaghan had warned that in order for there to be a termination, there would need to be a psychological report. 'But I'm eighteen ...'

'Quite so,' he'd said, curt, before asking if it was my father to whom he should send the bill.

It was Bea who'd suggested I see our father's doctor when my own local GP refused to provide me with a test. 'Are you using contraception?' She'd fixed me with a look so scathing I'd sworn that, yes, I was.

'Each time?'

I nodded, and as punishment for lying – wasn't my situation punishment enough? – she'd smiled. 'In that case your period is bound to come.'

I was six weeks late.

Now, after a full day of rehearsals, when the rest of our year surged down to the pub, all I wanted was to crawl into bed. 'Go with them,' I urged Nathan, but he insisted on escorting me to the bus, on leaping aboard, on spending the evenings in a cocoon of quilt, sharing meals bought at the corner shop: pitta bread, taramasalata, olives. Only occasionally did he lure me back to his, an unlikely cottage behind the Caledonian Road, discovered when, caught short, he'd slipped into an alley for a slash and found himself in an orchard, grasses, daisies, a canopy of branches, apples fallen, rotting on the ground.

'You should move in too,' he suggested. Winter was opening into spring as we waded through wet grass towards the house, half-obscured by blossom, its pleasing old brick face as beguilingly safe as Nathan had become.

'Maybe.' I took his hand and we stepped over the sill.

Nathan's room was stark, the bed a mattress, his clothes hung from nails in the wall. I sat down while he went to make tea, and then I lay down. I considered running over lines, but as always now, my eyes drooped closed. When I woke it was dark. I got up and creaked open the door, stepped carefully across the hall and peered into the main room. A huddle of shapes sat round the fire. 'I bet the bastard a fiver. Should have bet him more.' It was a story of Nathan's that I'd heard before. 'The little prick. I showed him.'

'Nate.' I bent to whisper in his ear. 'I really should get going.'

'Relax.' He gripped my wrist.

'I need to eat.'

The man who had the upstairs room threw a can into the fire. It spat and buckled. I pulled myself free. Nathan followed me into his room, watched while I scrabbled for my coat. 'I'll cook you something.'

I'd glanced into the kitchen. There was nothing. There was always nothing.

'I can get you a kebab.'

I turned away and retched. I'd meant it as a mime, to convince him how very much I didn't want a kebab, but a shoot of spittle flew into my hand.

'I'm going home.'

'Fine.' He shouted into the front room. 'Sorry, guys, I'm off.'

'Bye.' I put my head around the door.

In silence we walked through the streets. I found a tissue in my bag and wiped my hand, and not long after, Nathan took it, and squeezed the fingers tight. On Holloway Road we jumped aboard a bus. 'Prick,' he was caught up in his story. He kicked the seat in front.

At home we ate toast, and leftover spaghetti, and then, still hungry, a star-shaped biscuit Max had baked at school. My mother came in, stopping short when she saw the crumbs. She was wearing a silk print dressing gown, her hair loose down her back. 'Any chance,' she asked, 'of dropping Max at school for me tomorrow?' She had a job transforming waste ground into a garden. The project had started as a voluntary contribution, to this, our new community. Now a grant had been received, and with it a deadline.

'I could take him in on Thursday.' On Thursday soliloquies were scheduled, and as I didn't have one, I wouldn't be needed until lunch.

'Thank you!' She brushed all evidence of biscuit from the table, using her hands, the thumbs of which were seamed with earth. A bramble scratch ran raw along one arm.

'Night,' she said, and we answered, cheerful: 'Night.'

The next morning I received my letter. An appointment had been made for Thursday.

'Can't you take Max first?' My mother's voice rose, hectic.

'The hospital's on the other side of London.'

'Why?'

'I don't know!' We hadn't discussed my father's doctor. We hadn't discussed anything at all.

'What time?' she softened.

I conceded the appointment was at ten, and we agreed I'd drop Max early, and get straight on the bus.

On Thursday, I tucked Max into his coat, held him wriggling as I brushed his hair, and tugged him through the door. 'No!' he yelled, as he yelled every day, but once we were on the street, and I had hold of his hand, he began, in his passionate monotone, to tell me about a dinosaur that weighed fifty metric tonnes. 'It's from the same family as Tyrannosaurus, except most dinosaurs' front legs are short, the front legs of the brachiosaurus are long.'

'Interesting.' I was running over the twists and turns of the plot of *The White Devil*, the many varied ways in which enemies were avenged.

'Sauropod,' Max's voice broke in.

We turned into the road that led to his school. Two boys passed, swiping at each other with their bags. He pulled his hand from mine. *What even is a psychological report?* I leant in for a kiss. 'Don't.' Max reared away.

I watched him as he trudged, head down, across the yard.

'It is my job to warn you –' my case worker was a woman '– you may experience regret.' She waited, flicking through a form. 'Is this something you've considered?'

'Yes.' It wasn't true.

'And do you have support?'

'Support?'

'A boyfriend. Family?'

I nodded, *yes.*

'Are you under any pressure?'

'Pressure?'

'Ultimately …' she lowered her head so that her hair formed a screen between us '… it must be you who decides if you wish, or do not wish, to have this baby.'

There is no baby! I put a hand over my mouth. *Only a mistake.*

'You need to understand, if you make this decision …'

'I have made it.' With a sudden leap of hope: 'Can it be today?'

'Not today.'

'Then, when?' My stomach was swollen. My breasts stood out in cones.

'Paperwork first.' She leafed through a file.

'Did they talk you out of it?' Nathan caught me as I rushed into college.

'Shh!' Hadn't we agreed never to mention my predicament in public? I turned to wave at Nisha. 'Coming,' I called, and I hurried away to do a quick run-through of our deaths.

I was thirteen weeks, and the high sash of my costume accentuated the swell of my waist. 'Ye gods,' Roland from second year smirked as he waltzed by, 'methinks you are with child.' Roland was known for the theatrical stumbles he affected every time he walked through a door. I sucked my stomach in and glared.

'Ignore him,' Nisha sighed, 'he's tiresome,' and jutting out her lip she asked why she never saw me any more?

'You do!' But it was true, we used to spend whole nights together, lying on her carpeted floor, singing along to Millie Jackson while Nisha filled me in on the latest developments in her life. She was in love with the married boss of the bakery she'd worked in the summer before college, and we'd listen to *Caught Up*, the story of two women entangled with the same man. 'If loving you is wrong,' our voices rose, 'I don't want to be right.' The A side of the album was the mistress, and there was no doubting that we liked the mistress most. We *were* the mistress – fearless and desired – but the wife's story on the B side, with its weariness and wisdom, its raunchiness and outright lust, the shift – so tender – to when she was a girl, secretly melted our hard hearts.

I thought of Ted who'd moved to London. Who'd rented a room in the same house as Bea. Did they make breakfast in the mornings? Eat cereal together at the end of the night? I allowed myself to imagine the tangle of Ted's limbs, the curl of his wide mouth. 'Shall we meet?' I suggested to Bea when we spoke, but she was busy, or thought she might be. She was going to let me know.

I promised to make a date with Nisha, soon.

'If you can bear to be apart from Nathan?'

'Don't be ridiculous,' I laughed.

The next day another letter arrived. I'd passed the assessment. I could have cried, although tears were always pressing now, as was hunger, as was sleep. The procedure, as they called it, had been booked. I handed the letter to my mother and watched her while she read. 'I'll take you.' She surprised me, and the following week while the rest of my year was in the pub, celebrating a successful performance of *The White Devil*, I ran down to the Tube, where, after only ten minutes – a miracle of punctuality in the long history of her lateness – she appeared. Max, two dinosaurs clanking in his pocket, was hurrying behind.

The hospital was in Westminster. We'd visited Bea here when she'd contracted hepatitis, travelling from Sussex to sit by her bed, the whites of her eyes yellow, her black fingernails glamorously chipped. Now it was my turn. I closed the curtain and undressed, and once I was sealed between the sheets, my mother and Max pulled chairs up close and we played cards, a game of Fish spread across the blanket. When Max won for the third time, with a stack of matching stegosaurus, it was time for them to go. The woman in the next bed smiled, conspiratorial. I turned away. On the other side a girl was whimpering, her face buried in the pillow.

Hungry, I searched my bag for the sandwich that I'd packed, but I must have left it in my locker. I poured water from the plastic jug and drank it down. By nine o'clock the lights were out. I stared up at the ceiling. My stomach clenched. I closed my eyes. I opened them again. I couldn't stay here. I slid from the bed, and picking up my shoes, my coat, I tiptoed from the ward. The corridor was empty, the stairs deserted as I hurtled down. The night was fresh and welcome. A man in a wheelchair sat smoking by the door.

I set off for the main road. All around was glass and metal, cranes and corrugated iron. I ran, hoping for a shop, a café, the lights of Victoria Station, but I must have headed the wrong way because I found myself at Parliament Square, spires and turrets, the faces of Big Ben. Cars tailed, headlights fading as they swept away. I dashed from one island to the next and walked on to the bridge. Below me lay the Thames. A boat approached, lights and music spilling out, and in its shadow, from the opposite direction, a long, dim tug came crawling past.

I turned back the way I'd come. If I kept walking I'd reach the station, and if nothing else, there'd be the Cartoon Cinema with its kiosk of sweets. It was where I'd waited through my childhood for the train to Sussex, a pound note from my father tucked against my palm. Marina Colquhoun had once dropped me there as a favour. She'd been at Dad's when I arrived, had come with us for knickerbocker glories, and afterwards he'd picked out records, playing songs, one for her, the next for me, singing along, laughing. When it was time for me to leave, Marina had stood and stretched, tucking her men's shirt into her men's trousers, saying she might as well leave too. 'Must you?' My father looked both irritable and amused, and she kissed him lightly, fleetingly, much as he kissed me.

I hadn't known she was planning to escort me to Victoria. Bea and I were used to making the journey alone, but she'd hopped aboard the bus, sat with me on the top deck, entertained me with a commentary on the people that we passed. We'd arrived early, bought the usual supplies – Hula Hoops, a Curly Wurly – and then, to my surprise, two tickets for the cinema. Breathless I climbed the stairs to the first-floor auditorium while she issued a warning: never to sit beside lone men, to be alert for shuffling and rustling – and she didn't mean of wrappers. They were showing *Tom and Jerry*, and afterwards a film of *Superman*, so engrossing I missed the next two trains.

Hula Hoops. That was what I needed. The sweet salt of their crunch, their moreish rings, but as I stooped in search of change, I caught myself reflected in a window, the scalloped edging of my nightdress, my ankles rising sockless from my shoes. I imagined pushing through the late-night travellers, the pickpockets, the teenagers queueing for Big Macs. A wave of nausea caught me. I doubled over, retched, and when it was safe to rise, I turned around and ran. The hospital was dark and quiet. I pushed at the door and finding it unlocked I hurried up the stairs, across the ward, and ducking past the nurses' station, I climbed into my bed.

'How you feeling?' Smoke and spirits enveloped me as Nathan leant over for a kiss.

'Fine.'

He sank into a chair. There'd been a party at the cottage, he told me, once the pub had closed, and when anyone asked where it was I'd disappeared to, he'd informed them my grandmother had died.

Which one? My father's mother who I'd never met, or my nana in Ireland, praying for me anyway, whatever sinful thing I'd done.

I turned to ask, but Nathan was asleep.

It was afternoon when he woke. 'What are we waiting for?' Tall and suited, shoaled by students, the doctor was making his rounds. 'You said you were fine. Let's leave.'

We were sidling from the ward when Matron apprehended us, turned me back towards my bed, directed my 'friend' to wait outside.

It was late before I was officially dismissed. 'Free at last!' Nathan lifted me off the ground, and taking my hand we hurried for the bus.

My mother had made shepherd's pie, a dish usually reserved for birthdays, but my appetite of the night before was gone. I crawled upstairs and locked myself in the bathroom where I inspected the pad provided by the hospital, drenched and clotted, a taunt for all the months I'd prayed for blood.

'Tell him to go home,' my mother hissed as she did the washing-up. 'Just for tonight.'

Nathan's eyes turned hard at the suggestion.

'Doctor's orders …' I tried. 'He said we mustn't … not till I start the pill.'

'All I want is to hold you.'

'I'm just not …' I put a palm to my forehead and found that it was damp. 'Tomorrow, we … I'm sure by then I'll feel …'

Nathan curled his hand into a fist. 'Not once has a single person asked me how I feel.'

It was true. I gave a guilty laugh. That single person was me.

'It's entirely clear that no one gives a fuck.'

I had a great desire to yell: *What's it got to do with you?* I'd learnt early that when it came to babies the work was left to women.

'See?' The gentleness of the last three months was gone. 'You can't even bother to pretend …'

I shook my head, and too tired to withstand him we climbed into my single bed, and when my mother went to tuck Max up I forced myself to open the front door, shout goodbye and close it.

'What if she comes in?' Nathan nuzzled my neck.

'She won't.' I fell into a cavernous sleep.

In the early hours I woke to find him hard against me. 'You OK?' he whispered.

'I am,' I said, and although my heart was heavy, when he wedged a hand between my legs I found that I was burning. I covered it with my own.

Nisha looked surprised when I arrived at college. 'Wasn't the funeral in Ireland?'

Of course: my grandmother had died. 'My *father's* mother.' It was easier to lose a grandmother I didn't know. 'Golders Green.' But during Improvisation my tongue tied, my lip wobbled, and by the end of the day, when I turned the wrong way during a routine from *Grease*, I escaped to the girls' changing room and, like so many before me, leant against the basin and cried.

'When are you moving in, then?' Nathan asked. We were in the pub, celebrating the last day of the spring term.

'I might wait …' I was drinking brandy in an attempt to numb the pain. I'd taken paracetamol, I'd take more as soon as I got home.

'Don't want to leave Mummy?' he said, sour, and I looked away, knowing he was only cross that I was going on a holiday without him, to an island off the coast of Spain, to a guest house on a hill. We'd been before, lived there through the winter, the year I was four, and I had a memory of Bea syphoning seawater into bottles, pretending it was Fanta, stoppering it with sand. I'd chased her through the shallows, trudging after her up the long slope of La Mola, calling for her to wait. 'Wouldn't it be nice if Bea came too,' my mother said. I didn't answer. We both knew that she wouldn't.

The next day I took more paracetamol, doubling the dose. I would have mentioned the discomfort, called my father's doctor, but I was sure I'd be all right as soon as I was on the plane.

'You OK?' Mum said as we snapped the buckles of our belts. 'You do look pale.' She took my hand and held it. The plane was gathering speed, shuddering as it pressed us back into its pull. For all our travelling – Scotland, Spain, North Africa – we'd almost never flown. Max was on her other side, eyes screwed shut as we lifted from the runway. 'Up we go,' she tried, but the sinews in her arms were tight, her fingers biting as they gripped my own.

I waited until we'd broken through the clouds, were gliding weightless into blue, before I pulled away to gulp more pills. 'What's that?' I'd been seen.

'Bit sore.' I grimaced, a hand on my stomach. Today the painkillers failed to work. A dark sluice washed against the lining of my womb, tightening, releasing, screwing into coils so sharply it was hard to speak. By the time we landed I could barely walk. We collected our bags, and took a taxi to the ferry. All I needed was to get there, to the island, to the stretch of beach, the safe and shallow sea.

The ferry smelt of oil and fish and I struggled not to gag. People crowded on around us. Locals with cans and bottles, baskets, fruit. An American with binoculars. His wide-bottomed wife. Over the sea we churned. 'Lucy?' My mother's voice was far away. I shook my head, arms pressed against the pulp of my insides. There were eyes on me, a hush, the thud of the boat as it docked. I stumbled, half-lifted, and sank down on the quay.

'El doctor.' The American spoke Spanish. Cold sweat stood out on my face. 'Rapido!'

We were in the cool confines of a clinic, pale and scrubbed, my mother explaining how I'd had a 'procedimiento' two weeks before. Fingers prodded. I screamed. There was muttering, my trousers tugged away, a needle jabbed. Sweat broke against my skin. 'Half hour more,' the doctor's voice was surly, 'infection would have cause fallopian to burst.' He surveyed me, disapproving, as I was handed water, ordered to take tablets, and once I could walk, to transfer to the mainland. To register at the hospital. They would take over my care.

Back we went across the sea. The boat half-empty. The three of us in silence. From the port we made our way to the hospital, a building adorned with statues of the Madonna; the walls were peppermint, the nurses nuns. Into these clean rooms we brought disappointment. 'Aborto.' Lips were curled.

Max sat on the floor and walked his dinosaurs across the tiles while I was tested and inspected and given instructions on where to go for an injection, daily, made more painful by its dose of shame. I had no idea then that a termination was a hazard faced by almost every woman I knew. My sister, my stepsister, three half-sisters at least, Zara, her mother. Mine! I couldn't have guessed how many years would pass before I'd be free to disclose it, and when I did, invariably there'd be a confidence returned.

'My son was less than seven months …'

'I was still studying …'

'My husband worked abroad; I only have two hands, I told him …'

'Like you I was young.'

We found a room with two beds and a truckle, and once we were settled my mother took Max in search of food. I must have slept because a moment later they were back: bread, tomatoes, a bottle of water, three oranges in a bag. 'Eat.' My mother placed an orange on a plate, and when I protested, she turned on me, fierce. 'Now.'

A burst of scent streamed into my nose as I broke through the peel. Juice ran through my fingers, fat segments splitting with pips, three babies clustered at the navel. I ate the babies first, as Bea and I had used to do, and as I sucked at the fruit I was flooded with memories of that island winter, the pillowy sand, the dent of the bay, the scrub of hilltop on which our hotel sat.

Revived by the sweet blood of the orange, I reached for the dictionary we'd packed. Under *aborto* I found further definitions: *failure, breakdown, fiasco, bust*. I glanced at my mother sitting by the window, reading Max a chapter of *The Village Dinosaur* – discovered in a quarry, befriended by a local boy named Jed. She caught my eye and smiled.

'How are you?' Nathan had asked that day as he'd leant over me. 'Fine,' I'd answered. But I wasn't fine. I was ecstatic. To be alive, in England, in the eighth decade of the twentieth century, to be handed back my future, to be freed. I could have leapt from the bed, flipped into a cartwheel, sung an aria, burst into a shoot of flame. 'Thank you,' I'd exhaled when I rose from unconsciousness to find myself returned, miraculously, to myself, and there before me were the legions of women, of girls less lucky – was my mother at the front? – snaking away in a never-ending line.

V

I was in my second year of drama school when news came through Sir Hew had died. The funeral was family only. Or certainly, it never occurred to me to go. Neither did I think to ask Janey, to ask Ted – to ask any one of them – how they were. Was it seeing so little of my own father that made it impossible to imagine how theirs could be missed? Or, at nineteen, is loss too abstract an idea until it turns and catches you, head-on?

Ted inherited the title but it was too late for the house. It was closed, the land leased. Lady Frances moved into a cottage on the grounds. I did write, at least, to her. *Our new home is remarkably convenient*, she replied on embossed Craigmont paper. *Now we're settled in I can't think how I ever managed the big house.*

Janey was in London, at University College. She'd grown enviably beautiful. Long-legged and narrow-waisted, she wore her hair piled high much like her mother. We met most weekends to discuss our lives, the quandary of the younger sister – what to do when it had already been done. We'd share a bath, trickling in hot water when it cooled, and sometimes Ted would appear, his pupils pinpricks, his glamour beyond my league. He'd started a band. They were writing songs. Bea had promised to take photos at their gig.

'Right.' I hadn't known Bea owned a camera. 'When is the gig?'

'Soon.' He threw himself on to the sofa, elbowing Janey, squashing her with his hip. I looked on, hungry. 'How is she …? I haven't …'

'Who?' His face in the grey light looked worn.

'Bea.'

'She's great.'

Bea was living in a flat owned by a girlfriend of our father's. It was in a mews above a garage, furnished with outcasts from a larger house. Brocaded lamps, lined linen curtains, a cupboard stocked with sheets so wide they were impossible to fold. I'd visited often when she first moved in, eaten late-night cereal in front of the TV. 'Sleep here,' she'd say – we both knew there was a ghost – and I'd climb into her high bed, breathing her smoke and perfume scent, feel the jut of her hip, encased in men's pyjamas, her feet in socks against the chill. 'Night,' she'd sigh. 'Night,' I'd turn away, and we'd fall into a blackened sleep.

It wasn't long before the flat filled up. A girl she met at a party. Two men who made experimental films. Now when I called she was busy. The message was she'd call me back.

'Where will you play?' I turned to Ted.

'Not sure.' He'd rolled a cigarette, and as he bent his head to light it, the flame flared, singeing his hair.

Before there ever was a gig, Ted was shipped to South America. It was Marina who'd arranged it. It was what he needed, everyone agreed, to be removed from London. I tracked his progress, heard how he'd escaped the job in

Venezuela, had reached New Mexico, was taking a bus across the States. He had spent some weeks in a facility. Was staying with Daphne who was studying in Boston. That he was better. Much better. Was on his way home.

I was living in the attic of a house owned by a woman whose commitment to the arts led her to rent rooms cheaply to students. She was elderly, her husband was confined to bed. After three months she was struggling to accommodate my habits. Playing music at all hours, bringing 'men' back in the afternoon. 'You're not the only one.' She'd jumped out from the landing as I passed with a would-be actor, come back to rehearse a scene from *Entertaining Mr Sloane*, and when we'd reached my room we'd fallen about so uncontrollably she'd banged her stick against the floor.

Her patience was almost at an end when one late night the doorbell rang. I ran to the window, and there, standing, looking up, was Ted Colquhoun. He was taller, thinner, his grey eyes slipped, if that was possible, further sideways in his head. I flew down the three flights to greet him.

'Bea ...'

'It's Lucy.' I blushed.

'She wouldn't answer ...'

I led Ted up the stairs and made him coffee in the small, square kitchen. Bea, I told him, lived in Italy now; she had a boyfriend there, in Florence. I watched him, closely, but he only bit his lip, and restless, and too big for the room, he drifted out on to the landing where, before I could reach him, he'd knocked the telephone from its shelf. It trilled and clattered through the house. 'Ted!' I pulled him into my room where I threw a quilt over the unmade bed, slung assorted items underneath, and when I turned, he'd slipped a record from its case. 'Don't.' I stretched for it, but he held me off, letting the needle fall. Music shuddered through the floor. *Pressure drop, oh pressure drop.*

We were dancing when the stick began to thump.

'What's the racket?' He bent and flicked the volume high.

'Ted!' I turned it low. 'She'll throw me out!'

'Who?'

'My landlady. She's eighty-four …'

'And still not deaf?' We clung together, laughing, and then he crashed us both on to the bed.

'Listen.' Was that a tread on the stair? 'Christ. I'm sorry but you're going to have to leave.' I helped him up and out on to the landing, and slowly, fearfully, promising to visit him instead, I guided him down through the dark house.

'What a nightmare.' I called Janey. How could she know that I was boasting? 'I'm definitely going to have to move now.'

'Have you tried flowers?'

I had tried flowers. 'I'm not a landlady,' she'd responded; and informing me it was her Russian lesson I was interrupting, she'd closed her sitting-room door.

Ted heated up a tin of ravioli. 'Old times' sake,' he smiled, lopsided, but he didn't eat. Instead he drank the bottle of wine I'd brought and then, his mouth red-rimmed and cracked, he took me to his room. 'Come here.' He lay down in his clothes. His knees were bent, his feet hung over the edge of the mattress. Did boys keep growing? I'd stopped soon after our first kiss. I pressed myself against him.

'What do you like?' he asked.

Nervous, I laughed. I didn't know. *You*, I wanted to say. It had always been the case.

When we'd heaved and thumped for what felt like hours, he apologised, explaining how the drugs made it impossible to come. We gave up and lay side by side, and in the morning I got dressed – I couldn't risk being late for college – and even though I shook his shoulder, kissed his forehead, he failed to wake.

That night I had supper with my father. 'How goes it?' He was distracted, having failed to get backing for a project he was sure would make his name, and without mentioning Ted – anything connected to Marina made him sad – I told him I'd most probably be looking for somewhere new to live. '"I'm not a landlady,"' I relayed the conversation, and scrabbling for a postcard, he wrote, *You Are a Landlady*, laughing, cheered with purpose as the phrase unfurled, *You Are a Landlady, You Are a Landlady*, until he ran out of space.

'Please,' I begged. 'Don't send it.' He'd already pasted on a stamp.

That weekend I didn't ring Janey, and we didn't meet. I'd give myself away the moment that I saw her. I'd blush, or mention Ted unnecessarily. I was busy too – at least that's what I told myself – later – looking for a place to live. Instead I called Ted. In the mornings, late at night. *Just checking in … to see … How are you?* I practised. *Hello?* Had someone answered? No one had.

I was packing up when Janey called. I had a cardboard box and I was heaping in possessions when the phone rang, eerily cheerful on its shelf. Her voice sounded hollow. Or was it the line? At first I didn't understand what was being said. 'Ted?' I repeated. I couldn't follow. 'Craigmont? But I was with him, in London. I was with him, last week.'

There was silence.

'It can't be ...' I tried again. But even as I said it, I knew that it was true.

The service for Ted was in the chapel, even though the house was closed. I stared up at the mass of Craigmont, the double flight of steps that met at the front door, and as I tracked my eyes across its windows I thought of Ted breaking into his own home, curving past the husks of roses, the portraits, the drawing room where the Americans were entertained, and on up the attic stairs to where his drum kit used to sit. He'd left no note. Had taken a rifle from the gun room. Bullets from the drawer. Although he'd only needed one.

Marina wanted everyone to dance. Ted would have liked that. Daphne knelt and turned over the tape, and when Elvis's voice rose from the bare earth two Colquhoun cousins dutifully jived. I moved my feet, self-conscious, but I couldn't dance, not alone, and Bea was in Italy. She'd said she was unable to get back. Janey's friend Christel had arrived the day before. I'd come early too in case she needed help. But she hadn't needed help, or not from me, and I'd been shown into a bedroom in the old gamekeeper's lodge which I was to share with a member of Ted's band.

I didn't cry, not until the train home, when I lay my head on the table and sobbed. 'Why so distraught?' Christel asked from across the aisle. 'Janey says you didn't even like him. Couldn't wait to be rid of him, the last time you met.'

'No,' I spluttered. Why had I never said I loved him? Loved him from the day we met? I'd explain, one day, I'd try to, although it wouldn't be to her, and I might have, if that same summer Bea hadn't called to say Marina had swum out from the beach at Berwick. A tragic accident. That was what was being said. They'd found her three days later, her ears and toes nibbled at the tips, and I knew then, in the hard, sure, selfish way of friendship, that I'd lost them all for good.

PART TWO

I

He appeared that night, as he'd appeared before: the ghost. I was wriggling down, cold in the cold sheets, leaning across to switch off the lamp, when there he was, a pillar of black, pressing me against the wall. I froze. Unable to blink, my breath caught in my chest. If I could turn I'd see him, face screwed shut, his feet in the leather lace-up shoes that were there when I moved in. But I couldn't turn. That was his trick. The weight of him heavy as a slab. I didn't so much fall asleep, as faint.

I woke, as always, my memory erased. Nothing but the tap and drill of construction, the twittering of birds. I walked into the kitchen and looked out. My new, old car was parked on the cobbles of the mews, a wing mirror missing where I'd clipped a wall. I put the kettle on, slid bread for toast under the grill, swiped a cloth over the table, pushed a broom across the floor. I stepped back to appraise my work – Bea, sharp-eyed, a raven on my shoulder – who lived here when she flew into London, her luggage Italian, like her boyfriend, older than her by thirty years, his manners too refined to scowl, as she did, at my house-keeping, trailing her possessions over every dusty surface, sending out the laundry so that the sheets returned so stiff with starch they screeched.

I took my tea and climbed back into bed. I was two years out of drama school and I had a small part in a play in a large theatre. I was on my way.

That night, after the curtain call, we were going to a club. There'd be girls from my dressing room; Jay, an honorary member; Connor, the male lead. Usually they came back to mine, and when they did it was Connor who stayed latest. Dark-eyed, soulful, he had a girlfriend, last seen at the first night. Left alone, we made awkward conversation, until at two, at three in the morning, he got up to leave. His gaze was piercing, familiar from posters. It's possible he'd never had to make a move. 'Bye, then.' We'd stand on the step, and kiss lightly on each cheek.

It was late when the six of us squeezed into my car. 'What if they don't let us in?' Jay's membership at Joey O's allowed for two – but when we arrived, and Connor smiled his film-star smile – they'd watched him in *The Mercy* – they waved us through. We stood at the upstairs bar, a horseshoe glittering with glasses, and the barman, a boy who hoped to be an actor, congratulated us on our reviews. 'Good show tonight?' he asked, professional. He poured us drinks, we drained them. He poured more.

Connor was beside me, his fingers moments from my own. 'Will you have another?' The wine was singing, stinging through the emptiness of my insides, and when I said I'd better not or I'd never find my car, let alone get home, he lowered his voice: 'I'll see that you get home.'

Jay nudged my knee. I'd confided in him every glance and smile, now I couldn't meet his eye. I slipped off to find a bathroom, to splash my face, to wipe away the grin.

That was the night that I met Zac.

He was standing by the downstairs bar, and he spoke my name as I squeezed by. He'd seen me, he said, in an episode of *Firefly*, and he'd been looking for me ever since. I laughed, and shook my head. 'I'll be back,' I'd told Connor. Tonight was our night. We both knew it. There were rumours – and rumours were enough – his girlfriend had moved out. Zac laid a hand on my arm. He was tall, and easeful. A lock of hair, jet black, fell over one eye. 'What will it be? Champagne?'

'I'm … I have to …' I squinted at the floor above.

'Don't go.' Zac was insistent. 'Not now that I've found you.'

I was sipping, bubbles bursting, when I saw Connor hovering, his face dismayed.

We stayed until closing when we fell into the street. I was too drunk to drive, but I drove anyway. 'I could drop you, which way do …?' I glanced sideways as we nosed through Soho. 'Or maybe …' the flat loomed darkly '… you could come back to mine?'

Zac kept his hand on my knee as I careered round Hyde Park Corner, tightening his grip as I circled the deserted squares and, without braking, bumped along the cobbles of the mews. I drew up in front of next door's Rolls-Royce. 'Don't touch,' I warned. People had a habit of stroking the nymph that stood on the car's bonnet, but the nymph was linked to an alarm, and with the faintest nudge would siren through Belgravia, forcing my neighbour, a chauffeur, to trudge down and switch it off.

I showed Zac up the stairs, explaining how the flat belonged to an old girlfriend of my father's, she'd inherited it from her own father, whose butler had lived here until one or other of them had died. At the back of the garage were stalls that might have been for horses; there were carriage tracks that curved into the street. 'How come it's empty?' I'd asked Bea, and she'd sworn me not to mention it, or someone might remember, and we'd have to move. At night the flat was very cold. I'd pinned a curtain to catch the draught from the French doors, stretched cling film across the window that led on to the roof. I knelt before the gas fire, clicked the button till it caught, and when I rose, Zac was there, behind me. 'Two years I've been waiting.' His lips were warm on mine.

I thought nothing of the ghost as I led Zac to the bedroom. I flicked on a lamp, swung shut the cupboard, barely noticing the shine of the black shoes. The bed in here was low and wide. We lay in it and kissed, and talked, and kissed again, and marvelled at the time it had taken for us to meet. 'I was waiting too,' I told him, although I hadn't known.

The drilling alerted us to morning. 'So,' I swivelled in his arms, 'what will your girlfriend be doing?' He paused, and glancing at the clock he said she'd most likely be heading into work.

'You're not serious?' When he looked as if he was, I thought of Connor and how I'd promised to be back. 'You'd better go.' The room felt damp. Condensation snailed down one wall, and as he dragged his clothes on a loneliness engulfed me, so crushingly I couldn't move.

That night there was a red rose at the stage door. It was sealed in a Perspex box, a card attached: *Call Zac.*

'I'm free,' he said when my coin dropped through the slot.

'Tonight?'

'Forever.'

So this was it. I stood with the receiver in my hands.

On the way up to the dressing room I passed actors, heading for the stage. Connor was among them, in costume, a brown jerkin, a feather in his cap. 'Hello,' I mouthed, apologetic. Connor said nothing. He was in the first scene and he needed to warm up.

I had a theory, gleaned from much research, that anyone can impress you for three months. After three months their true character cracks through, and after six, if you're still not disappointed, there's a chance. Zac and I had made it to eight months. We glided through summer, walking across London, laughing at our own concocted jokes. We drank late-night drinks at Joey O's where we stood at the bar, entwined. 'You're ruining my chances,' he teased when we'd talked only to each other, and I asked if he'd been testing his chances on the night we met. 'No,' he said. 'I was looking for you.'

That summer I had a part in a new play. It was the story of a girl whose parents – in flight from Nazi Germany – had placed her in an orphanage during the war. By the time they came to take her out she'd turned fourteen. Zac had advised me to embellish my credentials, lop several years off my age, tell them I was the child of refugees, keep quiet about my convent-educated mother, even though she'd been sent to board aged four.

On the opening night there were a dozen roses. *Love, Forever*, the card read, and Ruth, the author of the play, who saw me as herself, examined the inscription. 'It's serious?' She frowned. 'I didn't know.' When the roses wilted, their rims fringed round with black, I took them home and put them on a shelf.

Zac was less lucky with work. 'Actors need definition.' Tall and lean, his face was full. It was the reason, he insisted, he was rarely cast. I squished his warm flesh between my fingers, kissed his sulky, laughing mouth, while other, fuller faces flitted before me, swollen with success.

On my birthday, my twenty-fourth, there was a red rose for every year, and when they faded I tipped away the water and set them to dry with the rest. 'Do you know,' we lay on the lopsided sofa, 'we've never argued once.'

'Is that right?' He was unbuttoning my dress and we imagined our first row, and how we might make up.

That autumn I went north, to a repertory theatre, while Zac stayed in the flat. 'If Bea arrives, I'm sorry, but you'll have to leave.'

'Of course. It's not as if I'm homeless!'

I'd never asked. Where had he been living when we met?

On weekends when he visited I asked about his chances at the club. 'Not good,' he'd tell me. 'It's obvious I'm taken.' I imagined him, standing alone at the bar.

Then, one day, it happened. Zac got a part. Not just a part – a lead, in a film. It was a horror film, low-budget, set in New York, and when I'd finished with the repertory theatre I was to fly out and meet him.

'No,' Bea wailed when I rang to tell her. 'I can't stay there without you.'

I shivered. The echo of the garage. The shine of those black shoes.

'I couldn't face it. Not Christmas, on my own, with Mum.'

'Max will be there. Anyway, don't worry, I'll be home by then.' I wasn't leaving them together. I imagined the four of us around the table and my breath caught in my chest.

I wrote to Zara to tell her we were coming.

I don't believe it! she wrote back.

It was snowing when I landed in New York. Sharp flakes that melted even as they fell. I took a taxi, peeling off my woollen tights in the confines of the back, rolling on the stockings Zac preferred. But Zac was out. 'You can wait in his room.' The man on reception wished me a good day as he handed over a key, and I took the lift to the thirty-seventh floor where a sign on the door read: *Do Not Disturb*. My heart leapt. Was this Zac surprising me? The room was empty, save for a club sandwich congealed on a tray, and his underpants strewn across a chair. The bed was unmade. I lay on it. Was this nine months? I must have dozed because soon I was dreaming – the man – the tips of his black shoes. I snapped open my eyes and there was Zac. I held out my arms. I needed to feel him, draw him close, but he had his coat on, and his hands, he said, were icy. 'Look at this city!' Flinging up the blind he revealed a mass of white.

The other actors, and the actress – there was only one – were having supper at the hotel. 'Let's walk.' Zac didn't want to join them. 'See the theatres, find a bar.'

We stepped into a snow globe. The flakes were swirling, men rushed for taxis, women tucked scarves around their hair. 'Isn't it fantastic?' We hurried through the blizzard. I nodded, tipping back my head.

We fought our way along Fifth Avenue, keeping close in against shop windows, the snow thickening, muffling the city's sounds. Times Square was bright as day, the snow here churned and melting. I inched towards a pretzel stand, lured by its caravan of warmth. 'Let's get to the next block,' Zac urged, but we found nothing on the next block, or the one beyond. The windows here were darkened; there were potholes, and cracked kerbstones. *A knife, a fork, a bottle and a cork.* It was a song Zara used to sing. A song about New York.

It was three o'clock in the morning, at least it was for me, and I couldn't feel my feet. I stopped outside a pub with a shamrock sign, lit up. 'For Christ's sake,' Zac huffed. A blast of heat enveloped us as I tugged the door, and without waiting, I stamped in. We sat at a round table, snug against upholstered seats, and I watched Zac drain his pint. 'I missed you.' We still hadn't kissed.

Zac smiled. 'You know what I've been thinking?'

I wriggled. Here we were together. In New York.

'Use the money from this job, get a place to live.'

'Really?' I hadn't thought we'd move. Not with the mews mostly to ourselves. Not when there was barely any rent.

'I'm going to start looking.' He chewed at his thumb. 'I only need a small place. A studio would do.'

My smile wavered. 'So you …?' Questions flared and fell away. 'When we …?' I didn't want the answers. Not here. Not now.

'Somewhere of my own.' He picked up his empty glass.

By the time we arrived back at the hotel I was too tired to eat. I crawled into bed, and the next morning when I woke, Zac was dressed. 'Have a good day,' he twanged. He was gone.

'How the hell are you?' Zara hugged me, the familiar spring of her hair, the soft press of her chest, and she led me up a polished staircase, past a suit of armour, doors opening on to empty, wood-panelled rooms, and up again to an apartment at the top. Here there were beanbags and a coffee table with the mess of last night's supper. Pizza, and roaches, crumpled cans of beer. She and her boyfriend were minding the place for an uncle, a job that involved patrolling the building nightly, checking the casement windows and the doors.

'How's love?' she asked when we sank down.

'OK.'

'OK? I thought this was it?' She began to sing – 'Forever and ever, Amen' – and with a smile so wide it split her face, she told me Mackenzie had proposed. I screamed, as she did, and we clasped hands, but once I'd recovered from the shock of her news I asked: 'Is it what you want?'

'Don't you?'

What I wanted was for things to go back to how they were.

'Where is Zac anyway?'

'Filming.' They were working on the final scene: Zac in a tuxedo; the actress – Serena – stretched out on a marble tomb, her white skin (I'd seen a Polaroid) illuminating the shot.

'Then you'll come and stay? We have to go upstate, just for the weekend. Mackenzie's mother …' She made a face. 'You could mind the place for us. You'll get time for yourselves.' She took my hand and led me down to the next floor where she showed me into a wood-panelled room with nothing in it but a bed. Adjoining was a marbled bathroom, a glass-walled shower, steps leading to a gargantuan tub. 'You two are going to have such fun.'

We spent the afternoon catching up on news. Zara's sister had abandoned tennis and was retraining as a physio. Her mother had split from her most recent boyfriend, the son of a neighbour who'd moved home after college.

'And how is *your* mother?' she asked. 'I love your mother. Remember how she never minded what we did?'

'She's well,' I said, and I told her she'd taken up dancing – salsa and tango. That Max was still unhappily at school.

'And Bea? Is her boyfriend … is he actually ancient?'

I said he was, but also, not at all. He wore tailored suits and hand-embroidered shirts, and sometimes Bea dressed in his clothes, and they walked through Florence, crossing back and forth over the bridges, buying trinkets in the gift shops, taking photos with his Leica which they developed in the bath. I didn't tell her, as I'd told no one, that in the afternoons they locked themselves into a darkened room, and when they emerged, in time for evening drinks, they were mellow and languid. 'It's not sex,' she'd said as we stood with a group of tourists staring at Michelangelo's *David*, examining the neat curl of his cock, and she explained how the opium, hardly a drug at all, was not, in fact, addictive: Federico had been taking it for thirty years.

When it was time to go Zara pressed a key into my hand. 'Don't forget to check the house, last thing.' The key was tiny for such a giant door. 'See you Sunday.' She stood on the step to watch me as I walked backwards, waving, over the grey, packed ice.

Zac was exhausted. 'What a day.' He stood for a long time in the shower. We ordered room service and watched TV and Zac phoned down to reception and asked for a wake-up call at 5 a.m. 'Sleep tight.' He turned his body to the wall.

I woke in the early hours to find his arm draped round me. I eased it tighter, catching at the smell of him, disguised as it had been by distance and the scent of the hotel. When I next woke he was gone.

On the last night of filming there were drinks at the bar. Zac suggested that afterwards we go out and eat, just us. 'We'll walk, so wrap up warm.' I wore wool trousers, and a thermal vest under my shirt, and a pair of boots I'd bought in a sale. The first person I saw was Serena. 'Lovely to meet you.' She took my hand and squeezed it and I regretted we'd not met before. She had red hair, and troubled skin, but her arms and legs were elegant in a black, backless dress.

'You live here in New York?'

I shook my head.

'So how do you know Zac?' She seemed intrigued, and when I said I was his girlfriend, her hand went limp in mine.

In silence we walked the ten blocks to a Chinese restaurant. 'What's up?' Zac asked.

'Nothing.'

'Good.'

There was silence where there might have been a row, if we did row, which we didn't. 'I thought maybe —' if I didn't speak I'd scream '— we could visit that toyshop, the one with the piano?'

'Great plan.'

As we ate, duck rolled into pancakes, Zac talked about the flat he hoped to buy. He could sublet it while he was away, working, which he hoped to be, more and more. If he could find another agent. That's what Vince advised. 'Who's Vince?' His conversation was littered with people, with worlds I wasn't part of. I did my best to draw him back to ours. 'How was it?' I asked. 'Living in the mews these last few months?'

'Great.' He shrugged. 'Apart from the damn drilling. And your sister of course.'

'My sister?'

'She walked in on me. Unannounced!'

'I didn't know she'd been in London.'

'She wasn't there for long.'

'Was she alone?'

'Only for five minutes. Then her friends started piling in.'

'You never said.'

'I thought you knew.'

We glared. If this was our row it was easier than the one we might have had.

'So you met Bea?' I waited, eager, for a review: her beauty, the glamour of her style. Silk and cashmere. I smiled, indulgent. The musky perfume that she wore.

'By the time she left,' he rolled another pancake, 'the place was a dump.'

'It is her flat! I said you'd have to leave if she—'

'I did leave! I wouldn't have stayed if I was paid.'

I gasped.

'Sorry,' he said then, and he leant across and stroked my hand.

I didn't describe the mansion. I wanted it to be a surprise.

'Bloody hell.' Zac ran up to the landing, and stopping before the suit of armour, he lifted its visor and peered in. 'What is this place?'

We took a tour around the building. It was still morning but the green-paned windows cast a watery light. Most rooms were empty, some were lined with books. There were two kitchens: one in an alcove, its cupboards bare; the other a narrow galley in the attic. Here there was ketchup, soya sauce, a scattering of plastic cutlery. 'It seems no one in New York cooks.'

'Why would they?'

Everything I said now seemed absurd.

I left our bedroom to last.

Zac dropped his bag and embraced me. 'Let's get breakfast. I'm starved.'

The Happy Donut topped up our coffee and served such large portions of hash browns we didn't need lunch. All day we roamed Manhattan, trailing through department stores, travelling to the top of the Empire State Building where we gazed out over the city. When we got home we fell on to the bed. I pressed my foot against his socked one. He pressed back and gave a wide-mouthed yawn. Zac was still asleep when I ran myself a bath. The tub filled slowly, and when the water reached halfway, I switched it off. I peeled out of my jeans, my sweater, the tights and vest I'd been wearing underneath. My body looked winterish in the yellow light. I searched for soap and found none, only buttons on the side of the bath, one of which I pressed. Nothing. I pressed another. Bubbles rose. I lay back to enjoy the swirl, and then, curious, I tried a third. The water scooped and flung into the air. I pressed again in the hope that it would stop. It twisted into a whirlpool, spray cascading round the room, streaming down walls, drenching the floor. I jabbed at the controls but the speed increased, the water diminishing, what was left roiling high into a boil. I was standing in the empty bath when Zac opened the door. He looked at me. 'What the ...?'

'I ...' I was buckling with laughter. 'I thought it might be ...' tears stung in my nose '... romantic.' Gulping, I clambered out and reached for a wet towel.

It took almost an hour to mop the floor, dry the walls, wipe down the basin. When I'd finished I found Zac watching TV. He was reclining on a beanbag, drinking beer. 'Where did you get that?'

'Don't worry, I'll replace it.'

From far below came the clang of the front door. We looked at each other. They weren't due back till tomorrow. There was a clatter on the stairs. 'We're home.' It was Zara, her face stormy, Mackenzie behind her, carrying their bags.

Zac leapt to his feet. 'Thanks so much ...' He gestured round. 'I can't tell you ...' He hooked an arm around my waist and pulled me close. 'It's been so great, to get this time, just us.'

'You are welcome.' Mackenzie was tall and preppy with a sportsman's muscled frame. He put out his hand, and when we'd shaken, he backed out of the room.

Zara fell on to a beanbag. 'I actually hate him.'

Calm flooded through me.

'He's an asshole. It's official.'

My spirits soared.

Zac nuzzled my ear.

'A spoilt, lazy motherfucking—'

'Should we go, I mean, we could …' The truth was that we couldn't.

'Don't leave me alone with him, for Christ's sake.'

'… look for a hotel.'

'No!' She wiped her eyes. 'I've been longing to have you visit.' She sniffed and laughed. 'Anyway, it will do him good to see that some couples can be civilised, and still be happy.'

Zac kissed the side of my head.

'He's gorgeous,' she whispered later. 'And one thing's clear, he's crazy about you.'

That night I cuddled close against Zac's back. 'You still tired?' How long had it been? I stroked a thumb against his stomach. He made an indeterminate sound, shifting imperceptibly. I swallowed, and Serena's limp hand was once again in mine. Zac said nothing. Could he be asleep? I withdrew my fingers, rested my palm on his hip, and released, he rolled on to his front.

I lay awake with the sounds of the city. The blare of horns, the shock of an alarm – *Your property has been violated* – from the house next door.

The smell of coffee greeted me as I ambled up to the top floor. 'Hello, angel.' Zac drew me in. Zara was red-eyed and ragged.

'So, what do you lovebirds have planned?' she asked when Mackenzie had slugged milk from the carton and retreated, and she suggested we go skating in Central Park.

'Don't you two want …?'

'We're fine. We're always arguing like this.' She raised a goofy grin. 'When we make up, it's worth it.'

The queue was long, and by the time we reached the front my feet were numb. I pushed them into the unyielding boots and tottered out into the crowd. A family breezed by – mother, father, two children between them – wearing matching stripy scarves. I hurried after, I had a need to see their faces, but my skate caught at the tip. I fell. Mackenzie flew by wearing his own skates. A moment later Zac had hold of my hand. 'Hey, speedy.' He tugged till I was standing, and on we went, jingles blasting, as we wove round and round.

That night we offered to do the late patrol. Walking through the mansion we slid our fingers along ledges, tapped at the stained glass. We checked the locks and latches and continued to the next floor. The hall was echoey, the state rooms dense with quiet. 'Nothing in here,' he called from the kitchen, and I skidded out to join him. We walked down to the basement. There was a laundry room, and an outside door which I pushed against, hard. A low moaning drifted through. The hair rose on my neck. 'Stop that.' I spun around but Zac wasn't there. I dared myself to step through into a storeroom. There was a camp bed draped with a rug, and a wooden clotheshorse hung with hangers. I pulled open a cupboard and the coiled trunk of a Hoover fell against my leg. I screamed and put a hand over my mouth, and pressing it back, I ran for the stairs. The light was out. Was this the way we'd come? I took a breath, retraced my steps. There was the clotheshorse, and the camp bed. I turned, and a shadow shot out from between the fringes of the rug, a hand clutched at my foot. I flung and writhed and threw myself against the wall as nails scraped my leg.

'What's up with you?' Zac flicked on the bar of a light and looking down I saw a wire coat hanger caught in the wool of my sock.

'Where were you?' My heart beat fast.

'Looking at the moon.'

I stood out in the yard with him, and stared up at the sky. 'You OK?'

Still shivering, I said that I was. 'You?'

He gave me a tight smile.

Singing floated with the scent of coffee as we heaved up the stairs. 'Hi, guys.' Zara's face was creamy, wreathed in smiles. She said she'd rung in sick. 'How often do I get to spend the day with my best friend in the world?'

'And Mackenzie?'

'He had to go in early. Poor guy,' she grinned. 'He didn't get much sleep.'

Over breakfast at the Happy Donut she made us promise we'd be back. The wedding was in June.

'It's a date.' Zac offered me a forkful of his waffle.

'Of course,' I said when I could speak.

We spent the afternoon with her in Greenwich Village, loafing in and out of cafés, wandering through a warehouse of plaid shirts, leaving Zac to flick through racks of records while we went into a shop that sold lingerie and toys. I bought a black silk slip, while Zara asked so many questions about dildos I retreated to the street.

The weather had turned fine, the melt of snow running into streams as we travelled back uptown. That night it was warm enough to walk unclothed across our panelled room. I released the slip from its wrapping. Sheer and lace, I held it against me. If Zac noticed, he didn't say. 'Early start,' he yawned, although it wasn't true.

To fill the last hours we coiled our way round MoMA's central stairs, keeping each other in our sights, choosing careful postcards in the gift shop: a reproduction of *The Scream* for Bea. *It's too Munch!* A Picasso for my mother. Magritte for Max.

In a chocolate shop we filled a box with truffles which we left in the apartment with a card. *Love, Forever*, Zac scrawled, and I thought of the playwright: *It's serious? I didn't know.*

It was only once we were on the plane I discovered I still had the key. It was so small it fitted in my fist and I squeezed it hard against my palm as we soared away from land. I kept my face turned to the window. The moon was a crescent, tilted sideways, its angle altered from the moon I knew from home. Beside me Zac leafed through an inflight magazine, I could hear the swish of the pages, and I wondered how I'd find the flat when I got home. The gas fire blasting, the wreckage of Bea's friends, undisturbed by drilling, oblivious of the man. The sky was dark now, thick with cloud, the lights a haze below. At my back Zac's shoulder loomed. If I could turn I'd see him; if I could breathe, or blink, or shout.

'Nothing for me,' I said when the air steward passed, and I stayed staring out.

II

At first I waited on the street. Then I climbed back into the car. After fifteen minutes I rang the bell again. 'One sec,' Bea's voice came, distorted, through the grille.

It was raining and the paving stones were slick and black. Paint flaked from the pillars of the porch, the terrace stained and sooted as it neared the roar of the main road. I tipped my head and looked up at Ace's building. A light flickered on the second floor. I considered shouting; instead I walked, counting the uneven numbers until I reached the corner, where I counted myself back.

I rang the bell again. There was a high whine of interference. 'I'm coming, now.' The intercom smacked as it slapped against the wall.

A traffic warden appeared as if from nowhere. 'My sister ...' I flung myself behind the wheel. 'She's on her way ...'

Bea had two cases, and a jumble of bags. I was sliding out to help when Ace, in socked feet, and holding an umbrella, lunged from the doorway and pulled her back into the porch. After interminable minutes I beeped the horn, and when she didn't extricate herself I put the car into reverse.

'Sorry.' Bea was grinning as she slunk into the front seat. 'What time's your plane again?'

Her eyes flew open, the pupils two black pins. 'We can't be late.'

I accelerated fast.

The departure hall was quiet. All around Air Italia desks were shutting up. Bea scrabbled for her ticket. 'Florence.' Her hair sprang from a knot of her own making, her passport fluttered to the floor.

The attendant smiled neatly. 'I'm afraid the gate is closed.'

'It's not!' Bea swung round. The details of her flight were on the screen. 'Please, I have to—'

'Do you wish to rebook for tomorrow?'

'I don't!' she snapped. 'I wish to go tonight.'

We stood together in the huddle of her bags. 'You're going to have to call him.'

'Me?' It was true I'd taken a wrong turn, that there'd been traffic as we'd doubled back.

'He can't be angry if it's you who calls.'

'He won't be angry.' I thought of Federico, his manners, his immaculate starched cuffs.

'If no one tells him, he'll drive to the airport, he'll wait, he'll keep on waiting …'

I could see him, the last man at the gate, his hat at a humiliated tilt. 'So call him, then!'

'He likes you.'

I shook my head.

'If you do this for me …' She was searching for incentives: to replace the bikini that she'd borrowed and then lost, to never be late for anything again.

I was primed. Of all the things I'd done for her – stealing lip gloss when I didn't know what lip gloss was, throwing a brick through the window of a house which was not, as she'd maintained, deserted.

'You have to. Please.' She took my hand. 'I'm begging.' Her bones were light and brittle as a bird's.

'*Pronto.*' Federico's voice came formal down the line.

'Hello. It's Lucy. I'm so so sorry … I said I'd drive Bea to the airport and I took a wrong turn. Now they won't let her on the flight.'

I glanced at my sister who raised a championing thumb.

'The plane hasn't left, but they're refusing to allow her through the gate. She's terribly upset. That's why I'm calling …'

Federico gave a sigh. 'That is most unfair.' I swivelled round, tilted the receiver so that she could hear. 'Most inconvenient.'

I stuck out my tongue. Bea's shoulders shook.

'Is it a possibility to rebook?' he was asking.

'Rebook? I'm sure. One minute …' I pressed more coins into the slot. I was not going to be the one to explain she'd chosen not to. 'She's here. I'll pass you over. See you soon, I hope.'

'I also hope. Ciao, Lucy.'

'Ciao, Federico. Grazie.'

'Prego.'

I held out the phone.

Bea's Italian rippled, fluent – un disastro, un incubo – until, with the promise of another call – a domani – the receiver was plumped down.

We didn't speak as we drove into London. Bea was smoking, gloomy, her feet up on the dash. 'You might as well drop me back at Ace's.'

'Sure.' I thought of the reunion, too soon after the goodbye.

When I pulled over, she leant across for a hug, and quiet, I crooned into her ear: 'I don't know how to … hate you.'

'You're the worst,' Bea brightened. 'You're just the worst.'

'And I've had so many sisters before …' Our voices swelled in the canopy of the car. 'But … you … are … just … the … worst.'

She slithered out on to the street, and trailing her luggage disappeared into the porch.

When Bea delayed, and delayed again, Federico suggested they reunite in Paris. It is beautiful, he said, in the fall, and Bea agreed to meet him there in a week. I imagined her at Ace's lying on a sofa, phoning her friends, as she phoned me – 'What news?' – while I rummaged around for scraps with which to entertain her.

'I'm seeing Clive again.'

I'd first met Clive the summer before college. He was unprepossessing, his hair the same dun colour as his face, and when, at the end of my first shift, he'd leant across the bar where I was working and asked me on a date, I'd laughed.

Rather than take offence, he'd leant in closer. 'I'll wear you down with my devotion. It'll only be a matter of time,' but he hadn't needed to wear me down. Only to touch me. A finger on my wrist and a shiver shot through me so fierce it raised my scalp. Then he disappeared. Three days. Four. When I next saw him he was leaning against the wall of my work, and as I stretched in greeting, my shirt rose and his thumb brushed against my waist. The rest of that summer we spent every spare minute in bed, and it didn't matter, when he kissed me, that we had little, if anything, to say. 'I'll call,' he'd promise when we parted – he was forever staying with some numberless friend – and although he usually did call, there were days, a week, when he couldn't be reached. 'Where were you?' I hung around his neck. He'd look perplexed. Where had he been?

Once I started college I knew the relationship was doomed. Even his unreliability could not compete with the sheer drama of drama school: the intensity, the terror and the hope. He'd gripped my hand when I told him it was over. 'Don't do this,' he insisted, but I kept to my resolve. Now, since Zac's departure, he was back. Although he'd never entirely gone away. Sending notes, calling to check how I was getting on, advising me against Nathan, consoling me after Ted, and then when I lost Janey, sitting by my bedside when I couldn't get up for a week.

'How is that?' Bea yawned.

I was at the smiling stage. 'It's good.'

'About later ...' She had her ticket for Paris. 'The plane leaves at seven ...'

'No.' I was determined. 'Get the Tube.'

'I've got so much stuff ...'

'Ask Ace to take you.'

'Ace?' she laughed, derisive. 'How about I bring my bags round now, and we leave early, as early as you like?'

I was home again, and pinning a paper pattern on to silk – a shirt, long-sleeved, to hide the eczema that had flared since Zac – when the phone rang in the next room.

'I can't face it.' I'd known it was Bea from the first ring.

'Where are you?' My mouth was bunched with pins.

'Airport.'

'What, still?' It was four hours since I'd dropped her off.

'In Paris.' I extricated the pins as she told me how she'd been standing by the carousel, waiting as every last piece of luggage was reclaimed until there was only one case travelling round. 'Then I realised –' she let out a strangled laugh '– it was mine.'

Even without the pins I had no words. 'Bea …' I tried.

'I can't bear it,' she was crying. 'Federico, he'll be out there, and he'll be so fucking kind.'

I held the receiver, breathing my support, until, with a clunk, her time ran out.

I was still seeing Clive when Bea flew back for Christmas. She arrived with a girl she'd met roaming the galleries of the Pitti Palace. Porcelain-skinned, eyes wide beneath the tendrils of a fringe, Sally had nowhere else to stay. 'For Christ's sake, it's freezing.' Bea flicked on the plug-in radiator in the hall, and disgusted – 'What were you thinking?' – she forced me to inspect a stain on the veneer of a three-tiered table that stood, incongruous, beside the broken sofa. Sally made a conciliatory face behind my sister's shoulder, but when Bea turned, she slunk, languorous, against the wall.

Clive chose that moment to appear. He'd rung the bell in the early hours after an absence of three days and I'd left him sleeping as I cleaned the flat. 'Afternoon.' He'd spiked his hair. His shirt was unbuttoned pitifully to the apex of his chest.

I tensed for the scorn of Bea's appraisal, but to my surprise she smiled. 'Meet Sal.' A look passed between the three of them.

I walked Clive to the end of the mews, and on, around the crescent. 'See you tonight.' He slipped his hand inside my coat.

'Maybe.' My nerve ends tangled, and I watched as, head down, he set off towards Hyde Park.

Back at the flat the windows were flung open and dust from plumped cushions hung in the air. Bea beat and blasted, while Sally nozzled the Hoover's snout across the floor.

'I've hoovered already,' I shouted, and Bea ordered me to go back out, we needed cleaning things. Scourers, bleach. I hesitated – the local shop was prohibitively expensive – but she drew a fistful of lire from her purse, thousands, millions, plucking from within their folds a five-pound note.

'You don't mind, do you, if I stay?' Sally whispered. 'I'll go to my own folks on Christmas Eve.'

This year, for the first time, Bea and I were hosting Christmas. She'd ordered a turkey, and it was my job to collect Max and our mother once it was in the oven. I woke early. The day was mild. Not even a frost for the occasion. I flicked off the radiator turned high in the hall. Bea's bedroom door was shut; her shoes, and Sally's, lay heels up outside.

I'd never cooked a turkey. Bea was going to be the one to do it, but when, at midday, I inched open her door, all

I could see were two heads, dark and fair, buried in the pillows. 'Morning.'

'Morning.' Sally's voice was small.

The turkey was monstrous. Too big for the pan. I squeezed it in, its legs around its ears. In a cupboard I found thyme from some prehistoric era, a shaker of pepper. I rubbed in butter, sprinkled it with salt. The potatoes I peeled and set in a pan.

'I'm off.' I stood at the foot of the bed. 'To get Mum.'

From Bea there came a low-spirited grunt.

'The turkey will be done in two hundred …' I persisted. 'Two hundred and ten minutes.'

'Happy Christmas,' Sally's voice came back.

The sun was shining in Stoke Newington. My mother's upstairs neighbour had dropped in for a drink. The last time I'd heard, they'd fought so fiercely the woman had slammed Mum's arm in the door, but now, in the spirit of Christmas, they'd effected a truce. They sat at the table, clinking glasses, while three curly-headed children jumped from chair to chair. Max sat below a lamp, reading *The Guinness Book of Records*. 'We'd better go,' I urged them.

'Have one drink,' the neighbour tried, but I was tense, the image of the turkey crackling. Or worse, its beige skin cold.

It took some time to cajole my mother into the car, Max regaling us with facts – the woman with the world's longest fingernails, the man who'd smashed the most amount of watermelons with his head – and when I did, the engine firing, I was seized by an unwelcome vision: my door key lying on the kitchen table, at home. I slumped against the wheel.

'What?' My mother was alarmed.

'Nothing!'

Even Max looked up.

'Is Bea all right?'

'Bea's fine!' Then taking pity, 'She's asleep, that's all.'

The curtains were still drawn when we arrived. I pressed the bell and when there was no answer, my mother tried a series of short bursts. 'Wake up!' Max crouched before the letter box, and I nudged him from his post and shouted, 'Saaaaally.'

'Who's Sally?'

'Just, someone. She might not even be there.'

We kept on ringing, long and short, while Max flipped open his book. 'The record for eating mince pies in one minute? The largest group of Santas to go surfing?' Our mother slid down against the garage doors. 'Happy Christmas, darling.'

I squatted beside her. Our first Christmas in London had been worse. She'd met an old friend, a man we'd known in Spain, and finding him somehow dispossessed, she'd invited him to lunch. Pauli. That's what we'd called him then – he'd chased us as we raced across the sand – although his name, it seemed, was Paul. Paul was drunk when he arrived. Soon he was drunker, and by the time my mother lit the pudding he'd climbed on to the table, muttering obscenities, before passing out.

'Mum invited Pauli?' Bea said, quiet, when she rang. She was spending Christmas at Craigmont, and it was late before she called. 'What the …?'

'How is it there? How's Janey? How is Ted?'

'Fine,' she muttered, and when I asked if she wanted to speak to the others – Max was still awake – she hung up.

'Who was that?' Mum called from the kitchen, and unable to bear her upset, not tonight, I told her it was Dad.

'Happy Christmas,' I said now, and pulling her up I suggested we look in at the local shop. Leaving Max, we walked to the end of the mews. We peered along the crescent, crossed the road and stared in through the closed window. 'What's up with Bea anyway?' Mum asked.

I looked at her reflection. The rapid blink, her nervous swallow. Surely she must know? Our eyes met, and I considered taking a brick as my sister had once ordered me to do, and smashing it through glass.

A greasy, roasting smell was drifting out into the mews when we returned. 'Bea!' Max yelled through the letter box. I squeezed in beside him and pressed my thumb against the bell. I held it there till it was white. Mum struck the door with the side of her fist. 'Is there no one else who has a key?'

I was shaking my head, when I remembered that there was.

Zac's mother lived in a flat off Harrow Road.

'Hello?' her surprised voice came travelling down.

'It's me, Lucy ...' I'd always liked her and I rushed the words in case she imagined I'd chosen Christmas Day, of all days, to inveigle my way back in. 'I've locked myself out and I was hoping Zac still has a key?'

Minutes later Zac was standing in the street. Tall and handsome, the ease of him was like a blow. 'I do have your key. It's at my flat.' There was nothing else to do but drive there. He slid into the passenger seat, and we set off, up on to the Westway, past King's Cross. I could sense the weight of him, the lock of hair that fell across one eye. 'How's it been?' Careful, we swapped news of work, of friends fallen on either side of the divide, as we sailed down Essex Road.

His flat was small, as promised. One room. The bed tipped vertically into the wall. I stood in the doorway and took note. His familiar possessions. The dust in a gratifying layer. 'Got it!' The key was in amongst the contents of a box, attached to its red thread, the thread I'd wound for him from silk. We were halfway home when he pulled on a glove, black, and leather. He lifted an arm to admire it.

'So where's the motorbike?'

Zac laughed, hearty and for much too long. 'My Christmas present from …' The name formed, precious, on his lips. 'Yvette. I'm always borrowing hers, which is fair enough as she keeps stealing my jacket. Which fits her, well, obviously not quite …' Was this how love looked? Delirious. 'We're so alike. It's actually uncanny.' I glanced at him, his smiling mouth, the desire to mention her too strong to resist. 'Once, we were mistaken for twins.'

I pulled up in his mother's road. 'Bye, then,' I clipped. 'Sorry for the interruption to your day.'

There was a moment of hesitation. Was he going to lean in for a kiss? 'Happy Christmas,' he said instead, and he leapt from the car and, gloved hand raised, he loped across the road.

Laughter burst as I came up the stairs. I'd left my mother and Max dissecting a chocolate orange in the street, now they were sitting at the kitchen table with Bea, her feet up beside an open bottle of advocaat, Sally between them spooning peanut butter from a jar.

'Thank God!' Bea said. 'We need to know, when did the turkey go in? We've been basting it non-stop.'

'Twelve-thirty.' It was a quarter to six.

'Sally has made the most delicious stuffing.' My mother beamed.

'My pleasure.' Sally bobbed her head. 'It's so kind of you to have me.' Beside her was a stack of exquisitely wrapped gifts.

'What happened to *your* family?' I muttered as I retreated to the bedroom where I allowed myself three rasping sobs before rummaging through the cupboard. At the back I found the New York slip. Unworn, it lay nestled in its tissue. I scrawled Sally's name across the paper, and on my way back to the kitchen, I slung it under the tree.

We'd finished eating when the doorbell rang. Plates were piled in the sink. Wrapping lay scattered on the floor. No one moved. 'Who on earth …?' Mum said, and Max hissed, fierce, 'Shhh.' *Jurassic Park* was playing.

Slowly I walked down the stairs. 'Hello?'

There was a shuffle.

I swung open the door.

'Happy Christmas.' Clive had a bottle of brandy, its neck wrapped with a bow. He kissed me, and a distant shiver ran along one arm. 'Aren't you going to ask me up?'

Bea and Sally had bolstered the sofa with a quilt. They waved, remote. I took Clive into the kitchen and offered him turkey, but he poured himself a slug of brandy and drank it down. 'How's it been?' I asked. His parents were home from Hong Kong. The first time in five years.

'Excruciating.' He poured himself more.

Jurassic Park was still not finished when Bea sloped into the hall, stretching the telephone as far as it would go, murmuring, indistinct, while Sally gathered up the debris of the day and stuffed it into a black bag. 'Night,' she yawned, 'thank you for a lovely day,' and bundling up the duvet she retreated with Bea, only to reappear, thirty minutes later, to seize the bin bag and heave it into the street. 'Forgot,' she blushed.

Max's eyes never left the screen.

Clive leant towards me as the credits rolled. 'I could kill for a bath, would that be rude?'

'Of course, I mean, not at all.' I readied myself to rise, but he laid a hand on my head. 'I won't be long.'

It was the three of us then, eating chocolate, spooning up cold Christmas pudding. My spirits had revived with so much sugar, and we danced to Robert Gordon as we did the washing-up, 'My gal is red hot', while Max read out grotesque and record-breaking facts.

'I hope he hasn't drowned in there,' Mum observed when we sat down to watch a rerun Christmas special of Morecambe and Wise.

I traipsed along the hall and knocked, and when there was no answer I twisted the handle. The door swung open. 'Clive?' The bath was empty, but there, crouched on the toilet seat, was Sally, a syringe hanging from her arm. 'Sorry,' she mouthed. A spray of blood was flecked across the tiles, and with her best effort she reached across and tugged the needle out.

Silent, I backed away. I listened, and hearing nothing I pushed open Bea's door. She and Clive were on the bed, crouched over the bowl of a spoon. They jolted apart, turned – the same, pained expression of regret – and when no one spoke I retreated to the sitting room where I sat on the floor between my mother and Max. 'Bring me sunshine,' Eric and Ernie sang, their bow ties an echo of their smiles, arms akimbo, legs in the most casual of high kicks. I pressed my back against the broken beam of the sofa as the laughter rolled over me in waves.

III

I gripped the receiver, pressing it so hard against my ear it burned, while Marlene described in whispered gulps how Ian had pursued her with an axe.

'Where are you now?' I asked, assailed by the image of a poster for *The Shining*: Jack Nicholson leering, his victim screaming, his axe slicing through a door.

'At work.'

Of course. I recognised the echo of the bathroom. She'd been crying there when we first met. 'I packed a bag, but now I can't decide … should I go back?'

'You mustn't!'

'Or maybe could I stay with you?' And when I said she could, she went on to describe the bedroom window, the drainpipe she was sure would break as she escaped, while I imagined the relish Bea would take in my retelling, before remembering, we no longer spoke.

Marlene arrived soon after six. She was wearing a maroon polo neck and a mac in muted pink and even with her swollen nose, her red-rimmed eyes, she managed to look stylish. It had always been the case – however casually thrown on, everything she wore looked dazzling – and I had to stop myself reaching out to touch the cloth of her coat. 'What was Ian doing with an axe?' I shook myself and Marlene sighed, explaining how Ian liked to roam the streets of Kilburn to find old furniture, left out, to chop up for a fire.

I ran her a bath. Usually I'd stay while she stepped in, watching as her shoulders slid under the foam, but tonight I didn't trust myself to look away from the bruises on her arms and legs, the imprint of a fist, yellowing above her breast. I went to my old room – I slept in Bea's bed now – and lifted down a blanket, careful to avoid the laced-up shoes, still shined, amid the dust and hangers of the cupboard floor.

That summer I'd redecorated the flat. On first glance it appeared as sleek as a hotel, but as soon as you sat on the ruined sofa and felt the breeze through the warp of the French doors, the illusion crumbled – it was as dilapidated as before. I'd come to know my neighbours: the chauffeur, whose employer seemed never to go out, who spent his days polishing the car; and opposite, a moustachioed couple who roared in and out on matching motorbikes, who'd taken to waving if they saw me in the kitchen, who once said they'd been worried I looked sad. To my left the flat was empty, although bodyguards from the house acquired by the Crown Prince of Kuwait would use the garage, slipping surreptitiously in and out. The bodyguards worked in shifts, manning the mouth of the mews, twenty-four hours, seven days a week. At first we'd nodded, moving on to greetings – a short good morning, a hurried goodnight – until they'd taken to commenting on every aspect of my life. 'Cheer up,' they'd shout, whether I summoned a smile, or not, 'he wasn't worth it.' Anyone would think they'd witnessed Zac striding out on Christmas Eve, his belongings in a duffel bag while I stood, stricken, in the street. 'What do you expect,' they'd sigh, whoever I brought home, 'if you hitch up with a hopeless lot like that?'

I shook out the extra blanket and laid it on the bed, and I told Marlene she could stay however long she liked.

The next morning the bodyguards were waiting. They wanted to be introduced to my new friend. Marlene chatted easily, her hair tied back, a lilac scarf she'd uncoiled from her bag shimmering as it caught the light. 'We'd better go.' I had a day's work as a receptionist, and later, an audition for an advert for a biscuit. I hurried her round the crescent and up towards the Tube.

After the audition – my attempt to bring enthusiasm to *Jam and cream, share the dream* negligible – I walked through Berwick Street Market, wondering what I might give Marlene for supper. She had an endearingly sweet tooth, ate Milky Ways and Twixes instead of meals, and I wanted to surprise her. Loaded with shopping, I caught a bus on Piccadilly, but when I arrived home there was a message: Marlene was off out with friends. Stupidly disappointed, I stood by the phone, and when it rang I jumped.

'Bless you …' it was Marlene's mother '… for taking in my daughter.'

She talked for more than an hour.

I was in bed, embroidering a pillowcase, when the key turned in the lock. I heard the clack of Marlene's shoes coming up the stairs, the hurry of her in the hall. 'Hello!'

She was flushed from running, and I thought how I should warn her the cobbles bit into high heels.

'Your mum rang.' I tucked away my needle. 'Ian's been phoning, wanting to know where you are.'

Marlene steadied herself against the wall.

'It's all right.' I sat up. 'He'll never find you here.'

She smeared a palm across each eye, glanced, anxious, behind her.

'Sleep in with me.' I shifted over, and grateful, she peeled off her clothes.

'So ...' she wriggled '... where's this new boyfriend? Henry, is it?'

'Busy.' I yawned, breathing in her city scent, cigarettes and perfume, a sharp spice in her hair. The last person I wanted to think about was Henry. 'Night,' I said, and when she echoed, 'Night,' we laughed at the sound of our voices so close together on the pillow.

Within minutes she was asleep. Her breath sweet, her leg warm against my own. I turned on to my side and she moved too, the spring of her hair tickling. I lay, wakeful, wincing as I recalled the hurt on Henry's face. *I'll call*, I'd said, *when I've had time to think*. Was it a month already? Was it more?

Marlene was in the bathroom when I woke. I watched her through the open door, fresh as daisies in a yellow top, socks with one small pom-pom at the back, and I thought of her mother and how frantic she'd been when we spoke. 'Tonight,' I called as she swiped on mascara, 'let's meet up for a drink.'

'But where?' she said into the mirror.

It was a joke between us, the dangers of London. How, if she wasn't careful, there'd soon be nowhere safe to go. She refused to set foot in Maida Vale for fear of meeting her first love, and after two regrettable entanglements in Camden she had to skirt the Heath and travel down through Kentish Town. In Balham she'd been trapped by a man who'd turned psychotic after one last beer, and now, for reasons that were hazy, Cricklewood, the Angel, the Elephant and Castle were all out of bounds.

'Leicester Square?' I suggested. If nothing else, she'd be hiding in plain sight, and when Marlene agreed, I waved her off, and with nothing else to do, I got back into bed.

All morning I listened for the phone, hoping it might be my agent with news that the director who'd checked my availability for a touring production of *All's Well That Ends Well* needed me at once, but no one called, and restless, I ran over the places I avoided: Caledonian Road where Nathan was still rumoured to be living, the street in Stoke Newington where Zac had bought his flat. It wasn't often that I found myself in Battersea, but I dreaded passing the house where I'd last visited Ted. If only I'd gone back, if only I had stayed – it was a familiar loop – even though I knew I was a fool to imagine it was me that could have saved him. I got up and slipped into my old bedroom, and in an effort to shake away these thoughts, I opened the cupboard. Marlene's clothes hungneatly. I tried a cherry-red shirt, but it drooped shapeless, and the dress I'd coveted – polka dots in blue and white – looked drab.

It was late when the phone rang. 'They've asked me to stay on at work.'

'But that's … They can't make you, can they, without warning?'

Marlene sighed, resigned.

I got up to put a potato in the oven, and unable to think of anything else to do, poured a sachet of blue dye into a saucepan, and folding in a stained white skirt, I stirred it idly while it baked.

'One of the bodyguards is actually quite dishy,' Marlene whistled from the bottom of the stairs. I woke with a start. I'd fallen asleep on the sofa and a loose spring was jammed against my ribs. 'They've asked if we'd go out with them one night.'

I looked up to check this was a joke.

'Might be fun.' She put her head on one side. 'There's a quaint old pub not far, that's what they said.' I picked up the cold remainder of my food and scraped it into the bin. 'Seeing as I'm free and single.' She skipped through to the bathroom to get washed.

Marlene was warm and scented when she crawled into bed. She turned towards me, closing her eyes, her mouth a little open, lips bright as if with gloss. 'Night.' She snuggled down and a hand brushed against my hip. I swallowed, and I thought of Henry, and how conscientious he'd been in his efforts to please. 'We could marry next year,' he said after a fumbling afternoon, resulting, eventually, in success. 'Start trying for a baby, have our second the year after that.' He looked at me, our lives arranged, our family complete.

'We could.' I'd been trained for struggle, and I wasn't sure it was worth it, if it came as easily as that.

'Night.' Marlene's black lashes fluttered. She was sinking, her milk breath in my ear, and I imagined her fingers with their frosted nails trailing across my skin.

'Ian's stopped calling.' It was Marlene's mother.

'Isn't that a good thing?'

'What's he up to?'

'Maybe he's tormenting someone else?'

'I wish!' She blew her nose. I wondered if she'd seen the bruises, her daughter's fingers in a splint the time he bent them back.

I took a breath. 'She's safe with me. He couldn't …'

'Something's not right. I feel it. I feel it in my bones.'

Now, as I approached them, the bodyguards struck self-conscious poses, hands in pockets, shoulders back. 'Where's your friend?' they grinned, their mouths out of control.

I stopped, and they drew close. 'If anyone comes looking for her …' I described Ian, his sandy hair, his blameless face. 'Don't let him through.'

'Got it,' they touched the hoods of their parkas, 'leave it with us, boss,' and I thought how monotonous it must be, with the Crown Prince so rarely in residence, guarding the gold leaf of the railings three hundred and sixty-five days a year.

Marlene arrived home that night with flowers. Roses and chrysanthemums in a plastic sheath. I reached for them, ready with my thanks.

'Lovely, aren't they?' She held tight. 'A girl from work – Roxie. She didn't have to! I only covered for an hour.' She rolled her eyes to distract from my embarrassment, and I lifted down a vase.

We ate in front of the gas fire, toast with cheese and salami, and a bottle of white wine. 'Tell me.' Marlene sat cross-legged. Her socks were sparkly. They caught the flecks in her eyes. 'What's going on with Henry?'

I drained my glass. 'I'm just not …'

'He sounded perfect!'

'He was. He is.' I'd been hoping I might miss him.

She poured more wine and crawled closer. 'That cute bodyguard. Why don't we all go out?'

'No!'

'He can't be worse than … bloody hell, than Clive?' We lay on the carpet, swapping stories, eating biscuits, trailing back over our adventures, until Marlene began to reminisce as if she and Ian had been apart for years. 'He used to find me heart-shaped stones, paint our names on them …' She smiled, swoony.

'You'd never get together again, though, would you?'

Wine spurted from her nose. 'Are you mad?' She coughed so hard I had to thump her on the back.

That night I woke to find her arm around my waist. Her breath puffed in small hot gasps as her fingers grazed my breast. 'Sweet …' She pressed her mouth against my ear and I shifted in her arms. 'Babe …' Her lips were nuzzling, a hand dipping down between my legs. 'Ian … don't …'

I swallowed, and as slowly, as carefully as I could, I twisted away.

I stayed at home on Friday. I'd been offered work – three months maternity cover for a firm of accountants. They were giving me until six to confirm. I leant out of the kitchen window, strained my eyes along the mews. We were out of milk, but there were the bodyguards, smoking, shifting their weight from foot to foot. At five o'clock the phone rang. I sent up a prayer: *Let it be my agent.* It was Marlene. 'Don't get the wrong idea, but I've been invited away for the weekend.' There were other girls from the office going, they hadn't thought to ask her, not till now, because usually she was busy, with Ian. 'It's some sort of spa hotel.'

'Won't you need to come back here first?' I could see her washbag, the pear shape of her hairbrush, the lotion she smoothed on to her skin.

'Roxie will lend me what I need. Sorry!' She was gone.

That weekend I visited my father, walking across Hyde Park and down through Kensington Gardens to where he lived on the far side of Shepherd's Bush. 'How are you?' he appraised me, and I told him I'd heard nothing about the advert, or the tour. I started to cry. He waited, and when, inevitably, I stopped, he opened the fridge and lifted out a lobster. It was scalded orange, its pincers bound. He used his hands to break it open, a tumbler to smash apart a leg. 'Please,' he offered.

The more I ate, the hungrier I became – crushing claws, sucking juice, teasing out the sweet metallic flesh. When we'd finished, and there was nothing but the debris, he brought a bowl of water to the table, tossing in a slice of lemon, dipping in his hands. I dipped mine too, and we were scrabbling, sea creatures, determined, squeezing the last sharp grains of fruit. I pushed him to the side, he bolted back, and we were laughing, fighting, he for supremacy, me for my place in the world.

Afterwards he made a pot of tea, loose smoky leaves, and while it brewed I sifted through his records. Nina Simone. George Formby – which I played – singing along to our shared favourite, the story of a man waiting by a lamp post for the girl he most loved to appear. Why he waited, he was clear, and he wanted to inform us in his twangy, optimistic voice that the girl was … absolutely beautiful, and marvellous, and wonderful. My father joined in on the chorus. Anyone would understand the reason that he waited. Anyone could tell.

'How's Bea?' he asked.

The last I knew she was living back in London. I'd been in Soho when I'd seen her, walking along Gerrard Street, and too surprised to care we'd fallen out, I'd run to catch her up. She took my hand, excited as a child, and asked if I'd like to see her room. I would, I said, as long as I didn't have to share it, and laughing, she led me through a ribboned door, nodding to the man who sat in the booth, up the stairs to a room on the second floor. There was a bed and a wardrobe, a window that looked on to the street. The walls vibrated with the thud of bass and a dancing girl in neon flashed through the thin curtain, red, then white, then red. 'Is this … Does it mean you have to …?'

'Don't be an idiot. It's good, though, isn't it, to live right at the centre of it all?'

This wasn't my intention when I'd threatened to leave the mews. Said that I couldn't live there with her, even for a week a year. It was the day after Christmas and I hadn't slept. She'd looked at me, her eyes were blank. 'No one should have to live with me,' she'd agreed. She was going back to Italy. She didn't want a lift.

On our way out we met a girl who asked if we'd like to watch her act. The girl was pale, in court shoes and a leotard the same peach colour as her skin. We followed her to the basement where she slid a tape into the cassette, and when the music started she pranced and pirouetted, peeking out between her legs, rotating her pink tongue.

'Not sure.' I looked over at my father. A month had passed since then.

I continued to inspect each album. Fats Waller, Debbie Harry, Edith Piaf inscribed with a message from Marina. *Je ne regrette.* With the *ne* crossed out, and replaced with a smile. I traced each letter before moving on. My father had the newspapers spread over the table. He was, as ever, on the lookout for a word, an image, that might lead to inspiration, although his most lucrative invention had come from an idea supplied by Mum. It was a record player, portable, that fitted under the dashboard of a car, and although you had to change the 45s every three minutes, risking your life to do it, he'd succeeded in selling the patent to Chrysler.

'Anything hopeful?'

'Nope.' His best ideas came to him in the bath. A bath, he believed, had the power to shift your mood. Occasionally – he told me – he had five a day.

We drank tea, scooped peas from their pods, demolished a packet of vanilla wafers, and as it neared midnight we drove to Marble Arch. I leapt out as the Sunday papers were delivered in bound bales, buying him a copy of each issue, dashing through a downpour to where he waited, the engine running, sliding them across the seat. He dropped me home, stopping, at my insistence, on the corner of the mews, where he leant across and pressed his lips against my forehead, delicate and permanent as a stamp.

I was woken in the early hours by a crash. I jolted from my bed. A shadow loomed at the window. A jacket, flapping. A parka. Blue. I raced past, seized my keys, bolted down the stairs. I could alert the bodyguards, ask them if they'd spotted Ian. But what if it *was* the bodyguards? From the flat next door they had access to the roof. I slid behind the wheel of my car, kept my head down as I crawled through the arch. At first I circled the square. Then I edged on to Hyde Park Corner. Where to go? I drove up Piccadilly, turning on to Shaftesbury Avenue where a woman with a bag on her head did her best to flag me down. I parked on Wardour Street, ran towards the nightclub door. Light filtered through the strips of curtain, music rose up through a grille. 'Can I help you?' the man called from his booth. I backed away and looked up at the window. 'Bea!' A car slowed. I had to see her. There was a grid of bells. None of them said *Bea*. A man came hunching out. I called again. 'It's me.' Her room was dark. I looked round for a stone to throw, but there were only fag ends and one flattened sock. I retreated, turning every other step to check her window, the red light washing, flimsy, as the girl's legs flashed off and on.

Dawn was breaking as I crept up my stairs. I glanced into the kitchen. All was still. The sitting room was as I'd left it, Marlene's make-up spilling over the floor. I pressed my nose against the window, no splintering of wood, no shattered glass, and there in the gully was the maiden where I'd hung my skirt, the blue-dyed tangle of it, blown down from the roof.

I lay on the sofa, covered myself with my coat, and unable to sleep, I got up with the sun and drove to Brick Lane. The streets were quiet, the market stalls were only half set up. I rifled through a mound of curtains, floral, striped, fishing out a linen panel and a square of lace.

I bought bagels from the all-night bakery, cream cheese, the off-cuts of smoked salmon, and drove to my mother's. 'How's Bea?' she asked as she made tea, and when I didn't answer, she stayed staring out at the garden, waiting for the water to boil. Max devoured a bagel. Then another. He was dressed for battle in a helmet with horns. 'How does he find them?' I asked when he'd set off for Turnpike Lane.

'The dungeons and the dragons?' Mum didn't know. 'I'm just relieved that he has friends.'

It was a damp autumn day, and my mother lit a fire. She was hemming a skirt, red with a pattern of parrots, and as I sorted through her sewing box, stirring for buttons, she told me how she'd signed up for a dance camp in Devon. Could I move in for a few days and keep an eye on Max?

'If I'm not on a world tour,' I told her. She smiled, and tightening the thread, she snipped it with her teeth.

It was dark by the time I turned into the mews. 'You have a visitor,' a voice called as I slowed. I rolled down my window. 'Someone most eager to see you.'

Henry. My spirits quelled, but there was no apologetic shape lingering by the door. That's when I remembered – Bea still had her key. 'Thanks.' I bounced over the cobbles, braking inches from my neighbour's car.

A shadow moved across the window, light from the kitchen pooled into the street. 'Hello?' I slid my key into the lock, and looking up the slope of the stairs my eyes met Ian's.

'It's all right.' Marlene was beside him. 'It's not what you think.'

'She's been so upset,' Ian said, earnest, 'about deceiving you. She was on about it all weekend.'

'At the spa hotel?' I realised my mistake.

'We've talked things over.' She had hold of Ian's hand. 'We've decided it's best if I go home.'

'She's really sorry,' Ian added. 'She hates to lie.' They smiled at each other. 'Thanks so much for putting her up.' Down they came towards me.

'It meant the world.' Marlene enclosed me in a scented hug, clinging to me a second too long, before Ian took her hand and led her out into the mews. I stood and watched them, waiting until they reached the corner where the bodyguards raised the red tips of their cigarettes, called good luck as they turned into the street.

IV

We recognised the three of them as soon as we walked in.
Dark hair, light eyes, the wolfish shoulders of the eldest, the
dip of the youngest's chin. They were seated at the back
of the long bar, had pushed two tables together, gathered
enough chairs.

'Here goes.' I gripped Bea's arm.

They introduced themselves, although we knew their
names – Nick, Jamie, Peter. Knew it was the middle one,
Jamie, who worked in hospitality, who'd met a friend of
Bea's at the opening of a hotel.

'There's a boy who's saying he's our brother,' she'd called
me, and when I tried to interrupt, 'he's one of three.'

'Three what?'

'Three children.' There was a pause. 'All Dad's.'

Jamie went to the bar for drinks. I watched him as he
walked away. *It's usually the firstborn who looks most like the
father* – I'd read this somewhere – *it reassures the male the
child is his.* But in our family, like theirs, it was me who
looked like Dad, a useful deviation, much needed when my
mother's protestations had fallen on closed ears.

Nick and Peter, Bea and I, smiled at each other. It was too early for alcohol – we'd decided on the unthreatening choice of tea – but all the same, Jamie returned with a bottle of white wine.

'Not for me.' My sister put a hand over her glass. It was a year, more, since she'd been sober, but all the same I watched her, nervous as we drank it down. 'Did you ever … meet him?' she asked.

'Dad?'

What name were they supposed to use?

Jamie and Peter shook their heads, but Nick's face brightened. 'I saw him. He was wearing a dark coat. I woke up and I must have walked into the kitchen. There he was, backing out.'

We laughed, too fast. Nick frowned.

'No …' I tried. 'It's just … That sounds like him.'

'We probably *did* see him,' Peter explained. 'When we were small, before we moved.'

'Moved where?' I asked.

'The council, they offered us a house. Before that, we were …' Jamie looked to the others for support '… round the corner from wherever it is he lives.'

We were silent, and I thought of our mother appealing to the council to be housed, how the closest we'd come was sharing with an old man who lived on the estate above the village. His house was squat and comforting, a front garden planted with poached-egg plants, and in the back, behind the plank-board toilet, a gate that led on to a lane the locals called the Twitten. When he dies, I thought, we can have this house and every day an ice-cream van sent its spangled song across the close. But the old man didn't die. He sat in his chair, complaining he'd not received the plot of land he'd been promised for fighting in the war, complaining in the morning, complaining in the afternoon, until one evening he took hold of his stick and staggered up. 'I could jump high as the moon.' He made a lunge for our mother, and with nothing to defend herself except a glass of Ribena, she threw it over his head.

The next day we'd had to leave. We'd stayed with a woman who'd recently had twins. Her husband had moved out, but after a few months he moved back in. That was when Mum found Gorse Cottage. Three bedrooms and a garden on the edge of the Ashdown Forest. I still remembered what it cost. Five thousand, two hundred and fifty pounds. So much. Too much. Our father must have thought the same. No, he said. He couldn't stretch to that.

'What's he like?' Jamie was asking.

I looked to Bea. How could we explain our father? Fearsome, funny, the most dazzling, daring, ruthless boy at school. 'We didn't see him much when we were young. He isn't good with babies.' He'd told me once they frightened him. What if they needed something he couldn't provide?

'Why have so many?' Nick scowled. 'What is it? Thirty-four?'

'Don't be ridiculous.' Bea's offence did nothing to deter him.

'Sometimes I worry,' there was a vein of menace in his voice now, 'what if I meet one of my sisters in a nightclub, what if I don't know?'

There was silence. Jamie filled our glasses.

'For years we didn't see him,' I tried.

Peter looked bruised. 'But now you do.'

We'd failed to hide our luck.

'How about,' Bea cut in, 'we tell our life stories?'

The three heads were still.

'We could meet at weekends, take it in turns?'

I volunteered my flat. I'd recently moved, and although I was short on furniture, I'd painted the walls with tubes of Naples Yellow paint and hung curtains that I'd made myself, rough linen, scoured, and dyed in the bath – leaving a permanent blue rim. I'd patterned each panel with the leaves of the limes that overlooked the building, cutting out their shapes, stitching them, one by one, on to the cloth.

The following Saturday they arrived. I ran down to let them in and was struck again as they stood on the doorstep – a hip, a jaw – by their familiar shapes. I reached out to greet them, holding myself awkward as their hard boy bodies pressed momentarily against my own.

Nick, it was decided, should go first. We settled on the floor and watched him while he talked. His memory was both unreliable and detailed. He'd won a scholarship to an independent school, had learnt to ride, control a lab-induced explosion, recite *The Rime of the Ancient Mariner* by heart. Despite its excellence, he'd left without qualifications, embarking on an apprenticeship – for what he didn't say. He'd worked in the garment industry, on boats, as a welder. He was married now. His wife ran a company importing jute.

What about your mother? I wanted to ask, thinking how she must have overlapped with ours, but Bea had started on her turn. She described our travels – Spain, and then Morocco – the moves, the schools, the man our mother had moved in with when we were eight and ten. How he'd said no, Bea couldn't bring her cat, an outsized tabby, the only thing she loved. Right from the start, she said, he made it clear that we weren't welcome, that first Christmas when we'd been given stinky Afghan hats, while his daughter, Cora, got a bike. Bea's childhood was almost unrecognisable from my own. I'd loved that Christmas. The brandy leaping on the pudding, the tree so tall it brushed the roof, how we'd decorated it with roses made from tissue, apple rings threaded on to string. I'd worn my Afghan hat all winter, and through the one that followed. I might still have it if it hadn't been mislaid in the hurry when we left.

Bea didn't tell the brothers – as she'd never told me – why she'd turned her life around. Finding a therapist. Attending sixty meetings in as many days. Was it Daphne, who'd cut off all communication? Or Sally, who'd smuggled drugs into prison for a friend and been locked up herself? I'd arrived to meet our father at a restaurant, and found Bea there, beside him. No less pale, or thin, but calmer. Wise. 'No thanks,' she'd declined the wine he ordered, and when he pressed – 'It was never drink that was a problem, was it?' – she'd said from now on she'd be keeping her head clear.

'Are you insane?' Bea said when I explained about Jamaica.

'It's not just me and Jamie, there are others going, and anyway ...' I rolled up a sleeve to reveal the crease of my elbow, raw with eczema '... I need sun.'

The rain, when we arrived, was sleeting. *What will we do here for ten days?* I glanced at my brother. Was he really my brother? At his girlfriend, Lin, in pedal pushers and a pink cropped top. I leant forward to the driver. 'Does it rain here often?' Cheerful, he slammed a cassette into the player. 'One Love'. Bob Marley's voice rose up. 'It does.'

It was still raining when we reached the hotel. The manager was there to greet us, sleek and young, his name – Fleming – on a badge across his chest. 'Jamie.' He grappled him into an embrace, and I stared as they collided, squeezing shoulders, slapping backs, until I felt Lin's eyes on me as she untangled sunglasses from the highlights of her hair.

Fleming looked us over. 'While you are here ...' despite his youth, his whole, honed self was managerial '... everything is complimentary. Everything, that is, except the bar.' We turned and surveyed the bar which was in the middle of the garden, people gathered, drinking cocktails in great bowls of glasses, shielded from the rain by its rush roof.

Lin and I were shown to our rooms. Mine was sumptuous, a king-sized bed, an armchair upholstered in chintz. Could it only be a fortnight since I'd called my new-found brother to ask where might be cheap to go, for sun? I stared now at the dry backs of my hands and indulged in a frenzy of delicious scratching, catching at the edge of pain.

By the time I stepped on to the terrace the sky was blue. Guests lay on loungers, a speaker fluted jazz across the lawn. I walked through gardens to the beach. The sea was azure, minnows flitted in the shallows. I hitched up my dress and waded in, my toes sinking into sand, my tendons stretching, my head raised to the horizon, the sore backs of my knees ignored.

That night Fleming joined us for dinner. He sat beside Jamie, swapping anecdotes and jokes. 'What happened to the dreads?' Jamie cuffed his friend's shorn head, the kinked ends of his hair, oiled down. 'Hotel policy, they don't want me to be black,' he checked his manager's badge. I turned to Lin, asked about her family, her work, leaving no space for any questions she might have for me. I hadn't told either of my parents I was here. 'Going away with friends,' I'd said to Mum, and I'd told Dad the same.

'How are you finding our hotel?' It was Fleming.

I'd patted foundation across the rough skin of my cheeks, blotted it over the backs of my hands. 'Heaven.' I was safe in the soft light.

'It's what we aim for.' He flashed me a smile. 'Let me know if there's anything you need.'

'Are you flirting with my sister?' Jamie reached across the table for the wine. I'd reached out too, our bare arms brushing as the bottle tipped. I blushed, as he did. 'Sorry,' we reared away.

After that first meeting it was decided that Bea and I would tell our father – their father – about the existence of the sons.

'Three?' His eyes shot open.

'Nick, Jamie, Peter,' we recited. 'Their mother. Helen. She lived near.'

He nodded, neither in agreement nor dispute. 'Three of them?' He poured water, gulped it down. 'I did occasionally drop by.'

Out on the street relief sent us reeling. 'Three of them!' we repeated. 'Occasionally!' We laughed so hard it hurt. But he hadn't denied it. He hadn't denied them. All we had to do was arrange a time, a place, so they could meet.

On our second day at the hotel I found the beach was cordoned off. I was walking along the shoreline when I saw three boys on the far side of a fence, their knees tucked under their chins. One of them sprang up as I approached. 'I have nothing.' I showed my empty palms although they hadn't asked, and I thought, disgusted, of the juice, heavy with umbrellas, discarded by my plate. I turned back, turned again to see a man in uniform hurrying towards them with a stick. The smallest boy flipped into a cartwheel before all three scudded off across the sand.

I dropped my towel and walked into the sea. The sting was like a slicing. I held my breath, pushed forward, dipping under until the water closed over my head. When I emerged I peered back at the beach. There was a family, two children digging in the sand, and a couple, polished to mahogany, broiling in the sun. Lin was standing on the terrace steps. She wore a bright pink sundress and a hat to shade her face. I closed my eyes and floated, imagined myself drifting, washing up against an island, uninhabited, surviving on guava, spearing fish. I'd be happy there. I lay against the swell, and I pictured an explorer, falling for my missing, printed face, arriving on a boat to bring me home. *I have nothing to go home for.* I'd had enough of London. The diminishing auditions, Mum fearful when I caught her eye. 'What's wrong with Bea?' she'd ask — was it out of habit? — while I sat at her table, my body tensed, too cowardly to tell her that I knew: that Bea had told me. Soon after she got clean. How, when we were living off the coast of Spain, she'd been woken early by the sun. It was beating through the orange curtains, did I remember, they were striped? She'd crawled into our mother's bed but there was someone else there. Pauli. The man who chased us on the beach. He'd lifted her nightdress … If she'd relayed the details I'd wiped them from my mind. 'Stop it,' Mum had told him, and when he didn't stop, she'd looked away.

I snapped open my eyes. Lin was a bright speck, sitting upright. I lifted an arm to alert her but the current was too strong. Swim sideways from a rip tide, but what if there was no rip tide, I'd be wasting precious moments as I was swept away? Hard and fast, head down, I swam. Legs straining, arms arcing, sweeping away the water with each stroke. Gasping, I looked up. The beach was a stage set, its figures miniature. A desert island! I wouldn't survive a night.

By the time I reached the shore my limbs were rubbery. Goosebumps prickled on my arms and legs, and with a last effort I stood upright. 'Hey!' Lin was waving from her lounger. I dragged my feet across the sand.

'Do you swim professionally?' She patted the seat as I sank down, and I saw that just like yesterday, the sky was thickening with cloud. 'Or did you, as a kid?'

'Hardly.' It was Dad who'd taught me that first summer at Craigmont. It was a rare warm day and the others had thrown themselves into the lake while I'd lain kicking in the shallows. He'd taken pity, stripped off his clothes and waded in, placing his hands flat against my stomach, his touch so unfamiliar I'd used every ounce of strength to flip away. 'You're swimming!' Bea applauded, and too busy to answer, I'd beetled across the pond.

I asked Lin if she'd been to this hotel before.

'Hardly,' she smiled, and we sat side by side until the rain came pelting down.

———————

The next night Fleming stopped at our table. 'Anyone up for an adventure?'

'Why not?' Jamie squeezed Lin's shoulder.

'Yes,' I agreed, eager.

Our trip was to a waterfall. We clambered into a hotel van and ground out of the drive, down the hill, through green sweeps of vegetation, into the local town where market stalls were stacked with fruit and a stand sold saltfish fritters. I peered out of the window, hopeful, but we drove on, out and up through another swell of hills.

'I love your costume,' Lin said as I stepped out of my dress. It was a navy one-piece with a flounce around each cup, and I thanked her, sure all she was seeing were the raised welts on my arms and legs where I'd given in and scratched. Fleming and Jamie wore matching fuchsia shorts. They yanked off their T-shirts by the scruff and slung them on to the back seat.

The rumble of the waterfall made it unnecessary to talk. Jamie climbed ahead. He was taller than our father, his hair lighter, but I recognised his calves, the turn of his ankle, the twist of my own thumb. Lin was beside him in a white bikini. He tugged her up boulders, threatened to push her into gullies, and when she squealed he clasped her, undeniably tender.

Fleming's fingers at my elbow made me jump. 'Careful,' he said. I moved in against the rock.

At the top of the next steps was a pool. Fleming sprang on to the ledge above and dived. Jamie took a running leap, a bomb designed for the maximum splash, while Lin slid in, feet first. I glided, relishing the cold, ignoring Fleming's sleek dark body circling below.

We dried as we walked higher, the sun beating, the rush of water in our ears. A last scramble up sheer rock, the air was wet with spray, the river gushing at such speed it formed a cave. Fleming led the way. 'Tread slow,' he warned. Light scissored in as if through glass, the slate floor glinting, the rock face cool as I edged against the shelf. Jamie stepped in behind me, one foot so close we touched. The hairs on my arm stood upright. I quivered, and I felt him quiver in return. I took a breath, the scorch of our damp skin, and as the rock shelf tilted I thought how we'd been born six months apart, in the same West London hospital where my mother had laboured for two days, alone. 'I always wanted a sister,' he'd said that second Saturday when we'd swapped stories, and his eyes, so familiar, caught mine. I took a step. The walls were warping. The floor turned to sand.

'Keep back!' Fleming gripped my wrist.

Jamie took my other hand. He eased me in against the rock. 'You all right?'

'Yes,' I swallowed. Our fingers laced. We stayed there watching the waterfall until Lin complained that she was cold.

We were silent as we drove back across the island. We passed through the town, the tiers of mango, a woman ladling jerk chicken. Fleming kept his eyes ahead, and I thought of the warnings we'd been given – gun crime, dog bites, unaccompanied travel – when I'd enquired about leaving the hotel. Fleming drove in through the gate.

'Thanks, mate.' Jamie leapt out, and his arm clasped tightly round Lin's waist he hurried her away.

It was Nick our father met first. Bea went too on Dad's request. 'He's saying now he's qualified to fly a plane.' She sounded troubled when she rang. 'Could we have forgotten?'

I was there when he met the youngest brother, Peter, a DJ, his references hip hop and grime. 'I'm not certain …' Dad turned to me as we watched him strut away '… if it mightn't be too late.'

'No,' I protested. I knew from our life stories that Peter had been shy at school. That he could cook, and play the clarinet.

Supper with Jamie was delayed. First he was abroad, inspecting a ski resort, and then on his return our father developed ailments – a cough, a limp. It was months before we found a date. Bea and I tossed coins. 'Best of three. Heads, he's yours.'

'Heads it is.' She looked relieved.

I was nervous as we waited at the restaurant, but when Jamie entered – the same graceful movements, the dip of the chin – our father rose. 'Hello.' They spoke in unison, and through the meal every subject was covered, except one.

'That's that, then,' Dad exhaled when the last goodbye was voiced, and he kissed me, tender, on the forehead, slid into his car and sped away.

I was on a lounger, staring out to sea, when Lin passed, elegant in a sarong. 'That waterfall was treacherous.' She kept on walking. 'Jamie's lying down.'

I swam, and read my book. I walked to the end of the drive, looked left and right, wished that I could find my way to town, stride through the market, order fried plantain and a beer. My mother would have hitched a lift by now, my father would have summoned up a car. I retreated to my room. My cheeks had calmed, the flaking skin above my eyelids smoothed. I dressed in loose trousers and a vest, and after only the most cursory of scratches I went out to the bar. Music clunked from a cassette player – *Get up, stand up!* I ordered a rum cocktail, baulking at the price, insisting on passing over cash when the barman offered to put it on a tab.

'How you doing today?' A man was leaning up beside me.

'Great.'

'Nev,' he stretched out his hand, and when I introduced myself he wanted to know – was I enjoying his island?

'It's beautiful, not that I've seen much.' I asked if he knew of any transport, buses, or a tour. 'It's not that it's not nice at the hotel.' The rum was strong, and I took another sip. 'It's strange, that's all, to be … If I could find someone with a car …'

'You've found someone.' He was drinking a beer and he raised it.

'Really?'

We clinked glasses, made a plan to meet the day after tomorrow, at midday, on the road. I slid from my stool and skipped back to my room as the sky darkened and the rain came down.

I didn't mention my arrangement to the others. I didn't want to be asked what price I'd fixed, or even who Nev was, so I continued as before, swimming, reading, walking up and down the beach, swapping small talk. Avoiding the big subjects. Each night we sat at our usual table, and I made sure not to sit beside my brother, preferring Fleming, even when he slid his thigh against my own.

At five minutes to twelve I stood on the road. I had a hat, sunglasses, a bag with an orange in it, and my purse. A taxi slowed and the couple in the back, elegant in white, glanced curious in my direction as it turned into the hotel. 'I am allowed to leave,' I muttered. My heart was thumping. A battered car came into view. 'Get in, then,' Nev said, 'if you're coming.' There was a man in the back, and in the front a woman.

'Where is it you're wanting to go?'

'The town?'

He looked unimpressed.

'Montego Bay?' I should have brought a map. 'How about we visit ...' I glanced at the man beside me. Where was there? Who was there? 'Bob Marley.' There must be a shrine.

Nev released the brake and the car began to roll. We drove along the coast road, the sea stretching until it met the sky. With a screech we veered inland, climbing steeply into hills. The track was narrow, twisting blind round bends. I held tight to the door. What if a vehicle came racing down towards us? I tensed for the scrape of metal, the smash as we went up in flames. 'You all right back there?' Nev caught me in the mirror.

'Yes.' I swallowed so loud the gulp jumped in the car.

We climbed higher, the road uneven, the blue tips of the hills above. The woman, Cecile, was singing in the front. It was a song about a man who loved his food. Jackfruit. Callaloo. He'd bring it home to cook. The man beside me joined in, low. Cassava. Breadfruit. Nev was speeding, one hand on the wheel. 'Okra. Ackee.' We veered off into grassland. The ignition petered out and stopped. 'Nine Mile.'

I unpeeled myself stickily from the seat. The air was cooler here; the hills, red clay and gentle, formed a plateau. A wooden shack sat in a dip of green. There was a man standing on the step. He raised his hand, a reefer flaming. 'Welcome,' he said as he walked towards me wreathed in smoke. 'Terence.'

Terence was tall, and his sandals, bound with cloth, bounced him taller on their car-tyre soles. This place, he told me, was where Bob was born. Where he'd returned when his first child was born. He gestured for me to survey the view. The slope of treetops, the sweetness of the air. Butterflies flitted among flowers. Terence led me into the shack. There were two small rooms, one furnished with a narrow bed. It was where Bob lived with Mama Marley till he was thirteen.

'And the father?'

Terence kissed his lips. He sucked on the reefer and let the smoke coil into the room. Captain Marley had given nothing but his name.

Backing out, we looked again at the blue mountains, the roll of the hills, the scattering of goats. Birds were scrapping in a patch of earth. Terence began to sing 'Three Little Birds', and as if to order, a bird hopped on to the stoep. 'You hear them songs?' He cupped his ear.

I did hear them, the melody was sweet, and with my eyes open, and my ears, I followed him in an arc until we stood before Bob Marley's grave. Terence leant in close. 'Murdered.'

I jumped.

'In Miami. Murdered.' He said it again, rolling every 'r'.

Head down, I stood in contemplation as Terence told me how his hero was buried with his guitar, a football, a ring gifted by the son of the Emperor Haile Selassie, a stalk of ganga placed there by Rita, mother to four of his eleven children, and a Bible open at Psalm 23. 'The Lord is my shepherd,' he recited. 'I shall not want. He makes me lie down in green pastures, he leads me beside quiet waters. He restores my soul.' I thought of my nana and the solace of her faith, the letters she sent from Ireland, suggesting that I visit. 'I will dwell in the house of the Lord forever.' Tears streaked Terence's face. Then he turned to me. 'Do not be sad. Bob lives on here among us.'

We were quiet on the drive home. 'I thought Bob Marley died of cancer?' I said when we reached the safety of the main road.

'Cancer of one toe.' Cecile didn't turn. 'Why was he not saved?'

'Why?' The man beside me spoke for the first time.

Nev stopped beyond the hotel, and I paid the agreed amount, and more. Cecile, he explained, had taken time out from her busy day, as had her cousin in the back.

I hurried down the drive. It seemed I'd been away for years, but here all was the same. Jamie and Lin were at the bar. 'Join us,' Lin insisted. She was wearing a leopard-print bikini and her nose was pink with burn. They were drinking margaritas.

'What'll you have?' Jamie asked, glancing my way so briefly there was nothing but a blur.

'Same.'

The margarita fuelled me. The sweetness of it, the crisp of salt around the rim. Soon I was ordering another, fishing the last notes from my purse to buy a round. Lin too had sprung alive. She was talking about her job and how she hated it. She wasn't cut out, she said, for events. Next winter she'd go to Switzerland, find work as a chalet girl, ski the season, save up to travel to Japan. Jamie drained his drink. 'You could visit,' she tried, but we all knew he wouldn't.

'It's so weird.' She was on her third margarita. 'You two!' She looked from me to my brother. 'You're so alike, and sort of, at the same time ... not alike at all. Aren't you going to ...' She shrugged so violently she almost fell from her stool. 'I don't know ... talk or have a fight, or ...' She began to giggle.

I glanced at Jamie, and we were in my flat, that second Saturday as I took my turn. I'd recounted the travels and the moves, the three of us, together, me, Bea and Mum. I told them how I'd searched for a family with every job I'd done. How often I'd adopted one, only to find it more precarious than my own. I'd chosen men – I was starting to discover this – loved them in direct relation to how likely they were to leave. Accepted the subjects that were out of bounds. Children. Marriage. Home.

Nick had laughed. Peter too. 'Have fun, why don't you, while you're young.' Jamie remained silent.

I smiled at him now as Lin lit herself a cigarette. 'I don't know about you,' he looked away, 'but I think we'd better get something to eat.' We peered out from the shelter of the bar. The light had faded, the scratching of the crickets was a roar. I shivered. 'I'm getting this,' and I raked through my purse before Jamie could add it to his tab.

In my room I gulped water. I needed food, and a shower, but more than that to lie, for a moment, on the bed.

I was woken by a tapping on the door. My throat was dry, my head throbbing. I slid to the floor and felt my way across the room. 'Jamie?' I twisted the lock. *I'm sorry*, the words were in my mouth. I had tried to arrange another meeting but our father seemed always to be busy. Three of them? I saw his startled face. Was three too many? It was also true I'd given up.

Fleming stood in the dim light of the porch. 'We missed you at dinner.' He took a step inside, and I cast behind me at the mess of clothes, the cream I used to soothe my rash, the pots of foundation that acted as a shield. 'We hope you are still enjoying your stay at the hotel?'

'I am.'

'I hear you went off campus. You should be careful, a beautiful woman like you.'

'Do you show this concern for all your guests?'

'I don't.'

We looked at each other, and for a flicker of a moment I considered taking his hand, leading him through to the marble grandeur of the bathroom where I'd switch on the shower, watch as he unbuttoned his shirt, kick away his trousers and step in with me under the flow.

'Leaning over the ledge like that, you gave me a fright.' He looked so serious, I put out a hand to touch his badge. 'I could have lost my job. If you had slipped.' And as if I might be in danger he drew me in against his side.

———

On our last night there was a party. Lights were strung between the trees in a clearing by the river. Cecile sang from a small stage. Nev accompanied her on drums. Lin danced, her midriff bare, her fingers quick as flames, while Jamie sat watching her and drank. Fleming stood to attention, one eye on the proceedings, giving orders, directing staff; the other ready to catch mine.

'How lucky are we to know this man?' Jamie said the next morning when we met in the foyer. He took Fleming's hand and pumped it. 'He's saying now that *everything* is complimentary. It was a joke about the bar.'

Jamie hugged him and so did Lin, who said she wished that she'd drunk more.

'Thanks, Fleming.' His embrace was discreet.

'It was my pleasure.' He signalled to the doorman. Our bags were carried to the car.

On the plane I was directed to the back. It was how the seats were allocated. Jamie and Lin were near the front. 'It's fine,' I told them. There was a prospectus for a textile course at Camberwell I'd been carrying with me everywhere I went. I was flipping through it, imagining the liberation of never again having to audition, when Jamie was there, standing above me, looking down. Would this be the moment that we spoke?

'I don't know how you were brought up –' his face was pained '– but your behaviour, on this holiday … it was a disgrace.'

I opened my mouth and closed it.

'After all his generosity, could you not show some respect?'

'What? I …' We held each other's stare.

'Fleming. There's no excuse for not leaving him a tip. Even my mother, when I brought her out, managed a few pounds.' He turned and shouldered his way along the aisle.

I was still running over explanations when the loud-speaker crackled into life. 'This is your captain.' His voice was careful. 'There is no cause for alarm, but we'll be making an emergency landing, touching down at John F. Kennedy Airport as soon as we have clearance.' A rush of chatter rippled through the plane. 'I see smoke,' a woman shrilled. Noses were pressed to the windows. The *No Smoking* sign flashed on. 'We'll be landing in approximately fifteen minutes.' I stood up. An air steward pressed me down.

I didn't see Jamie until we were on the concourse. 'Wait!' I called to his disappearing back. If I'd known how to behave. If I'd known him. I flooded with the others out into the day where coaches were waiting to take us to a hotel. A bank of payphones ran along one wall. 'Zara?' I breathed. 'You are not going to believe it …!' We arranged to meet at the Happy Donut in an hour.

V

A mystic had set up shop on the Portobello Road. Bea discovered him when she went to buy a cactus. 'I see challenges,' he'd told her. 'Breakthroughs, and applause.' Three years into recovery, she was working as a stills photographer on a film. Bea resisted asking the mystic about love, and neither did he mention it. She didn't want to hear her relationship with the producer was a sham.

The next day I went in search of the mystic myself. Past the halal butcher and the launderette, the heel bar and the florist. He was sitting alone in the bow window of a house. He handed me a deck of Tarot cards, instructing me to shuffle. My fingers fumbled. What if I chose The Devil? What if I chose Death?

'You've changed direction.' We were gazing at the Ace of Pentacles, and I was as impressed as if I hadn't known I'd graduated from Camberwell, was selling my designs from a stall under the Westway. Next came the Two of Cups. 'A new, sustaining enterprise.' The third card was The Lovers.

'Am I going to meet someone?' I stared hard at the card. Two figures, naked, on either side of a divide.

'You already have.'

An image of Lex Maybury flashed into my mind, stooped in Nisha's kitchen, helping with the washing-up. 'I don't think so.' The mystic laughed as if to say: *What choices do we have?* I laid down three more cards.

When I'd paid, and I was halfway through the door, I remembered what I most wanted to ask. 'Is ...' My chest constricted. 'Will there ...' I seized my courage '... be a baby?'

He stood and reached for my hand, and like schoolgirls we faced each other as he inspected the side of my palm. The seconds passed. 'The line is faint,' he hesitated, 'but yes, I see a child.'

What if he'd seen the one I'd given up?

I walked back to my flat, and once inside, I lay down on the floor. Through the window stretched the branches of the trees, great knotted limes whose roots had woven their way beneath the building causing cracks to open in the walls, so wide in places I could prise in a finger, the littlest finger, the one below which sat the faint line of my child. After an hour I called Bea. 'I've met someone.'

'That was quick.' We'd spoken first thing, and I told her how the week before a man had arrived at Nisha's thirtieth, hair tousled, clothes ravished by moths. 'The kind of handsome you think no one has noticed?'

'They're the worst.'

'I know!'

I'd been so distracted by him I'd left the party early. Had taken the folding chairs I'd brought and stumbled with them down the stairs.

'Exciting, though.' She sounded wistful, and I hoped, against all odds, that the producer really was about to leave his wife.

For the next three weeks I thought idly about Lex Maybury, entertaining myself during discussions about the state of the building, nodding, serious, as the options were put forward: bore holes, piling, pollarding the trees. Maybe it was someone else the mystic had predicted? That friend of Zara's who'd sent a postcard after I'd kept him company on a tourist tour of London, suggesting I come out to New York so he could acquaint me with landmarks of his own? Hoping it wasn't the director of a play who said he wished I was the girl who'd removed her clothes in the last act.

And then I saw him. Lex Maybury. He was browsing through the market, stopping by a stall of world-war paraphernalia, helmets, jackets with RAF lapels. 'Which one do you think goes best with stripes?' I'd been attempting to sell a cushion to a woman unable to decide between the plain fabric and the patterned. I couldn't speak. Lex had captured all my attention. I knew now why I'd left the party early. No wonder I'd tried to put him from my mind. I suggested the plain, and forced it into a bag. When I looked up he'd gone.

'Can you mind the stall?' My neighbour sold handbags stitched from boiled wool, and I dashed away through the square of stands, round its perimeter and on to the road, searching the crowd, straining my eyes for a glimpse of his blue shirt. There were blue shirts everywhere. Of Lex there was no sign. Defeated, I walked back. I'd have to call Nisha, ask her for his number, and I regretted my insistence the whole of this last year, that I'd found the key to happiness: being on my own.

Lex was standing at my stall. 'It's you,' he said, and he stroked a strip of moss-green velvet that I'd dyed myself.

'Yes,' I agreed, idiotic, and we talked about the party, charting a trail of mutual friends, the hilarity of Nisha's engagement to Tavish, a man she'd been introduced to by her parents after a decade of refusing to countenance a single one of their suggestions. 'It could be nice to have family who considered it their job to supply husbands.' I flushed. Would he think I was desperate? I added that my own parents were too busy chasing love affairs of their own. Lex was laughing when we were interrupted by a couple fingering the fabric, asking questions about block printing and batik, and then, once they'd moved off, a girl who wished so loudly she could afford a pincushion, one of a dozen I'd embroidered, I almost gave her one so she would leave.

'I'll be going.' Lex backed away. 'I can see you're busy.'

The girl had tipped out her purse, and as she scrambled for the rolling coins, I watched him moving through the market, the nape of his neck, grooved and tender above the collar of his shirt.

'Excuse me?' My neighbour was smirking, and she asked if I could mind her wares while she went to inspect a rival stall of boiled wool.

The following week I walked to the end of Portobello Road and glanced through the window at the mystic, shuffling his cards, alone. He cut the deck, withdrew a card, and laid it down. The Fool, reversed. I hurried on to the haberdasher's, the proprietor hiding behind bolts of cotton, stubble layered with pancake, shoulders brawny as she reached for drapes of lace. There were squares of felt in every colour, tassels, buttons, zips. I bought a half metre of fake fur and two glass eyes. I'd make a bear for Zara's baby, due in a month's time.

I waited five more days before calling Nisha. 'Come for supper?' I suggested. 'Tavish too, and if he's free, maybe you might ...' She interrupted to ask if she could bring a friend, someone lonely, who needed cheering up.

The minute Lex Maybury stepped through my door I was lost. The pie crust singed, the potatoes were half-raw. The green beans I discovered the next morning in the fridge. We didn't speak. But he was everywhere. Filling my head. Clumsying my fingers. I watched as he examined the trestle I'd pushed into a corner, my mother's old Singer at one end, the electric sewing machine brought by my father at the other. I saw him glance at my books, my music, squint at the pencil lines that bridged the widest of the cracks, following one that snaked up a wall, bursting apart the plaster, travelling across the ceiling to the central light.

It was midnight when the others left. The air was close. The windows on to the canopy of trees flung wide. 'I'll get going too,' Lex risked a smile, and I walked him down the narrow stairs, along the hall. He lingered on the step.

'Lovely night.'

'It was.'

He reached out a hand. Warm with promise, it was better than a kiss, and when he squeezed my fingers a wealth of possibilities shot along my arm. 'I don't have your number,' he was looking at me, and when I told him, he repeated it, said he'd repeat it until the moment he reached home.

With everyone I'd been involved with, I'd known, from the start, how it would end. They'd leave me. Or I'd leave them. And I'd been right. With Lex my vision was obscured.

Three days passed in which he failed to ring. I worked, feverish, cutting lengths of linen, whirring seams on my machine. I set up a burner on the terrace off the landing and boiled them in a pot too big for the hob. 'Maybe he lives on the other side of London,' Bea said as we took turns to be the man at Rock'n'Roll with Ricky, the dance class we'd signed up for at the local gym. 'By the time he arrived he'd forgotten half your number. He's been calling combinations ever since. Now he's working overtime to pay the bill.'

'And twist,' Ricky called from the front.

It was early the next morning when the phone rang. I crawled from bed, pressed the receiver to my ear.

'It's me.' There was the lovely unexpected rattle of Lex Maybury's laugh, his shortened vowels, his voice with all its cadences and burrs. 'Sorry, I—'

'Let's meet,' I interrupted, and so we arranged it for that evening, a summer date enshrined into our calendar, celebrated for years to come, because although we'd met already, we both knew this was the start.

I was waiting when the bell rang, and I ran down to where he stood, formal, clutching flowers. 'Thank you.' I took them into my arms, and I led him up the stairs, his eyes – I could feel them – raking my neck, my hips, my ankles lifting out of heels. He followed as we pressed through the dividing door, realigning when we reached the kitchen where we turned and faced each other and smiled. We went to a film, sat, self-conscious, side by side, the story on the screen less vital than our own. Only afterwards did we begin to talk, marvelling at each connection, intrigued by the unknown. Like me he'd been raised almost entirely by his mother, his father dying early. Ill since he was small. He described the visits to his ward. How he'd be happy if he never set foot in a hospital again. How his mother was the glue. Coming, occasionally, unstuck. Alone, she'd raised four boys, all married with children now, except him.

'I'd like a child,' I said. We laughed. 'I don't mean now, but I wouldn't want to wait too long.' I waited. He was fine-skinned. Clear-eyed. No one in his family had been divorced.

'I've never thought about it,' and after another, longer pause: 'All right.'

We laughed. The ocean bellowed. I reached for his hand and he held tight.

That summer we hardly ventured out. We lay on the sofa, listening to favourite songs, discovering each other, unafraid of what we'd find. He worked as a lecturer at an East London university, was trying, had been trying, to turn his PhD into a book. Most nights he stayed with me. His own flat in Whitechapel was so crammed with books and papers it was hard to find a space to sit down. The table was a desk, the bed a table, the hall so narrowed by journals you had to twist sideways to slide in. 'How can you live like this?' I asked, admiring, and he looked around, surprised. 'Like what?'

Only when I had a commission to complete did we spend a day apart. That week there were curtains. I'd found a set of antique sheets in the market, scoured them, dyed them in the bath, hung them to dry from a contraption suspended from the railings of the terrace. The leaves I cut from the same cloth, dip-dyed a shade darker so that they floated against blue. I was up a ladder, testing them for light, when I heard the letter box rattle. There was a delivery I was expecting, and I ran down, but it wasn't hooks or loop rings, it was an envelope, my name in Lex's hand. I swooped for it, the scrape of his stubble fresh against my chin. *I love you, I love you, I love.* It was half an hour since he'd left.

'Is this it, then?' Bea flipped over the card. It was the end of the day and she'd come to help me hang the curtains from a pole, check the drop, the smooth line of each seam. 'Is he The One?'

The air was soupy, my bare feet sensuous against the ladder's rung.

'According to Mel –' Mel was Bea's therapist, and Bea was free with her advice '– we should be alert for patterns.'

'Patterns?'

'Make sure we're not just drawn to what's familiar.'

I shook my head and climbed.

'Unavailable.'

I took a step.

'Unfaithful.'

I ignored this. 'With Lex it feels different. Familiar. In a good way. As if it was meant.'

I looked down, expecting the dark roll of her eyes, but she was staring through the window at the people passing, the beaten pavements, the litter collected around each tree. The producer was in Sweden with his wife.

'Ready?'

Bea stepped on to a chair and as we hoisted, the room grew dim, the leaves floating on their panels, a flutter of the real leaves behind.

'Tea at mine?' she asked when the curtains were smoothed and folded and ready to be hung in their new home. Lex wouldn't be back until this evening. He'd ring the bell, and

I'd fly down, amuse him with the collision of our bodies, and later still – released, united – we'd set off on a walk, our steps aligned, the world a set, humanity all extras. This was our story, technicolour. There was no one else but us. Guiltily I picked up my key. 'Let's go.'

'What about America?' Bea asked when we were on the street.

On the urging of Zara's friend – the Postcard Man, as he'd been named – I'd booked some months before to fly to New York. Had I been curious, or simply obliging? Whatever else I'd meet Zara's baby. 'What about it?'

Bea arched her eyes. 'Will you still see him?'

'I'm not sure.'

'Not sure?'

'Maybe, one drink, so then I'll know.'

'I thought you did know?'

'I do!'

We ran across the road to where Bea lived, her floor strewn with photographs – the actress, beautiful in black and white; the producer, in full colour.

'Did you speak to Mum?'

'No.' She scooped up her cat, a snooty Persian with the sharpest claws.

'I just thought … her birthday?'

Bea tensed, defensive. 'I was working.'

'We went for supper. Lex came too.'

My sister ruffled down into a chair, a hungry bird ready to be fed. 'How was that?' Her cat eyed me, cool.

It hadn't been my intention to disparage our mother, but I needed currency with which to make up for my luck.

'She served us The Spaghetti. Watery as ever, although she did add olives as a special treat.'

Bea laughed and it was worth it.

'I bought her a swimming costume. Fifties, gorgeous – but it turns out she already has a swimming costume.' Maybe I did want to disparage her? 'Then she insisted on moulding it against her body, which reminded her that Cathleen had sent underwear – it's a tradition, the deprivations of boarding school, the greying knickers, the liberty bodice – which she then insisted on displaying, dancing them around …' I remembered Lex's face. 'All lacy and transparent.'

'Yuck,' Bea said, and I was overtaken by regret.

'Lex thought she was great.' There was a sour taste in my mouth. 'She is great. You know she's learning Spanish?'

Bea wasn't interested in Spanish, and instead she passed me, one by one, the series of pictures she'd embarked on, children from every corner of the world, Jamaica, Portugal, Morocco, growing up in this West London borough. When I'd looked at the last – a dark-eyed girl, defiant – she pressed a cassette into the machine and clearing the floor of prints she turned the volume up. Al Green, vowing that we'd stay together, whether times were good or bad, happy or sad. We sang along, our voices rising, schoolkids on the street below yelling at the window. 'Throw down a key!' We clutched each other's hands, we'd stay together, whether, whether, and she spun me round so fast I slipped from her grasp and, laughing, thumped against the wall.

That night, when I told Lex about America, he froze. Even when I said I'd arranged the trip before we met, even when I pressed myself against him, kissed his forehead and his eyes, he stayed cool as clay. 'You can catch up on your work,' I tried, 'you've been saying you need time to write your book …'

'True,' he agreed dully, and we lay together searching for sleep; a crack, as wide as the one that snaked across the wall, running between us down the middle of the bed.

Day 1. New York.

I'm on the downtown subway, writing this for you. From 110th to 18th I miss you, Lex. I'm thinking about you. I'm talking to you, can you hear?

Last night I stayed up late with Zara. The baby's sweet, and sleeps a lot, but Zara is exhausted. They've called him Mackenzie! 'How hard can it be, hey Mom?' she said while she was feeding him, and she asked if I thought he was unusually ugly, you know, for a baby? He's three weeks old and Zara's mother hasn't visited. Then I remembered the wedding which she was too busy to attend, although Zara's stepmother was there, griping about the weather – it was November, freakishly hot – and she'd bought a wool suit. 'At least you can wear it at Thanksgiving.' I was trying to be helpful, but she accused me of being A Little Pollyanna. It was a strange wedding. Or are weddings always strange? There's not much history of marriage in my family. My father was done with it before I was born. My mother hasn't tried it. Yet. Which reminds me, the night after Zara's wedding we went out to eat, and a conversation started about love. 'What even is love?' Mackenzie said – inappropriate! – and Zara, thin as a reed (not so now), her black hair tamed (ditto), asked if he was fucking joking?

Day 2. New York.

I tried calling. Did you get my message? Well, here I am on the subway again. I'm going for lunch with Cora (stepsister, keep up!), who's working on 5th Avenue, in some fancy office. Tomorrow I'm off to the country to stay with Ruth — I played her as a child — where I hope to hear your voice on the phone. I woke this morning early, thinking, thinking about you.

Last night Mackenzie (Senior) took me and Zara and the baby to eat lobster (it came with baked potato!). Mackenzie's in trouble at work. He took the day off to go bungee jumping at a place called Action Park where you queue for over an hour to go on death-defying forty-second rides. One ride was closed for ten minutes because someone fell off and broke their neck. Zara said he was also in trouble with her. That's no way for a father to behave. Really it's because she's tired. Mackenzie's hardly ever home, and though Mackenzie Junior spends the whole day sleeping, looking after him still seems to be a full-time job. 'How hard can it be, Mom?' she said again. Then she whispered: 'Hope he gets a bit more ... you know ... handsome.' Which made us laugh so hard the baby actually woke up.

Christ. A girl has boarded the train and announced she has the AIDS virus. She's holding out a hat and asking for money. I gave her a dollar and she wished me a good day.

Day 3. Upstate.

I don't know what I'm doing here. Although I also know Day Three is when you wonder what you are doing wherever you are — when you realise there's a lot to be said for being at home, for having your things around you, and the people you like (love). Earlier I was sitting by the pool when I heard the phone ring in the house. I leapt up, but it wasn't you. Are you getting my messages? It would be good to hear your voice. Every time I've tried you the answerphone picks up. Now I've decided you will ring, today, at 6 p.m. Please ring at 6 p.m.

Last night I dreamt about snow. Bea and I were sledging. We must have brought our wooden sledge with us from Sussex — and we dragged it to the top of the hill. She sat at the front (have you met my sister?) and I squeezed on to the back, and down we went, lifting, flying, we could see people fallen below us, and we were singing our song, the one from Jesus Christ Superstar, *about how much we hate each other, when we crashed into a snow bank. I dragged her up, pulling so hard a glove slipped off, and there they were, fresh cuts across her wrist.*

I guess the dream wasn't about snow.

Day 5. Upstate.

Yesterday, as predicted, was good. I didn't even need to write. We swam, then we went bowling. I won seven dollars at Zilch. I may buy you a present. I hope you're all right. I called Nisha and she said she'd seen you, and you were looking … quiet. I hope that's because you miss me? I've decided … I'm not going to keep calling, or listening for the phone. Ha! The phone just rang and my heart leapt. I hope you know how much I like you. Do you?

Day 9. Shelter Island.

It's early, and I'm sitting on the porch of a white plank-board house drinking tea and staring out across the lawn, past an oak tree, over the creek and across to a wooded slope on the far side. It's a house Mackenzie's family have rented every summer since he was a child. Tomorrow is the first day of September and in another month everything here will be blazing with shades of orange and red. But am I thinking about that? No. I'm worrying about the fact you haven't called. Did you get knocked down by a bus? Meet someone else? I'm also thinking, and maybe I should have considered this before, to what extent is a person capable of cruelty?

Sorry. I'm letting thoughts run riot. For all I know, you did ring, and we were rowing back across the creek. Row faster, I was willing Mackenzie. I felt sick at the thought of missing you – but when the phone did ring, it was my father saying he couldn't wait till I got home. 'I'm longing to see you' (he hates anyone to be away). 'I'm longing to see you too,' I said, and then rather hurriedly we put down the phone. We're not used to exclamations of affection, but London for him is the safest place to be, which it was of course when he arrived. He's hardly left since. Afterwards I had a thought: catching hold of my father's love is the biggest achievement of my life.

Now I am trying to imagine how you feel with your father ... without a father? Is there a chasm, a freedom? You don't behave like anybody's son. Maybe there's a shift – you become responsible – is that what it is?

Day 10. Shelter Island.

Tomorrow I'm leaving for New York. Then home. Tonight there's a party. There's always a party, and each party is full of girls with breast reconstructions and international accents and several marriages behind them. The day after I leave Al Pacino arrives! 'Change your flight,' they're all saying. 'Stay.' They don't know why I'm in such a hurry to get home. Mackenzie, who is 6 foot 3, is under strict instructions not to stand anywhere near Pacino in case it draws attention to his height. He wasn't allowed to talk to Paul Simon who was at a supper in Sag Harbor last year.

But as you know I approve of tall men.

I wonder … are you going to meet me at the airport? Or will that set a dangerous precedent (see When H met S*)? I'm arriving early. I'll be dishevelled from the plane, so if you're not there, maybe it's for the best.*

England was warm, and grey. Lex's car, also grey, had a dent in the passenger door, and the sandwich wrappers collecting in the footwell had been tossed into the back. We kissed as I came through the gate, our limbs self-conscious, our hair grown. Ten days. We'd have to start again. 'Why did you never call?' I asked as we drove towards my flat, and he turned to look at me. Tears, unexpected, filled his eyes. 'I guess I'm not good with … desertion.'

'Desertion!'

'You'll think I'm an imbecile, I couldn't get it out of my head – what if me and you, if none of it was real?' He took my hand, abandoning the gears. 'I should warn you, I do have a habit of messing things up.'

'Just you try.' I leant across and kissed him, and it was only when the car behind us hooted that we drew apart.

It was carnival the week before and my street had a rocked and empty look. Beer spills and urine stains, the heat of floats and feet. The air was ash, the asphalt steamed. Inside, the rooms were stuffy, and below the window, on the carpet, was the round black burn of a pan. *Sorry.* Max had left a note. *Popcorn.* I'd given him a key.

The answerphone was blinking. I determined to ignore it but the lure of its red light was impossible to resist. There was a message from the director of the play in which the actress had removed her clothes. There'd been an incident.

Could I take over for the last week of the run? Then a further message, desperate. And one more: he'd found another girl.

There was a query about upholstery. An order for three cushions. An invitation to take a stand at a hand sale at the Unitarian Chapel before Christmas.

'Are you still not back?' Bea sounded cross. 'You've been gone, literally, for yonks. And obviously I want to know, did you meet up with—'

I pressed erase.

I ran a bath and we climbed in. Lex's legs tilting sideways to make room for mine; his feet, high-arched, propped beside the taps. My body had been striped by my bikini: breasts, egg white, breaking the surface; the tanned skin of my stomach submerged. We grinned from either end, detailing the events of each missed day, how Lex had buried himself in work, and afterwards, draped in our towels, we kissed, damp, kneeling together on the bed while he reached for protection. Deft, he slipped a Durex from its foil, his erection comical – Punch with his truncheon – and to stop myself from giggling I eased my hand over the sheath, followed his own until our fingers met.

'Lex,' I asked, as we lay quiet. 'Have you ever had a test?'

He rolled towards me.

'For AIDS?' The capitals blared, however softly they were spoken.

He shook his head, but his arm, below my shoulder, tensed.

'I was thinking, if we both had one, then we wouldn't …' Was the inference that from then on we'd stay faithful? 'We wouldn't have to keep using … I know you'd prefer …' The puddle of the condom lay beside us on the floor.

Lex lay still. His last girlfriend was from Edinburgh, and Edinburgh, as everybody knew, was the AIDS capital of Europe. 'We could.' He ran cool fingers down my spine. 'Why not?' There was a clinic at his university. He'd go in, as soon as he had time.

'I'll find a place and do the same.' We agreed not to mention it again until it was done.

My clinic was on Charlotte Street. Nurses, no-nonsense, in a corridor of booths. I turned away as blood was taken, kept my eyes lowered as I waited for an appointment to return for the results in ten days' time. Travelling home, everything looked new. The shopfronts shone, the rooftops glittered, women sashayed in bare-legged liberation, their feet strappy in high heels. I walked through the park. Dogs raced, smiling. I took off my own shoes and ran. But as the days passed, my mood began to falter. The weather darkened. Gusts shook the branches of the limes, and another crack appeared above the window, so wide that brick dust trickled through. A surveyor arrived to take new measurements, adjusting the numbers, refusing to be drawn on whether or not I'd have to leave.

The first time I'd heard of AIDS I'd been sitting on the college steps with Nisha. We'd been whispering about herpes, horrifying each other with the facts – 'it never goes!' – when Roland, from the year above, who'd discovered the paradise of Hampstead Heath, bussing up there every night for sex, warned there was another, newer virus. 'If you catch it,' he was pale, 'you're dead.'

Eight years later we all knew people who'd died. Roland himself, and a boy from third year, the star of his term. Sally, who'd contracted HIV in prison, whose family insisted it was pneumonia till the end. I closed my eyes and saw her slumped on the toilet, the spray of blood across the tiles. I'd wiped the wall with a dishcloth. Had I washed my hands? I dared myself to think how Bea had put herself at risk.

On the fifth day I walked round to her flat.

'You'll be all right,' she said. I lay on her floor, and she lay beside me.

'What about you?'

'I'd know by now.'

'But don't you, wouldn't it be—'

'I'm fine,' she snapped.

Conversation shifted to the producer who'd invited Bea to meet him in LA. 'Maybe say no?' I counselled, but I was her younger sister and she wasn't in the habit of listening to anything I had to say. She skipped upstairs to pack. I followed and hunched down on the bed. 'What if the news is bad, and you're not here?'

'Don't be an idiot.' She held up a dress for my approval. I hesitated, and she threw it into her case.

By the end of the week I was certain I'd been cursed. The man who walked, ticking, down my street barked as I edged past: 'I'm sane as you.' The boy whose spiderweb tattoo covered half his face pinned me with an eye.

'Period pains,' I excused myself from Lex. Then I had the flu. On the tenth day I travelled into the West End. Head bent against the rain, I saw holes in the hem of my wool coat, which reminded me Lex had left a sweater on the bedroom floor, and as I'd bent to pick it up I'd found a patch more than a foot wide where the carpet had been devoured by moths. What did it matter? I held my umbrella like a shield.

I arrived at the clinic early, and sat beside a woman, a child on her knee. No one spoke. Even the child was silent. I slid a notebook from my bag, attempted a sketch, but the lines blurred, and when I looked up there was a pool of wet below my chair. I glanced at my neighbour. Did she imagine that I'd lost control? I was edging away from the incriminating drip of the umbrella when my number was called. I stood and moved towards a booth. The nurse was male. He looked at me, unsure. 'The test came back …' he glanced at the slip of paper '… negative.'

I waited.

He rearranged his notes. 'Anything else I can help you with today?'

I shook my head. 'Thank you,' and not glancing at the others, I stumbled back along the corridor, pushing my way into the street where I stood, arms stretched, face bare against the downpour.

As soon as I was home I called.

'Lex Maybury speaking?'

'I'm negative.'

There was a pause. 'Not always …'

'The test!' I told him. 'I'm clear.'

'That was quick.'

The endlessness of those ten days. 'Are you saying that you …?' We'd have to wait another ten. 'Book yours, now, and while you're at it, call pest control, the moths, they're …'

'Sex control?

We were laughing. Nothing mattered. I was negative. The chances were that he'd be negative too. 'Call them!' The future lifted like a barn. 'And stop pretending to be a grown-up – "Lex Maybury speaking" – and get over here as soon as you can.'

'I'm on my way.' Once again, and not for the last time, we began.

PART THREE

I

The Lookout was perched above the sea, a wooden house, a tower at the top. I'd found it while driving with Lex along the Norfolk coast, stopping at Blakeney for crab sandwiches, racing each other across the sands of Holkham Bay. I'd taken down the number, rain-lashed within its sheet of laminated card, and booked it for the following July. By then Lex was in America launching his finally published PhD, and I was heading east, with Bea.

'He's left her!' she said as we swung out of my road. After all these years the producer was separating from his wife, and high on good fortune we talked about the future: the script Bea was writing; how I'd organise my work around a baby; when, and how, we'd reconnect with Mum. Nauseous (me) and nibbling at crackers, we dissected the reasons for our rifts. The trouble had started with an interview. My designs were to be featured in the Simone Xa Home collection. Bea had an exhibition of her prints. 'Coming Up', the article was titled, and in order for there to be a story, it had emphasised how far we'd been … down. 'I never felt safe.' A quote from Bea was highlighted below an image of the two of us as children, eyes round, our partings scrappy, and although my only crime was in describing the regularity with which we moved, our mother was incensed. 'Write and tell them it's not true. You were safe.' It wasn't Bea she called – Bea, she knew, would slam her down, and much as I explained it could only make things worse, she became increasingly distressed – convinced that everyone was whispering – that all around were sneers. 'Why didn't you ask to read the article,' her calls came late at night, 'before you volunteered that photo?' And when we met she cried so hard her eyelids swelled, and her hands, so capable, hung, old. I'd tried my best to soothe her, pressed my cheek against the salt side of her face, stroked her arm, tracing the veins – so known – that ran below the skin. But she couldn't be consoled. She even had a letter from her parents: *the two of us, we should be ashamed, washing out our dirty linen* ... Finally – if she could smile – they'd come out in her support.

It was Bea who encouraged me to make the break. 'There's only so much you can take.' Hollowed out, and guilty, I was struggling to sleep. If I'd refused to take part in the interview. If everything had stayed as it was. Then Bea made a break herself. At first I was alarmed. She'd done it, and now I never could. But Bea had been in hospital – a lump was discovered in her breast, and although it was almost certainly benign, it had to be removed. Hostilities abandoned, our mother offered to collect her, bring her home. 'I was so pleased!' Bea's voice sang girlish down the phone, and my hope, ever present, leapt over battle lines, kicked a ball across the scarred and pitted earth. The day after the operation Mum failed to arrive. Bea waited, in a corridor, on a plastic chair, and when a nurse passed – 'You still here, love?' – she made her own way home.

It was evening when her bell rang. Weary, my sister traipsed down to the front door, and I listened, heavy-hearted, as she described how neither of them spoke. Bea, her thin arms crossed; Mum, whose face I knew better than my own, loved more painfully than anyone I'd ever known, clutching a spray of flowers to her chest. 'Sorry to be late,' she gave in, and when Bea didn't comment she suggested coming back tomorrow. 'No,' Bea shook her head, 'I'm better on my own.'

Our mother turned, the flowers wilting, and I followed as I always would, as she walked away along the street.

I clung on for another year, sitting at her kitchen table, my chest so tight I had to take my breath in sips. 'I wasn't such a terrible mother, was I? At least I didn't send you away to boarding school aged four.'

'You weren't!' I assured her, but her shoulders heaved.

'So write to them,' she pleaded. 'Issue a statement.' We were back where we'd started, and I'd arrive home worrying about Max, who'd taken to locking himself in his room on the pretext of revising for the resits of his A levels, and collapse, despairing, into Lex's arms.

One night as I lay sleepless, I saw that I would have to write. Not to the papers, but to her. I climbed from my bed, and before I lost the courage, I crept downstairs. *Dear Mum, I think it would be best, for a while at least, if we don't ...* I bit my pen ... *if we don't meet.*

'Christ!' Lex said, a month later when I told him I was pregnant. He sank into a chair. 'I'm not sure I'll know ... that I'll be ...' I stood before him, waiting, and when it was clear he had nothing else to add, I filled a glass with brandy and watched him as he drank.

———

The Lookout was much as I'd remembered. Boards weathered silver, metal windows, green and flaked. Inside, the rooms were striped with light, the furniture worn to comfort, rich with woodsmoke, smelling only faintly of damp. There were puzzles in boxes, a pack of cards, Cluedo with half the implements for murder missing. In the kitchen was a folder. How to read the meter. When to take the bin down to the lane. There were numbers listed in the event of an emergency: plumber, electrician, doctor. Guests had scrawled their comments at the back. *Magical spot. Trrfic holiday. Can someone please strangle next door's effing cock?*

We chose our bedrooms. Mine had a rush mat on the floor, and gave off the sweet, warm scent of hay. Bea's was mannish with a dark-wood chest of drawers. Across the landing was a room with bunks, a teddy peeking from between the pillows. A ladder led up to the tower. It was where I'd hoped to sleep with Lex, three walls of windows open to the sky. 'We can work here,' Bea said. There was a table with a chair at either end, and although we agreed we'd start tomorrow she laid out her papers and her pen.

'When are you thinking you'll tell Mum?' Bea asked as we walked along the estuary. There was a harbour dotted with boats, and beyond, a plank-board path that stretched through scrubland to the sea.

'I'm going to try and wait …' I crossed my fingers back and forth to counteract a jinx '… until I'm at twelve weeks.' In two days I'd reach nine.

Bea stretched. 'What bliss to get away.'

I looked up at the sky, the whole wide bowl of it, unbroken blue.

She didn't look at me. 'I mean from Mum.'

'Are you saying I should wait?'

She shrugged.

'What if someone sees me?'

'Like who?'

Had she forgotten I'd moved near? 'I'd hate it if she heard the news from someone else.'

Bea narrowed her eyes in the direction of my stomach. When, I wondered, would I start to show? 'It feels cruel, that's all ...' History, it seemed, was predestined to repeat itself, and I thought how Mum had kept her own pregnancies to herself. How Nana and Grandpa might still not know if that relative hadn't spotted her in London with two children. 'She didn't have a choice,' I mounted my defence. 'A teenager, unmarried ... who knows what could have happened – to us, to her.'

Bea said nothing, but I couldn't let it go. 'She's tried so hard ...'

'But has she ...?'

'If Dad had helped.' I was assailed by the vision of Gorse Cottage. Three bedrooms and a garden. A view over the forest. Five thousand, two hundred and fifty pounds. A fraction of the money he'd received from the record player our mother had dreamed up.

Bea stiffened. I could see it in her back. 'Dad had debts. He still has debts.'

It was the tug of war we played, attempting to drag the other over to our point of view.

A gull swooped low, squawking as it circled round. Bea and I walked on in silence, past a boatyard, a chart pasted to its door, and down on to the quay from where the ferry set off for an island when the tide was high.

'You might need longer,' Bea said. 'Is all I meant.'

'You're right,' I conceded. It was easier that way. 'I might.'

The next morning, after Bea had spent an hour on the phone – it was hard to ignore the gasps of outrage at whatever indecency the producer was subjected to by his wife – we climbed, single file, to the tower. Bea's script was inspired by a girl she'd seen in Florence who lured cats back to her hotel. 'I'm giving her our childhood,' she warned as her pen rushed over paper, her arms forming a cradle around which it was impossible to see. I laid out my pad, my paints and brushes, a sharpener, three pencils, a pen. I was late with a design for Simone Xa and I inspected a stalk of samphire, knotted at the joints, as my thoughts leapt back in time. Mum, hauling two babies up and down the stairs, estranged from family, our father's interest waning, turning her back on the inhospitable city she'd arrived in at sixteen, setting off for Wales, for Scotland, and later, stifled by the prejudice of Britain, for Spain, and Morocco. My heart squeezed as I remembered her chopping vegetables for soup, reading nightly from the same three tattered books, stitching dolls from scraps of wool found in the alleys of the souk. I sketched a sea pea, its petals fuchsia, tried a hollyhock, fallen on the path by the back door, but all I saw was the four o'clock flower opening in the court-yard of the hotel in the Medina where our neighbour, a woman who lived on the same landing, stole Mum's trousers, the ones she'd made herself. I glanced across at Bea. We'd played hopscotch in that courtyard, caught lizards by the tails, run screaming at the rumour of a scorpion, eaten curls of pastry, the syrup leaking, orange, down our arms. Why did she never ask me for my memories? I still had my kaftan, shortened at the hem, and hers, in swirls of blue and green, folded in a plastic bag. I had her schoolbook, and a twist of braid, three Arabic coins with which our mother threw the lines of the I Ching.

I stared through the windows, down the length of the garden, out over the harbour, past the skiffs to where the ferry was banked against the quay. Was it the mule she was remembering? The one who shifted rubble by the gate? We'd stroke its dusty, gritted coat, suffer the back break of its work. I dismantled a poppy, made a frilly ineffectual sketch.

'Lunch?' I suggested. Bea blinked as she came up for air.

Each afternoon Bea unrolled a mat and pushed up into downward dog, twisting sideways into warrior, flinging her legs against a wall where she maintained a headstand for the time it took to leaf through *Family Knitting*, a manual from the seventies I'd found on a shelf. 'Apparently it calms you,' her smile quivered, 'the more time you spend upside down.' I chose a cardigan modelled by a baby with a tuft of duck-blonde hair. Was it dangerous to start knitting? If it was, I'd wait.

'It must be nice to be so sure,' Bea said as we walked across the marsh. I'd never known her mention children. Never heard her offer up a list of names as I had: Heloise, Isolde, and later, more prosaic, Sam.

'Might you, one day?'

'No.' She shook her head.

I'd been given a doll when I was eight, life-size, with eyes that opened when you picked her up. I'd bathed her, and dressed her, amassing a collection of smocked frocks and crochet jackets bought at the local jumble sale where I'd tunnel my way between the bodies of the mothers and snatch items from under their slow hands. I'd thrown her over, the moment I saw Max. 'Ideally, I'd like three.'

'And Lex?'

'He'd prefer to see how we get on with …' Was his fear that once we had a child he'd descend into illness like his father? None. I shook away the thought. 'With one.'

Neither of us mentioned the producer, who already had four girls.

'I don't think I'd be any good,' Bea shrugged. 'Sometimes I don't even like my cat.'

'Your cat's a brute.' I took her arm. 'Whereas your baby, it will be the best.'

The next morning I sat and stared through the window while Bea read her script, scrawling comments, dashing off the occasional red NO! She didn't look up when I sidled from the tower, searching the back borders of the garden: cow parsley and borage, a fig, its fruit as hard as nuts. There was an iron roller abandoned on the slope, the V of its handle resting in the grass. I imagined it levelling some formal lawn. I lifted the handle and tugged. Its wheels creaked, its belly wheezing, rusty. It was heavy as a log.

I found a clump of daisies by the gate, but as I bent to pick one I saw the slash of Bea's red pen. Predictable. I straightened up. I took the path that ran beside the harbour, past boats, bobbing upright, others rotted, tipped sideways into mud. A woman approached, a child on her hip. She smiled, indulgent. Could she tell? I laid a hand across my stomach. Of course not! I walked on.

When I arrived back at the house, the car was gone.

Supplies x

'What the …?' I stared at the note, and gripping the sprouts of fennel I'd collected, I trudged up to the tower. The pages of Bea's script were neatly stacked. I flicked a corner. *Child. Waiting. Mother* … I backed away, arranged the fronds, knowing even before I'd started they were wrong.

By mid-afternoon I'd given up. I made a tomato sauce, and while I waited, as my mother never had the time to do, for it to condense, I leafed through *Family Knitting*, completed a puzzle, walked the borders of the garden, inspected the iron roller, peered with increasing irritation down towards the gate. 'Do you mind,' I remembered my father asking on a rare visit to our school, 'when she's so mean?' I'd been picking beech nuts on the steps, peeling back the skin to nibble the insides. 'Who?'

'Bea.'

'She's never mean!' I spat out the husks.

'I hope you're hungry?' It was evening when the door flung open. I'd been dozing, fitful, on the sofa.

'Where were you?' I was determined to be angry, but the sight of her, weighed down by bags, her footsteps light, derailed me. I followed her through into the kitchen where she heaped wrapped packages on to the table. 'You've been gone for hours.'

'Cromer,' she set fresh mint in a jug, 'was further than I thought.'

'Cromer?' I stepped across to reclaim my sauce, to take a sidelong look into her eyes. 'That's miles from here.'

'A meeting.' She turned away. 'It was the nearest one.' She handed me a lemon and suggested that I grate the zest. She was going to make fish pie.

We ate outside at a stone table, insects swarming in the fading light. 'Was it helpful?' I swatted a mosquito. 'This meeting?' What could she say there that she couldn't say to me?

'You should go sometime.'

'To Cromer?'

'Wherever. They have meetings everywhere, for anyone affected.'

'I'm not affected.'

She sighed.

'Do you think?'

She put down her fork. 'He called me.' She was very still. 'The man.'

'The … who?'

'Pauli.' Disgust rippled through her. She pushed away her plate. 'He was arrested, approaching children in a park. It seems he has a record.' A moth flew against the candle, its wings already ash. 'Now he's in recovery, waiting for his trial, and he was ringing me to make … to make amends.'

I reached across and took her hand.

'"You got it wrong." That's what Mum said.'

'You spoke to her about it?'

'All she had to do was ask: "Are you all right?"'

'I'm sorry.' Was that what Pauli had been saying?

'Fucking amends,' she clattered the dishes so hard one cracked. 'It was never his amends I wanted. You're meant to listen but I couldn't. I hung up.'

The next day when I woke I heard Bea, shouting. I sat up, my heart thudding, but she was in the tower, reading her script aloud. 'I don't know how to …' I sang, in case her words slipped through, and pulling on my clothes I ran downstairs. My sauce lay congealed in its pan. I scraped it into a bowl and put it in the fridge, and then, assailed by hunger, I took it out and spooned it on to toast. The sharp taste was ecstatic. I'm pregnant! If only there was someone I could tell. Lex. But Lex was in America, and anyway, Lex knew. I made another slice of toast, spread the sauce on thickly and stepped into the garden. The air was warm, the long grass shimmering with dew. I walked, barefoot, my feet sinking, clover, thistle, the purple bells of heather. I tugged open the gate on to the lane. There was no one passing, and I took the track that ran above the river, through shrubs and scrub, over runnels of dried earth, scrutinising sea pink, mallow, an overhanging bush of gorse, its flowers soft amongst its thorns.

'It's only a first draft,' Bea said when I came in, and she lifted the manuscript as if to test its weight, 'but even so I think it's done.'

My fingers bloodied, I held up my own prize.

'Gorse. I like it.' Bea stood and stretched. 'Let's celebrate.' And then, as if there'd been no break in the conversation of the night before, she said, 'You know what I've never dared ask Mum?'

I waited.

'Why, when we were in Morocco,' she fluttered the pages as if that's what they contained, 'why she left me behind.'

———

The ferry was in when we reached the quay. We sat at the front and motored out along the estuary, round the headland, to where the island was separated by a reef. *You asked to stay behind!* I argued. Mum had plans to cross the Atlas Mountains, to visit a Zouia, to take counsel from a sheik. Bea was seven, and she didn't want to come. An English couple we'd met in Marrakech had said they'd take her in. They had a baby who was spoon-fed mashed potato. When we'd visited they'd baked a cake. *Please let me stay here*, I could see Bea pleading. No one had expected our mother to say yes.

'When do you come back?' she was asking the skipper.

'What d'you reckon? Time for two more trips? Either way, we come in, on the hour.'

The island sand was white. The water clear. There were people clustered in the dunes, families with picnics, children forming messages with stones. We walked beyond them to the further shore. Here the sea stretched flat to the horizon. I slipped my shoes off and stood in the shallows. Cold clutched at my ankles, grains of sand dragged between my toes. 'Let's walk the whole way round.' In the distance was the rise of a hill. We set off, imagining the hour it would take to reach it and track past, arriving at the jetty as the ferry moored.

There was no one and nothing in our view, only a shadow, sloped towards the sea. As we neared, it took the shape of a man, arms tucked against its side, feet crossed at the ankle. He lifted his head and we saw it was a seal. We ran to the shore, cupped water in our hands, trickling drops over its nose. It closed its eyes and lay its head back down. *Leave me*, it seemed to say.

Unsure what else to do, we walked away. Fast as we marched, the hill only receded. We'd been walking for an hour when it turned into a cliff. Giving up, we crossed the beach and, heaving ourselves by fronds of grass, we climbed the dune. Now we were on a pebbled plain. The ground was ridged and rutted, sprouted with the stalks of plants. We picked our way across the island, tracking paths that withered into scrub, alert for adders, leaping over swamps. Soon our legs were striped with white. If only I'd brought water. If only I'd packed food.

On the far shore the picnickers had gone. They'd left nothing but a pebbled HELP. We scanned the estuary. The tide was high, or had been. Now it was running out. I walked down to the creek and watched it pulling, scraps of weed scudding on the current, shells and sand spinning at my feet. Bea was on the jetty. She shielded her eyes. 'Remember when we were lost on the beach at Agadir?'

'We weren't lost,' I shouted.

We'd been digging, and Mum had said to stay right where we were, that she'd be back. But we'd grown tired of waiting, and we'd walked towards our camp. The sun was sinking, scattering light across the beach. We'd skipped through the shallows, the rippled sand, happy to be on the move. But our camp did not appear, only a man, his outline dark, his hood covering his face. 'Mum was late, that's all,' I insisted. I wanted to be included in Bea's memories, but not, it seemed, if they differed from my own.

We'd run then, run and run, until the sun sank, red, and it was gone. We left the beach, walked on to a road, when there he was again, the man, his fingers gnarled, his toothless mouth, and our mother thanking him, for finding us, *Inshallah*, for letting her know where we'd gone.

'Let's wade across.' I'd found a path, three boulders in a row.

'Really?' Bea took my hand, and we stepped in.

The current was stronger than it looked. We moved forward, the water up over our knees. Mud seized our ankles, rising in spirals before it rushed out to sea. I braced my body, turning my back on the gape of the estuary, nothing beyond it but stripes of blue and green. I took another step and plunged to the waist. We should have waited. One falter, we'd be swept away. My muscles strained; my skirt, a sail, pulled taut. I held my arms above my head. Would it be safer to stay here?

'It's a love test. Do you know that?' Bea yelled as the water rushed between us. 'Being late.'

I flung out an arm, attempted to twist around. So why do you both do it? Fury whipped through me. My whole life I'd been caught in their dance. But the water was behind me, and however hard I dug in with my heels, the current was too strong. 'Why,' I dared, 'can't you just …?' I took a step and slipped. My skirt billowed. Bea caught hold of the hem, yanking me up to higher ground where we stood on a boulder, our arms entwined.

'Just … what?'

Forgive her? Was that what I wanted? We struggled across to the far bank where I lay on the grass, my hands on my stomach. It felt warm below the chill of the wet cloth. 'Nothing.' Together we stared at the sky.

By the time we reached the second creek, the tide was out. Children were splashing in the shallows, nosing canoes along the narrow stream. 'I'm sorry,' I took her arm. Gulls, their underbellies snowy, welcomed us with swoops and calls.

'Will you tell Dad about the baby?'

'No.' I'd taken enough risks. 'Just you.'

'And Lex.'

'Believe it or not Lex knows.' We laughed, and scratched and damp and happy, we tramped up the long front garden to our door.

That evening I began to bleed. The shock of it was like a punch. I lay on Bea's mat. 'Please, please, please hold on,' I begged. Bea had driven to a meeting in another town.

I was still muttering when she slammed in through the door. 'What are you doing?'

I could see her silhouette.

My mouth turned down. I pressed a palm across my eyes. 'Bleeding.'

Bea retrieved the folder. Plumber, electrician, doctor. She dialled, and when an answerphone cut in, she recited the out-of-hours number.

'The hospital? So it's not …' she trailed away '… normal?'

I padded myself with tissue and hobbled to the car. The night was black, the sky cracked sharp with stars. Slowly we rolled through the garden to the gate. 'Don't move.' She leapt out and opened it, left the gate hanging on its hinge.

Flat fields stretched away on either side. Churches wreathed in shadow, barns, the huddled mass of cows. There were houses clustered in around a pub, hamlets clinging to the bends of roads.

'How you feeling?' We were on a motorway, roaring across an open plain.

I shook my head. She pressed her foot down, hard.

At the hospital I was asked to describe the blood. Pigment. Texture. Strength of flow. With every repetition I cried harder. 'It's not uncommon to miscarry.' A nurse, perturbed by the volume of my tears, pressed Kleenex into my wet hands. 'It has no bearing on your ability to, one day, bring a baby to full term.'

They didn't understand. It was *this* baby I needed. Please God, I prayed. Was it a punishment? For earlier freedoms? For Mum?

By the time I arrived in ultrasound I was a sodden mess. I was wearing white trousers, and through the paper wadding, a stain of red had travelled through. 'Lie still,' the sonographer instructed as my breath came juddery in bursts. He smoothed on gel and rolled a probe across my stomach. Water rushed, a whirring. There was silence as he dug deep against my side, and then a small and regular booming came sonic through the screen. I dared myself to turn my head, and there within a canopy of coils was the shell of an oyster; at its centre, a pearl.

'Still there.' He gave me a tight smile.

The cock was crowing when we arrived back at the house. 'Effing bird.' Bea mimed a strangulation, and I clutched myself as I tried not to laugh.

That night there was another streak of blood. Brighter this time. Stronger. I lay on my rush floor with a pad between my legs. Below me the telephone was ringing.

'Lucy!' Bea's voice came spiralling up.

At the first catch in my throat Lex knew. 'Sweetheart …'

Again, tears gushed.

'We'll have another baby,' I heard him, faint. 'This pregnancy is not what's most important. It's you that matters. You and me.'

I snuffled, grateful. But it wasn't true. For me it *was* this baby. I needed its new life. 'I'm holding on. Tight as I can.'

'Whatever happens …' Lex was convinced. 'It will be all right. Remember that. And I'll be home.'

The next day the blood had thinned. By our last morning it was gone.

'Will you tell Mum?' I asked as we drove towards London. Bea looked at me.

'About the man.' I couldn't say his name. 'About him calling.'

Bea kept her eyes on the road. 'You know she came with me, to a meeting?'

I didn't.

'Mel thought it might help. But afterwards all she said was: "Why can't we stop talking about the past!"' Bea began to laugh. Her shoulders shook, her hands jumped against the wheel. 'Why can't we!'

'Maybe we can?' I was laughing too, but when I looked across there were tears on her face.

We drove on in silence.

'Will you be all right?' Bea said as she dropped me off.

'I will.' I hugged her hard.

The house felt echoey and cold. I stood in the kitchen and wondered who to call, but I didn't trust myself not to talk about the baby, and there was nothing else to say. I took a breath. Who invented such a lonely rule?

From outside came the rattle of the gate, a shout, the pounding of small feet. I ran along the hall and opened the front door. Our neighbour was there, unstrapping his youngest from the car. 'Merrie's repaying me for last weekend when I snuck off to play golf.' He looked generally delighted, and I stood and watched as he herded his boys along the path. 'The witching hour.' He smiled, and shut his door.

I walked back into the empty house. Lex would be waking up. I tried his hotel and waited while they put me through. He answered, sleepy, and when I asked what time he'd be here in the morning he reminded me he'd not be arriving until the following day.

Of course!

Yawning, luxuriant, he told me about the talk he'd given, the room the university had hired, too small for the students who had wanted to attend.

'That's wonderful.' I was settling in to listen – it was one of the things I loved about him, his pleasure in describing the details of his day – when he remembered he'd agreed to meet a colleague. He'd try me later. Better still, he'd see me, tomorrow.

The day after, I reminded him.

Of course! He was laughing as he set down the phone.

The next day our neighbour's wife was still away. The boys, he released into the garden, early. There was the whir of a hosepipe, their chatter and their squalls as the paddling pool was filled. 'Wait till I bring out a kettle,' he called, but the children couldn't wait and in they tumbled. I listened to the splashing and the screams. 'Stand back!' Hot water hissing into cold.

I caught his eye above the wall.

'Hi.' He was a shy man, who did something impenetrable in IT. 'Gorgeous day.'

The children were gleaming, bare and brown, and I had a great desire to scoop them up, press their silken limbs against my own. I stepped on to a stool. 'Hey, boys,' I said, but they ignored me.

Inside the shadowed house I flicked through my sketches. Sea holly. Stonecrop. The seed pod of a poppy on a long twined stem. I tore out a clean sheet of paper and painted the gold wings of the gorse, the dagger of its thorns, slanting each stem sideways, until I'd covered a whole page.

Dear Mum, I wrote on the other side, *I have some news.* Faltering, I drew a figure with a round, protruding belly. *Let's meet for tea, and a Large slice of Cake.* I considered superstition and wrestled from its grip, and slipping on my shoes I walked through the streets to her front door where I pushed my card through the letter box and waited, to be certain, as it fluttered to the mat.

II

My mother arrived, eyes glittery, her hair swept back. She'd
bumped into an old flame on the train from Bath who'd
asked her on a date. 'Someone I met when Max was …'
high spots of colour appeared on each cheek '… when we
were at The Laurels.'

'Mum!'

'Towards the end …' She glanced around, defensive.
'When it was all unravelling.' Proud to think she'd wreaked
revenge on Max's father, I pulled her into an embrace.

'Lucy.' She read my ribs like Braille. 'What's wrong?'

'I'm fine.'

'And Pearl?'

Hearing her name Pearl threw herself between us. 'Swing
me.' She took our hands and led us into the garden where
we skimmed her feet against the flowers. 'I'm just not sure
whether I should see him?'

'Who?'

'My date!'

'Nana, Nana.' Pearl was tugging at her arm.

'He is nice, but is he …'

'I thought you …'

'… really worth the trouble?'

'Nana!' Pearl had taken both her hands and was climbing up her legs, and I thought how often she'd despaired of never meeting anyone again. How bitterly she'd regretted the relationships that she'd dismissed.

'Flip me!' Pearl tried.

'The chances are …' she set Pearl down '… he'll turn out to be a psychopath. Or dull.'

Pearl gave up and clambered on to the wall and I watched her nervous as my mother weighed the possibilities. 'Catch me.' She flung herself into my arms, and dizzy with the strain of it I suggested we walk up to the park.

Later, with Pearl in bed, we sat in the dark garden, sipping spirits, watching the smoke from our shared cigarette float away in wisps. 'Tell me —' I gave her my full attention '— how did you meet?'

'I was pregnant.'

'Really?' And she told me how he'd flirted, how she'd resisted, until one morning — by now Max was nearly one — she woke, early, and unable to face another drudging day she'd pulled a coat over her nightie, climbed into the van, and driven into town. 'To spend a few hours,' she exhaled, 'with someone … who liked me. The look of surprise when I climbed into his bed.'

I squeezed her hand, the rings and bangles familiarly in place, imagining her long, lean body, how I'd craved the warmth of it when I was small.

'When I got home, Max, for once, was fed and dressed, you girls were in the garden, Bea was weeding — if you can imagine such a thing — and although I had an alibi prepared — Ginny, in need of emotional support — no questions were asked. I ran through the house and up the stairs. *I'm not sorry*, I repeated. The truth was, I was scared.'

'Of him?'

'Of being on my own. Again.'

A year later, when my mother left for good, I'd sworn I hadn't known anything was wrong. But now, as I considered it, the soundtrack of The Laurels rose like a refrain. My stepfather raging, Cora fretting, Carole King's *Tapestry* spiralling up the stairs, until I knew each word of every song by heart.

'How is it,' she lowered her voice, even though I'd told her Lex was abroad, 'with you?'

I looked up, sharp. She couldn't know?

'Is it any easier, with Pearl?'

'Oh, that.' I shook my head. The last time she'd stayed I'd confided how difficult it was when Lex returned from trips away; how Pearl punished him, stalking off, sticking out her tongue.

'Lex. He's …' My mouth was dry. 'He's giving a paper this weekend. In Prague. I have so much work, Simone Xa has taken on a new house. I'm making blinds for every window. Each one has to be hand-stitched, attached to batons … not that I'm complaining.'

She looked at me, unconvinced, and I ran inside and up the stairs to find a quilt to make up her bed.

It was three weeks since the letter had dropped on to the mat, my name in capitals, a sun rising in biro, its rays travelling as far as the stamp. *Your husband is not the man you think he is.* My insides slipped. *Want to know more? Want to know the reason that my girlfriend left? Maybe you should ask him? Or ask me?* There was an email address of asterisks and stars. *Make contact.* He hadn't left his name. Coward, I thought, and I caught myself. How easy it was to blame the wrong man.

It was Saturday and Pearl was watching cartoons. I took the letter and stood by our bed.

'What?' Lex blinked, and even before I handed it over he saw it in my face. He blanched, and his features fell in on themselves, his cheeks hollowing as if his teeth had been removed. I watched from far away. A land unclouded by loyalty and love. How strange he looked from there. I snapped into the present. 'I don't understand.'

Lex swung his legs out of the bed and put his arms around me. 'I've had letters too. Threatening—'

'You've had letters?'

'This woman. It's nothing.' He felt me flinch. 'It's not nothing, but it happened a long time ago, not even last year, maybe the year before. A girl, in the department, a woman … she … there *was* something between us, I'm not denying that, and she used it as an excuse to finish with … I don't know why it's taken him so long but he started writing, saying he'd read our text messages. He knew a way to retrieve them, make them public.'

'Text messages?' I was shaking. 'Like …?'

'We were in touch, you know, sometimes we met up—'

'Texts, arranging to meet?'

'A bit more than—'

I turned away and ran.

Downstairs I looked in on Pearl. Her eyes were attached to the television by strings, the figures on the screen whirling in animated assaults. 'What is this?' I tried to intervene but she shouted 'Mum!' so vehemently

I retreated to the kitchen. I stood by the sink. Last night's dishes floated in a watery scum. I flicked on the kettle and waited, leaning into its whisper, attempting to decipher what was being said, but before I could catch even a fragment, Lex was there, his jeans on, the T-shirt he'd slept in, frantic. He had the letter, and he waved it at me. 'Don't make this about us. Look, he's not even signed his name, and as for her … I was an excuse. She'd wanted to leave him, wanted a change. She's not even in the faculty any more.'

When I didn't move he took me by the shoulders. 'There's always some kind of flirtation in a workplace. It's different for you, working alone, but it's part of it … it's how people get through the endlessness of the days.'

I could believe that. And Lex was Lex. Why wouldn't women flirt with him? I imagined myself in a meeting, the headiness of anyone's attention lightening the hour.

He held me then and I allowed myself to be held.

'I love you,' he said, and I nodded, my head twisted as it was, painfully, against his chest.

It still surprises me how little time there is to talk when what you need to talk about is dangerous. The day of the letter passed in a haze. Lex set off for football – he played a vicious weekly game with a team of academics – while I made clay animals with Pearl. We'd planned to meet, as we often did, at a café on the far side of the park. The owner greeted us with warmth. 'You all right?' Tall and motherly, she approved of our small family. 'Yes.' I forced a smile.

It was a blustery day, and the glass door shuddered each time anyone pushed through. I dreaded his appearance.

Dreaded even more he mightn't come. After half an hour Lex slid in beside me. 'What's it to be?' He wielded the menu although we rarely diverted from our choice. Pancakes for Pearl. A full English for him. 'Toast?' His eyes met mine, briefly, and I said yes, although my throat had tightened to the width of a hair.

'I spy,' Lex took it upon himself to distract Pearl with a game, 'something the colour of ...' he looked helpfully towards the sponge cake on the counter '... yellow.' After several guesses – 'that lady's hair, that lady's jumper'; was everything to be contentious? – Pearl seized on the cake.

Now it was her turn: 'I spy ...' and when it transpired Pearl had chosen the blue stuffed elephant in her bedroom, her peals of laughter rang out so deliciously I rose up from the depths where I'd been floundering, and breathed. By the time the food arrived I'd sunk again. I cut Pearl's pancakes into strips – that kept me busy – but as I stared at the wedges of my toast, my mind began to track over the events of the last years, stumbling each time I came across a clue, a late-night coldness, Lex's phone switched off, until, sickened, I gave up on any attempt at eating and retreated to the loo. There were two cubicles, and between them a small basin. I ran the water and watched myself in the mirror. There was our holiday in Greece. Lex had been there for a week already, holding workshops, when I flew out to join him. It was an early flight and I'd kept Pearl in her pyjamas, red and yellow, a Rupert Bear design. I'd hoped the pyjamas might coerce her into sleepiness but they seemed to have the opposite effect, freeing her to race across the concourse, toddle raucously down ramps. We'd changed planes in Athens, waited through the hottest hours of the day, arriving on the island late in the after-noon. 'Daddy!' Pearl had hurled herself against his legs, and it was clear, as he untangled her, that he'd rather we'd not come.

I dried my hands. Had *she* been there? Was that the reason for his coolness, for the empty fridge, not even a pint of milk for Pearl who still napped with a bottle? Or was there someone else whose company he'd been enjoy-ing? My stomach hollowed at the image of the woman in sandals and a sundress, who ran the writers' centre, who'd pressed Lex to attend.

A woman with a baby bustled from the cubicle. She held the door for me. I shook my head, but when I saw there wasn't room in the small space, I squeezed in and locked the door. I sat on the closed seat and waited until I might know what to do, knowing all the time there was nothing to be done but bear it.

'You OK?' Lex mouthed as I reclaimed my seat. The bloom of his post-match triumph had receded, and I saw his father in his face. The picture – the last taken – that he kept on his desk. Was it there as a reminder? Of frailty? Of time? How often did he glance at it as he worked into the night?

Bea didn't answer when I called. I left a message – *ringing for a chat* – but by the time she rang me back I was upstairs, wrangling Pearl into the bath. I could hear Lex through the floor, his laugh, the roll of his voice. She liked him. Loved him. As we all did. I squeezed shampoo on to Pearl's wet head and lathered the foam into a peak.

That night we'd been invited to a party. It was the party of a couple whose house backed on to ours, and even though we could have heard Pearl if she'd screamed, I'd booked a babysitter who arrived at eight.

I chose a dress I rarely wore – tight and red. I'd seen people's eyes, as mine had, slide across a woman's frame post-children to assess how successful she'd been in hauling back her figure – but since that morning I'd shrunk. It had happened with the shock of Lex's face. Not the letter. I'd reserved judgement on the letter. It was the proof of it that had contracted my insides.

The walk was mercifully short. 'Sweetheart ...' Lex tried.

I spun around. 'Don't think just because this is the one thing I'm hearing about it's not clear to me that there've been others.' *Deny it*, I begged, *swear on your child's life*, but Lex was battling for control, and rather than wait for his response I walked ahead. 'At some point we'll have to talk.' All I wanted was to run. To find a spell. Unknow. 'About what's been going on.' I'd read this in a woman's magazine, that there was nothing more dangerous than imagination. 'Then we can ...' What if there *was* something more dangerous? What if it was the truth?

He didn't meet my eye.

We turned the corner and walked along the parallel street. Lex said nothing. He was scared of me, and surprised to find I liked it, I strode ahead in the armour of my dress.

It took us weeks to find the time to talk. That first weekend Pearl kept us in a loop, food and fights, walks and games and tucking up – a ritual that involved three songs, two books, a made-up story, and a hand-holding session that could never last long enough. 'No,' she pleaded as I prised away my fingers, 'you didn't say hand-holding had started,' and I knew from experience it was quicker to begin again – three minutes – than to argue. By the time she was asleep I was too tired to talk, although I was awake again in the middle of the night, adrift against the wall of Lex's back.

The next week Lex was away – he was taking part in a seminar on the Great British Short Story – and when he called from a city in Romania it was supper time, or bath time, or once, I was at the Foundling Museum, examining their collection of textiles, snippets of eighteenth-century material left by mothers in the hope that one day they might be reunited with their children. What if a woman's own segment of material went missing? I scrutinised a scrap of voile left with a baby named Eliza, but the information card stated that Eliza had died when she was five days old. I hoped the mother had been unable to return.

I told Lex I'd call back.

I waited until Pearl was asleep. His phone went to voicemail, and I was assaulted by a pain so powerful it folded me in half. Was this how it would be now? I sat in the kitchen, laid out my work, not sure which was worse, the future, altered, or the past. *Your husband is not the man you think he is.* I should have kept the letter. *Want to know more?* But to keep it was to honour it. I'd dropped the optimistic rays into the bin. Foundling 1,347 – Henry – had come with a square of lawn. I placed the sketch I'd made – fuchsia petals against taupe – beside a copy of a nightjar, its throat open in song.

The next day Mum and I took Pearl to the zoo. She wanted to see a camel, it was why my mother was here. As I sliced bread for sandwiches, filled a Thermos with tea, I ran over the possibility of remaining at home, alone: *Wouldn't you both … Mightn't it be fun …?* I spread butter, lumpen from the fridge, and saw the quiver of Pearl's lip, my mother's apprehension.

'Ready?' I rallied, and later, as we wandered from one pen to the next, I hoped Pearl wouldn't notice that the elephants looked sad, that the tigers stared at us with scorn. We saw pelicans and penguins, monkeys – their babies clinging to their chests as they swung from post to post. 'This way for camels,' my voice echoed through the hollow of the tunnel, 'race you both,' and as we ran I wished I could grasp my mother's hand, confide in her, allow my cheerfulness to dent. But I couldn't take the risk. I couldn't manage, not today, with any less than I had, and I thought of how I'd gone to her the day Zac left. 'It's over.' I'd collapsed in her kitchen, and she'd burst into tears. 'It's been years since I was in a relationship,' she'd wailed. 'The chances are I'll never be in one again.' All afternoon I'd consoled her as she cried.

'Exceedingly annoying, or the usual?' Bea called when Mum had gone.

'The usual.' I lacked the energy for elaboration, but when this was met with silence I mustered strength and tried again. 'Did you know she had a fling when we were at The Laurels?'

'What!'

I had her back. All mine.

Once we'd run through every detail – the wellingtons, the van – I asked her how she was. 'Still furious.' The producer, it transpired, had never entirely left his marriage, and now, despite the years of litigation, his wife was pregnant, again.

I'd rung the day after The Letter and found her too angry to talk. 'I'm going to cut off his balls,' she'd told me, and, relieved to relegate my troubles, I'd offered to help.

'How's Lex?' she asked now.

'He's OK. Away.'

'So popular!'

I saw him on the doorstep, his shame binding as a weed. I'd prided myself on keeping secrets. The least I could do was to keep his.

It was another week before we walked along the river and found a bench on which to talk. My heart was thumping, my chest tight as a balloon. 'So tell me,' I was gentle, 'what's been going on?'

Lex swallowed. Spread his fingers as if to help him count. 'There've been five …'

Pearl had just turned three.

'A girl at a conference. A kiss. That's all.'

We had to get this over with. Tunnel to the other side.

'Then someone. A PhD student. As soon as I realised I suggested she transfer. Insisted. It was nothing.'

Nothing was the word I clung to.

He checked his fingers. 'That stupid stag weekend for Franz. Tim got heavily involved, I wriggled out …'

'Greece?' I prompted when he paused.

'No.'

'Just grumpy, for no reason?' I kicked his leg and then I remembered and I sickened. 'Was the woman, from the letter … was it … when I was pregnant …?'

'No. She was – that was … before!'

Why was he writing now? I frowned, but he put his hand in mine. I needed to believe him. 'And?'

'What?'

'You said five.'

He searched, as if the events weren't seared into his brain. 'That's it.'

I was so relieved I kissed him. 'Let's forget the whole stupid business.'

'Yes,' he slumped. 'Thank you. Please.'

We stood and walked towards the Embankment. 'When he started sending me those letters,' Lex's voice caught, and he paused, 'I was scared. What if he destroyed the most precious thing I have?' He held me in the middle of the path, and as people passed, brushing against us, shadowy and soft, I allowed myself to be enclosed.

We had a month before the next letter arrived. The same sun, sending out its rays. This was more explicit. *Licking. Fucking.* He'd written down their texts. I studied the asterisks and stars of the address. Should I make contact? But even the 'hot' of the Hotmail left me and without showing it to Lex I slid the envelope into a drawer, buried it below a scatter of CDs, where it waited, ticking, an unexploded bomb.

III

A mother's love, I'd heard, could move a mountain, could pick up a truck and toss it to one side, and so I gripped the handle of the iron roller and I heaved. It was solid as a building, wedged, as if in stone. That's when I began to scream.

A woman must have run in from the lane. She stood beside me, and with every ounce of strength we had, we tried again. 'My daughter …' and she did what I was too cowardly to do, she squatted down and looked between the wheels. 'She's here.'

Pearl's dress was ripped across the middle, there was blood clogging in her nose. We eased her out, legs, arms, toes still sandy from the beach. There was nothing on her but a smear of dirt. 'Pearl?' Her eyes were wide.

That's when the woman's own daughter, whose ice cream had melted in a mess over her hand, asked why everything was going wrong that day? That's when Zara stepped out of the house. I could see her, shielding her eyes against the sun. 'Where's Mac?' She stopped, staring down the track, the solid round of iron, not where it had been before.

'Mackenzie!' She ran. I'd lain a towel over Pearl, was stroking the hair back from her face. 'Oh God.' She looked around, and there he was, in nothing but his trunks, crouching low behind the bush where Pearl and he most liked to hide.

I called an ambulance. Gave directions: 'The Lookout.' It was on an unmarked lane. 'I don't know!' Hysteria was rising. The woman prised the phone from my hand, instructed them to drive towards the harbour. 'Tell them,' she turned away, 'the child's been crushed. Tell them to come soon.'

I rang Lex from the ambulance. His answerphone cut in. Pearl was strapped on to a stretcher. I sat upright on a folding metal chair. Within minutes his name flashed across the screen. Had the shrill of the ringing reached him? The whir of the blue light? He was in Perm overseeing a seminar on Campus Novels, was due to fly from there to Yale, but he'd known, he said, the second that he saw my name, that it was bad, that it was Pearl.

'It's a miracle she's not more badly hurt.' I pressed the phone against my ear, and I listened while he explained the complications of travel from this most easterly corner of Europe, how he'd do his best to be with us, as soon as he could.

Call me, I texted Bea. She was on-set, in Florence. The last time we'd spoken it was from a landline. Her mobile had been damaged when she'd gone hiking – hiking! – with the director of photography, on her one day off. It must have fallen from her pocket, she hadn't even noticed, she'd found it cracked on the way down. 'Amir Malek. Have you heard of him? He's brilliant. And incredibly nice.'

'Nice!'

'Calm down.' She was laughing. 'I expect he has his moments. We can't all meet a Lex.'

At the hospital I was asked to hold an oxygen mask against Pearl's face. To answer questions. Name: Pearl. Age: five. How she came to be hurt. They watched me as I described the iron roller, knocking her under, pinning her against the fence.

I hovered close as blood was taken, as she was fed into a scanner, running alongside when she was wheeled into intensive care. Her spleen was torn. Her liver damaged. One lung had collapsed. 'The pivotal time …' three doctors were gathered round her bed '… is the next seventy-two hours. That's when a haemorrhage is likely to occur.' I counted forward to Tuesday afternoon, when if she was … I crossed my arms over my chest. If she pulled through, I'd never complain about anything again.

All night I sat beside her, waiting, willing, watching the clock, until the first light appeared in the sky. When a doctor approached I risked a smile, but he stood before me, solemn. We must prepare to be transferred, he said. There was a hospital better equipped if the worst should occur. Again, I climbed with Pearl into an ambulance, and we raced across the countryside at such speed the force of it held me in my seat. Once we arrived we were rushed down corridors, in and out of lifts and into an intensive care ward – for children only – with a border of animals high up on the walls. Pearl's eyes startled as if reunited with old friends.

The ward was muted. The raspy gasping of assisted breath, the rustle of the nurses. I sat by my daughter's bed, waiting, wincing as they opened an artery, inserted a tap in order to take blood. It'll be easier, they explained, than searching continually for veins. Three tubes ran from suckers on her chest, a drip was held in place by plasters and a splint. When everything was sealed stickers were produced, pressed against her skin, so that when I looked over her body my eye was caught, not just by tubes and wires, but by the button-nosed smiles of bears.

It was late when I was directed from the ward, down through the hospital, around the car park and across a courtyard, to a red-brick house. I was shown into a room with a blond-wood bed, a bathroom and a phone. 'Get some sleep.' The implication was that later I might need it. 'We'll call,' the nurse was firm, 'if there's any change.'

I undressed and stood in the light of the mirror. My eyes were dark with disbelief, and on my arms were two circular bruises where I'd clutched them with my thumbs. I didn't risk the shower – what if I missed their call? – washing myself at the sink, brushing my teeth with the toothbrush provided. The bed was firm, the sheets cool. I stared at the ceiling, too agitated for sleep, but my eyelids must have drooped because I was taken down a chute of black, rushed through darkness, landing on the seabed in a wrap of weeds. I rested, rising, falling with the swell. My mother was there. She pulled me up and led me in the tango, head up, back straight, our arms outstretched. As we turned she opened her mouth but instead of words, bubbles rose, and in each bubble was a ringing bell.

The telephone jerked me out of sleep. 'You'd better come.' It was Matron, her voice terse. I ran so fast my brain knocked against my skull. Tripping in my shoes, buttoning my shirt. I'd never asked to leave!

There was a scrum around Pearl's bed. Her bloods had changed. White cells were outnumbering red. 'This may be the start.' A nurse made a movement with her hands. A cloud puff. Disintegration. I wanted to attack her but how would that have helped?

Pearl's eyes were searching, frantic. 'My mum,' she said. She'd found me.

'Yes.' I squeezed her hand.

We waited. Doctors, nurses, hurrying, testing. My phone chimed in my bag. I snatched at it to switch it off – the signal could interfere with the machines – and saw fifteen missed calls from Zara. A text message swam across the screen. *Tell me P's all right?*

I pressed a fist against my mouth.

There was nothing from Lex. Not a word from Bea. I let the phone drop to the bottom of my bag.

'Sorry.' It was Matron. 'Must have been a mix-up. Blood count seems normal enough now.' She gave me a stiff smile.

The morning was slow. I drank a cup of tea, and later, while Pearl slept, I dashed to the canteen. Stew and rice and mashed potato. Sandwiches glistening with cheese. My stomach heaved. I bought a banana and forced it down, and then I ran outside and switched on my phone. *Landed.* Lex's text opened with a ping. There'd been a train, two planes, a wait in Moscow. He was heading home to fetch the car.

I sent him the name of the new hospital.

XXXXXX, he texted back.

The afternoon was close, although Pearl's body, dotted with wires, the idiotic grinning faces of the bears, was cold. I leant in and kissed her shoulder, breathed the biscuit and the sunscreen smell, the overlay of antiseptic. She held tight to my hand.

To celebrate forty-eight hours Pearl was propped upright with pillows and offered a bright blue lolly. The sweet ooze of the ice rolled her eyes. She was still sucking when Lex rushed into the ward. 'My darling,' he fell to his knees. 'How is my girl?'

Pearl stuck out her blue tongue.

That night we lay together on two chairs, our limbs entwined, sinking and swimming in and out of sleep. There was nothing between us but relief, and I pressed myself as close in as I could get, heat pulsing, our worlds conjoined, for once. 'What will happen about Yale?' I whispered. He was due to give a series of three lectures. 'They'll under-stand.' He kissed my neck, and we drifted back to sleep.

I woke early and wound my way outside.

I tried Bea. The tone was elongated and hollow. *Pearl. Accident. Intensive*, I wrote, then I erased it. At least my mother didn't have a mobile. She was in Buenos Aires taking a course in Latin dance. Salsa, paso doble, jive. She'd sent a postcard of a man with a rose between his teeth. My phone rang in my hand. 'Hello?' I answered before I'd had time to check.

'I don't believe it!'

'Zara …'

'I'm sorry,' she was crying. 'I'm so sorry.'

'It's not your—'

'I've been ringing the hospital …'

'There wasn't ever any news.'

'And now?'

I crossed my fingers, touched a piece of wood. 'I think she's going to be all right.'

There was a pause while the roller gathered speed, thudding over the humps of the rough lawn. Mackenzie's voice burst through. 'Mom. Don't cry.'

'We'll visit. Can we?' She blew her nose, and I was seized with hatred for his eight-year-old self. The way he mispronounced Mum.

'I'm not sure …' I looked at my torn nails, and I forced myself to ask, 'How is Mackenzie?'

'Shhh,' Zara was saying, 'I said we would.' Then back to me. 'I promised him we'd take a trip to the island. Unless we visit? Could we?'

'No … I mean …' I'd been gone too long already, and promising to call, again, I switched off the phone and ran.

At seventy-two hours Pearl was unharnessed from her drips and probes and moved to the children's ward on the ground floor. The ward was busy; relatives, as if on guard, in an arc around each bed. To our right was a girl whose head was swathed in bandage. Her family – parents, grandparents, sisters, aunts – had set up home. They laid out supper, a spread of Tupperware, and offered me a plate. For three days I'd subsisted on crisps and the occasional polished apple, and now, ravenous, I accepted – potato salad, crackers, cheese. A tin of biscuits came by from the woman on the other side. A bowl of cherries was passed hospitably back.

I'd hoped Lex might stay, at least another night, but once Pearl was settled in the ward he began to pace. 'I'll get going.' His keys were jangling. 'Check on the house. Talk to Yale.' The lectures had been in place for a year. His shoulders sagged, defeated.

A roar of love and fear shot through me. 'Unless you do go?'

'Really?' he spun around. 'Would that … could you …?'

My heart skittered. 'You'll be back in a few days, a week at the most.'

He held me so tight I thought I might crack. 'I love you.' His breath was fire, and it was worth it. It was my reward. 'Be a good girl for your mummy.' He stroked Pearl's hair, and kissing me, he was gone.

I lay on the camp bed next to Pearl and held her hand, and all that night I reiterated my promise: I'd not complain about anything again.

The next day I called my father from the nurses' station, a hall, separated from the ward by glass. 'I'm so terribly sorry,' he said when I'd described the accident, as thoroughly as if it was a birth. 'Is there anything I can do?'

There wasn't, but it helped, to have him listen. 'If you hear from Bea?'

'Of course.'

A nurse ran in and glanced in my direction. 'I'd better go.' Matron had told us we could use the phone as needed, but the nurse was counting. She began to move. Forward and back, she mouthed instructions, forward on the other foot, and back. She swung her hips, and with each step she gave a push. Now she was turning, marking out a square. She stopped and lifted an imaginary hat, once, twice, before hurrying out through the swing doors.

'What was that about?' The mother of the bandaged girl was at my side, but before I could answer she'd covered her face. 'I know it's not Melinda's fault, but when I see her stuffing food into her mouth, no manners, not so much as a please or thank you …' She dissolved, her shoulders shaking, and I looked through the glass at her daughter. They'd found a tumour pressing on her brain and although there'd been an operation, they'd failed to get it out. 'This afternoon she spat at me, and I just snapped.' Tears slid between her fingers. Her husband appeared with two cups of tea, and handing his to me, he led her away.

The next morning I was back in the nurses' station. 'They want to keep Pearl in for monitoring,' I told Lex. 'They're not saying how long.' Pearl was sitting up in bed, running a pencil round the lanes of a maze.

'Better to be safe.' He was distracted.

'When are you off?'

'Tomorrow. I'm packing now.'

'So when will you drive up?'

He stiffened, I could feel it. 'I have to prepare.'

'Then I won't see you.'

'Hey,' he said, gentle. 'You saw me, yesterday.'

Was it yesterday? Or had it been the day before?'

'Mum?' It was Pearl, standing shakily in the door.

I screamed. 'You're not meant to be walking.' But she *was* walking. She staggered over and I caught her in my arms.

'I have to go.' I was laughing, and I carried Pearl back to her bed.

That evening I accepted a plate of kedgeree from Melinda's mother, and a samosa from the auntie of a boy

whose grandma had arrived with a feast. I'd gone downstairs, leaving Pearl in their care, and scanned the canteen
and the gift shop, finding nothing I could stomach except
another apple and more crisps.

'Take our car,' Melinda's father told me. 'There's a super-
market near the station. Stock up.' The mother showed
me where the cups and teabags were. 'Help yourself.' She
pointed to their shelf in the communal fridge. 'We look
out for each other in here.'

I took the car and drove into town. How strange the world
seemed. The evening streets. The trees in leaf. Rainwater
from a downpour pooling in the gutter. I stopped at a red
light and stared out at the people. Lovers with their arms
entwined. An old lady with her dog. I found the supermar-
ket after three wrong turns, and taking a basket, I walked
along the aisles. It was cold in here, and bright. The choice
immense. I bought dried apricots, a tin of biscuits. A loaf
of bread, a jar of peanut butter. I chose a newspaper, and a
comic with a purple plastic unicorn taped to the front.

When I returned, Melinda's mother came and sat beside
me. It was some time before she spoke. 'We have a date.'
It's what they'd been waiting for, although the surgeon had
been clear: they weren't certain they'd get the entirety of
the tumour out. Her other daughters were doing homework spread out on the floor. The father was reading. His
father was staring into space. I knew their names, and
the ones that were at home. The grandmother and the
aunt, the brother-in-law, the nieces. Stewing and baking,
scouring the shops for sticker books, for cross-stitch kits
and dolls. They were usually the last to depart, leaving
the mother to climb into her child-sized bed, watchful

while the nurse on duty made a last quick round. Taking temperatures. Checking charts. 'You all right, Mum?' They patted covers. There was no child unaccompanied. Only a boy with dwarfism, waiting for an operation on his palate who'd been put into a room of his own.

Each night, once Pearl was asleep, I took my mobile phone and slipped along the corridors, across the hospital foyer and out through the revolving doors. I stood with the smokers and turned it on. The messages were all from Zara.

Call if you can. Anytime. Day or night xx

Longing to see you. Thinking we should just turn up????

Staying on here. That OK? X

And then.

You're not going to believe it! Met someone on the ferry! Any chance you guys are coming back?

I closed my eyes against the green-flaked windows of The Lookout, the tattered puzzles and loyally awaiting books. *Family Knitting.* No, I switched off the phone, we'd not be going back, and wretched, hateful, I switched it on again.

Stay. No problem. I added a kiss.

From Bea there was nothing. *Call me. Urgent.* Then I erased it, letter by letter, until the window of my phone was black.

Pearl and I discovered a crate of dressing-up clothes, and a shelf of books which I read to her, and read to her again. I found a ball of wool, but with no needles we resorted to making pom-poms, encircling a disc of card, snipping through the strands so that they sprang into a ball. Each day Pearl's temperature was taken, her blood tested, and at visiting time, when the doors were opened, we ventured into the yard. We rolled play dough, dug in the sandpit, swore, or at least I did, when the brother of a girl with leukaemia bore down on us in a plastic truck.

Each night there was a text from Zara.

Wish you were here. Sunset crazy. How is P? x

Went kayaking. Pearl? x

Man from ferry driving me insane. Not in a good way! xxxxxxx

My fingers hovered. *All good*. I switched the phone off before she took the chance to call.

Lex, I called briefly, guiltily, from the nurses' station. The lectures were a triumph. Students, faculty, a professor he admired had all remarked on his originality of style.

'And you?' he asked.

'They're letting us out on Saturday.'

'Saturday.' He was writing it down – was there a chance he might forget? 'I'll be there.'

Soft, we said goodnight.

Behind me three nurses had gathered. 'Forward to the right, back to the left,' Matron led them from the front. 'And clap, and clap, and turn.'

My mother had run a line-dance class before she'd moved away from London. She'd encouraged me to join, and when I'd resisted she accused me of not appreciating anything she did.

'I've tried it. I'm rubbish.'

'Maybe you didn't have the right teacher?' She'd raised her eyebrows, clicking her fingers in the most aggravating way, sashaying and stamping until I'd agreed to go.

The hall was hard to find, and when I'd arrived the class was beginning. I edged my way into a middle row but she saw me, waved, and pointed to a space at the front. She was wearing cowboy boots with jeans tucked in, and a shirt tied at the waist. She looked flustered, with red spots high on her cheeks, and the tape machine she'd propped up on a chair I recognised as the old cracked one from home. But her smile was wide, her moves precise, and together we stepped and turned. 'Good!' She clicked on the music, and we repeated what we'd learnt. Next we tried a double hop. Again she showed us, and again, until even I had mastered the step. From there we moved to a shimmy. Arms out, chest back, before sidestepping in a square. At the end of the evening we braved the routine, the whole floor swaying as she led us, to the right, the left, a turn, a hop, a shimmy and a stamp. We cheered.

'It's true,' I told her afterwards, 'I do appreciate you more.' I wished, for one swift second, Bea had been there too.

'See?' She swung her hip, and laughing, we'd walked arm in arm into the night.

Three more nurses shuffled into line. I peered through the glass at the sleeping shape of Pearl, and seeing me, silhouetted, Melinda's mother tiptoed out. There were nine nurses now. Ten, including Matron. Forward and back. They did a double hop, lifted an imaginary hat. Once, twice, they jumped on to the right foot, tapping the left forward before they scattered, gently clapping as they hurried away. 'They're operating first thing,' she held the door. *Nil by Mouth* was printed on her daughter's board.

'Good luck.' We didn't risk a hug, and I lay awake in the dim light of the ward and listened to her, twisting and turning on the other side.

The next morning they were gone. A nurse was stripping off the sheets. I went to make a cup of tea and saw their shelf was empty: there was nothing in Melinda's square of fridge.

When Lex arrived on Saturday we were ready, packed, and waiting to be discharged. I handed him the book Pearl and I were reading – a cheerful story about a boy flattened by a bulletin board – and running, I dashed out through the hospital. One last time I tried Bea. How strange to be leaving when she didn't know we'd been admitted. There was still no answer. I called Zara. 'We're going home.' I could hear the chimes of masts, the flutter of sails.

'Thank God,' she yelled back. 'I'm leaving too.' I listened while she regaled me with the details of her fling. Passionate for the first five minutes, then, typical Brit, reticent as hell. 'How's Pearl?' she asked, quiet.

The wind lulled. 'She's going to be all right.'

'I, do … so ….' Every other word was taken. '… love …' Her voice was strangling in her throat. 'Can you forgive us, ever … forgive me?'

'No. I mean, of course!' I had no tears. 'It was an accid—'

'You saved me, all those years … you even sang along to Meatloaf. There isn't anyone. I couldn't …'

'Zara.' I closed my eyes, and my heart as it opened travelled down the line. 'You saved me too.' There was silence, nothing but the call of gulls. 'Don't forget the key. Leave it under the blue pot. And will you do me a favour?'

'Anything.'

'*Family Knitting*. Steal it for me, will you?'

A last syringe of blood was taken, and when the results came through, Pearl's stent was removed, the wound sealed, and we were free to go. I walked the length of the ward, saying my goodbyes, writing a note for Melinda's mother which Matron promised to pass on.

'Take care now,' she was pulling on her boots. 'Last practice.'

The music started with a twang. Three lines of nurses moved in unison, stamping, tilting their hips. Children turned in their beds, parents pressed against the window. The father of the boy with the cleft palate arrived clutching a balloon.

'Wish us luck,' Matron called, flushed. 'We're competing against three infirmaries tomorrow.'

'Good luck,' we chorused back, and holding Pearl against his shoulder Lex led us out through the happy crowd.

IV

I didn't know Josetta well, but I couldn't resist asking: 'How did your marriage end?' We were driving across London to a party on a boat moored on the canal, and as she lived close by, Bea had suggested Josetta collect me on her way.

'We'd moved into our first house,' she sped through an orange light, 'and every evening once the children were in bed we'd bring in stepladders and redecorate, one room at a time. The ceiling in the sitting room had plaster moulding and a central rose, and the plan was to scrape away the layers of clogged paint and reveal the beauty of the work. We scraped in silence, the radio playing, and at night, exhausted, we fell into bed. One evening we were invited to a dinner and although my husband wanted to keep on with the cornicing I persuaded him to go. I hired a babysitter, dressed in my best, neglected clothes, and as we were travelling there I asked: "Do you feel lucky having such an exceptionally good-looking wife?"' She laughed, delighted, as if, even then, this may have been a joke, but she was attractive, still, twenty, thirty years on, her hair cropped short, her legs so long her knees knifed up against the wheel. 'He glanced at me, and he said nothing.' She paused to navigate the traffic, easing forward so that when the lights turned green she raced across three lanes. 'A month later, when work on the cornicing was done, I took the children and I left.'

I knew the next part of her story, but I willed her to go on. 'That's when I met Sol. We never lived together. I was done with domesticity. Instead we embarked on an adventure – ten years – although it seemed we'd just begun.'

She didn't tell me how Sol died. Maybe she assumed I knew. How they were walking, in winter, by a lake, when he'd suffered a stroke, so sudden he never spoke another word. I'd heard her on the radio, a programme about gratitude, thanking the man who'd appeared as if from nowhere, consoled her while she waited for help. He'd disappeared when the ambulance arrived, she didn't know his name, but it meant a great deal, the kindness of this stranger, when she'd needed comfort most. I thought of my own stranger. The woman who'd run in from the lane. A woman I'd never seen again, and how she'd stood beside me, our knuckles whitening as I screamed.

We parked, and walked along a side street towards a hump-backed bridge, pushing through a gate, the boat in the distance, a row of portholes, lit up.

'How's that gorgeous man of yours?' She turned.

'Lex?' He was in Bruges. Or was it Brussels? One heel skidded and I grasped the rail. 'Away.'

When Lex and I were first together we had a two-week rule. We'd never be apart for longer. With time it edged to four, then six. But since Pearl's accident the parameters had shifted. Now the rules were broken, we were broken, although we still clung on.

'My daughter, she's—' There was a burst of light and laughter as Amir Malek pulled open the door. 'I may have to leave early.' I thanked her for the lift.

I'd left Pearl lying on the floor. She was arranging her Sylvanians: rabbits, hedgehogs, a set of badgers, the squirrel family, and three mice. She'd been given a Bamboo Panda with a bottle and a crib when she'd first come home from hospital. Now a kingdom had amassed. There was a schoolroom, a tree house, a playground and a farm, and rather than the Country Cottage that she'd begged for, I'd recommissioned a doll's house, painted the floorboards, hand-papered the walls. Here they lived, a family to each room, equipped with bunk beds, a dressing table and a sewing room with fabric squares as small as stamps.

'I won't be late.'

'You're going out?' Pearl spun around. 'You never said.'

The babysitter stared into a saucepan, watching for the water which wouldn't seem to boil. 'Jessica is making you spaghetti.'

'Don't go.' She gripped my arm.

'You can watch *The Simpsons* ...' I searched for another bribe. 'We have ice lollies.'

She released me, for a second, and I ran. 'Have fun,' I called before I slammed the door.

Now I stood out on the deck and sipped my drink, looking over the water to the lights on the far bank. Why was I even here? I glanced around for Bea, but I couldn't see her in the crowd.

Bea had flown back into London the same week as Mum. They'd visited, together, arriving less than half an hour late, and I'd answered the door to find them allied on the doorstep, while I stood on the other side. We'd hugged, the three of us – they knew about the accident – and we'd sat holding hands across the table as I described in detail what had taken place. They were quiet as I talked, their eyes stretched, their mouths open, while I floated near the ceiling reliving every moment, recreating every beat.

'Tell me your news.' I shook myself. I was exhausted by my own.

Our mother stood and clicked her fingers. It was a relief to see her twist across the floor, and as she pirouetted she told us about the many things she'd done, the people she'd met, the places that she'd seen. When we'd applauded, Bea gave us the highlights of her shoot: the caterers, the extras, the brilliance of the crew. Amir Malek, the director of photography who'd brought her script to life. 'You've probably both seen his work.' She couldn't hide her smile.

'And is he …?' Mum asked. 'Are the two of—'

Bea got up and yanked open the fridge.

'What about the actress who played you?' I jumped in quick.

'Not exactly me.' She gave a warning look.

'And the children?'

'Adorable.' Bea lifted out a covered bowl, inspected and returned it. 'I still can't believe we got the woman from *The Wherry* for the mum.'

Our mother stiffened.

'She's an actual genius.'

'She is,' I agreed. 'Although not, of course, as beautiful as our mum.' I stole a glance to see if this had worked.

'The little girl playing you is honestly the sweetest.' Bea snapped a stick of celery and tore it with her teeth.

'And yours?' I asked.

Bea sighed. 'She was there without her family. She did have a chaperone, but even so, we were a long way from home.' The air in the room thickened. 'It helped that the other family, your family, they scooped her up.'

'And how is our precious Pearl?' Mum shifted tack.

'She's …' I closed my eyes. Sent up a prayer. 'She's fine.'

We walked to collect Pearl from school, the three of us awkward on the pavement only wide enough for two. I held back as they crowded in against the classroom door to spy her, sleepy, on the carpet, and when she came out they caught her between them, implanting kisses, promising gifts as soon as we got home. 'Sylvanians,' I'd warned. 'It's all she wants.'

'It's strange, don't you think, a weird coincidence,' Bea said later, watching Pearl who'd arranged her presents, three squirrels, a hedgehog and a mouse, and was allocating names. 'How Lucy was knocked down too when she was small.'

I remembered nothing. Only the story as our mother had relayed it. How I'd been hit, how I'd gone *roly poly*, that the man driving the lorry had visited me in hospital every day for a week.

'I suppose it is.' I hardly dared look at Mum. She'd been returning from the shops. My heart clenched to think of her, lugging bags up the hill when the ambulance raced past.

Mum got up to fill the kettle. 'I'd left you in the garden, you were playing with children from the flats, you often played there – the mothers kept an eye – but while I was gone a train came by and Bea ran out and straight across the road. You followed.' She looked at me, concerned. 'You always followed Bea.'

'When I was about two,' Bea crossed her arms, 'I was in hospital, with measles. No one was allowed to visit. We had to spend all day in our cots, but there was one nurse who was kind. She'd slip me biscuits, brush my hair. One day I found a switch. I flicked it, and my nurse – as I thought of her – rushed across and flicked it off. She frowned, in a funny sort of way, so I flicked the switch again. The third time she came past she slapped me.' I flinched as Bea flew into the bars. 'I didn't cry. I remember being determined that I wouldn't cry. It's the worst thing, don't you think, about childhood, pretending not to mind?'

Mum poured the boiling water. 'For Christ's sake,' her hand was shaking, a splash scalded her arm, 'can we stop going on about the past?'

Bea pushed back her chair so hard it fell. 'Sure,' she said in the iciest of tones, and gathering her possessions, she slammed out of the door.

For some minutes there was silence. Only the murmuring of Pearl busy with her register. 'Catkins? Bladger?'

'Where's Lex anyway?' Mum set down the tea.

'Denver.'

Pearl plucked a Sylvanian from its bed and placed it in the ring. 'You're late.'

It was busy on Amir Malek's boat and Josetta, Bea's long-legged friend, was on the deck, hooting with laughter, pluming smoke into the night. I edged into her circle and found myself beside a man, handsome, in a light grey suit. 'Meet Marco,' she said. 'Marco is recently divorced.'

'You too are divorced?' His accent was thick, his interest instant, and when I said I wasn't, he frowned minutely, and before I had a chance to ask one of the many questions I had stored, he'd turned to wave at a woman on the far side of the deck, and he was gone.

I'd taken to skimming newspapers for the stories of other people's lives. I skipped over achievements, ruthless in my desire to know whether the Nobel Prize-winning physicist, the war reporter, the environmentalist, had found love, second time around. I read about a silversmith who'd met her new partner when he'd come to interview her about the politics of her motifs. I tore out a profile of a folk singer who'd fallen in love with the woman who designed her outfits, how they'd blended their two families into a happy tribe of six. There was a piece about an artist who'd disentangled himself from the dealer who'd controlled him, only to meet his soulmate on a plane as he flew to take part in a retreat. My mentor, Simone Xa, the woman who continued to showcase my designs, was on her second marriage. Her first husband had been older by almost twenty years. She'd admired his charisma, the anarchic way he lived, the courage with which he faced his many ailments, brought on – she later realised – by the quantities of whisky that he drank, until she found herself the sole provider, in charge of their three daughters, rushing to the chemist for medication before hurrying to work. How could she leave him? If she did – he'd die. But one Sunday, after a trip away, she found she couldn't physically go back. She rang to tell him, mad with worry, only to discover later how he'd wandered out into a local park, sunk down on a bench, where, within an hour (this may have been my own exaggeration), a woman approached and suggested they'd once met. They'd studied together, architecture, and on hearing of Simone's cruel desertion, she'd taken him home, fed him soup and brandy, and dashed down to the chemist for supplies. Now they were married, while Simone lived with a man she described as her best friend. The children, rather than unsettled, had been relieved, and they'd continued to see their father, rushing to his side when he was on his death-bed, which, she told me, was more often than you'd think.

I made a file on my computer, a receptacle for my collection. Into it went the tale of the woman whose twin daughters were in the same class as Pearl, who'd found me at the bus stop quaking with exhaustion, reeling from the effort of forcing Pearl to school. We'd travelled into the West End together – I needed calico from Wolfin's – and on the way, high up in the bounce of the front seats, she told me how she'd come to be separated from her children's father. 'You say that again …' It wasn't the first time he'd threatened to leave her, and although in the past she'd begged him, sometimes on her knees, to stay, now it occurred to her his going might be a relief.

'"Say it again … " I can't even remember what *it* was. But I said it …' she made a triumphant gesture '… and he left.' Soon after she was forced to move, and as her possessions were being unloaded into her new home, Glen appeared from the building opposite. 'The rest,' she blushed, 'is history.' When Glen moved in, all they had to do was carry her clothes and her guitar across the road.

Sometimes the stories refused to slot into my criteria. I took a break from work to have tea with a newly divorced sister-in-law of Nisha. I asked how, and why, her marriage had ended. Radiant, her hair cut short, she said it had simply run its course.

'It's lovely to see you,' she smiled through a froth of marshmallow. 'And how is Lex?'

'Away.'

She didn't take the bait.

'I hear he's a big shot on the circuit now. Did I tell you I'm thinking of doing a PhD?' She talked about Milton, the subject of her intended thesis, and hard as I tried to get her back to the thesis of my own, she wouldn't shift. She had no interest in a new relationship. Why would she? She'd been married since she was nineteen. 'So, your sister was filming in Italy?'

'Yes.'

'And the story, it's autobiographical?'

'Semi.'

'Based on your childhood, Nisha says?'

'Not really.' Italy wasn't anywhere we'd been. 'There are flashbacks. To give context.'

'I can't wait to see it. Did they film in Puglia, do you know?'

Unaccountably lonely, I drove home.

More and more often now, Pearl refused to go to school. She played with her Sylvanians, arranging them into family groups, taking them on trips, the farm, the playground, places she refused to go herself. When I looked in she was lying on her stomach, sliding the hedgehog children down the tree-house slide. I left her there and stared into the fridge. I had a commission for a nautically themed lamp-shade that was overdue, but Pearl had promised not to disturb me if I stopped at lunch, so here I was examining leftovers: three sprouts of broccoli, a square of lasagne, the corners curled. She slid through on socked feet. 'How are you doing?' I turned. Her cheeks were pink, her eyes bright, but she halted as if I'd thrown a spear. She knew my tricks. The minute she rallied I suggested school. Or a walk to the park. I watched her fold in on herself. 'Don't know.' We both looked out at the garden, the small lawn over-grown. I forced work from my mind – I could continue once she was in bed – and I suggested we spend the afternoon marking out the pond she'd been asking me to dig. She hopped and yipped and caught hold of my hands. 'Before we do that, though …' it was not the first time that I'd threatened it '… we'll go to the pet shop, check to see if they have fish.'

She pulled away.

'On Saturday, then.' I used my most determined voice.

On Saturday it was the thirtieth wedding anniversary of the dean of Lex's college. What's thirty years? I wondered. I had to look it up, and even when it was discovered to be pearl, Pearl refused to come. I hired Dora, a favourite teenage daughter of a neighbour, but Pearl clung, damp fingers, nose pressed against my dress, and I had to peel her off and slither out to Lex waiting in the car. We were halfway to Richmond when there was a text. 'She's fine,' I told him, but Lex was listening to his home team failing yet again to score, and he only smiled, briefly, as if to say: *of course*.

The night before, Lex's plane had been delayed, and by the time he arrived I was asleep. I'd woken with the shift of bedclothes, the draught of his limbs as he slid in. 'You awake?' In answer I'd inched myself against him and we'd lain curled together, his hardness flickering, waiting for one or the other to make a first move. My body tensed, my brain flailed. It wasn't as if I didn't like sex, but the jump was a chasm, and we lay immobile until he withered into sleep.

The party was at a cricket pavilion, decorated with roses and balloons. I'd worn white, as if the theme was bridal. 'You look lovely,' Lex remembered. A couples counsellor had suggested we try compliments. 'Thanks,' I forced a smile, and when the speeches started I manoeuvred myself as far away from him as I could get. 'We are delighted,' the dean raised a glass, 'to celebrate this day with you.' He *looked* delighted, as did his wife, vital in a burgundy lace dress. I searched their eyes for lies, but all I saw were the dedicated husband, the capable wife. Their son and daughter regaled us with memories, of holidays, of anniversaries, of jokes.

Halfway through, my phone fizzed in my pocket. Fearful as ever, I eased it out. *Chattable?* There was a text from Bea.

My thumb was hovering when a woman spoke into my ear. She wanted me to know that she adored my fabric. She had cushion covers in Clover, the curtains in her bedroom were Gorse. I took her outstretched hand, hungry beyond imagining for her warmth, but the toasts were being raised. 'To the happy, lucky couple!' Lex was behind me, and when he nudged my arm I lifted the champagne to my lips.

Later I sat beside a woman eating alone, who told me the dean had been her husband's friend – her second husband, she offered with no prompting, although the marriage was cut short. 'We had twelve good years, laughing and dancing. Camping, hiking, doing all the things people do.' I listened to the calm rhythm of her voice. 'Just the other day a friend described his death as tragic, but he'd been ill, and he was ready.' She looked at me and smiled. 'We'd said everything we needed to say, lived our fullest lives. When there's no unfinished business it's easier to grieve, it leaves a softness. I'm sorry,' she paused. 'Maybe you've lost someone yourself?'

I forced myself to shake my head.

The following week it was the Paris trade fair. I'd given Lex the dates six months before, but now it transpired he had a keynote speech in Amsterdam to deliver. 'Don't go,' Pearl trailed me as I packed a bag. She wound her fingers through my hair and pulled. I sat down on the bed and held her. A stand was booked, a hotel room reserved. I allowed myself a flash of its interior, the sliver of chocolate on the pillow, before promising to come straight back.

Jessica was working, but when I pleaded, she swapped her shift at the vet's in order to collect Pearl from school. But only if Pearl went to school. I felt so brittle I might break. Lex would have to take her before he caught his flight.

'Could your mother not help out?'

'No.' She'd used the money she'd extracted from my father – after thirty years she'd threatened him with court – to set up a dance centre in Bath. 'Before you ask, Max isn't an option.' He was building a computer, and was even more than usually absorbed. No one mentioned Bea. Bea was editing her film.

That night Pearl crept round to my side of the bed and lay pressed hard against me. I shuffled towards Lex, who shifted away until he was clinging to the edge. Could I have survived – it was the familiar tormenting question – if Pearl had not? I saw her small, shocked body, the rip in her dress. I'd been too lucky. I had no right to complain. Not even when, last month, I'd glanced at Lex's phone, unguarded, and seen a row of *xxxx*'s flash up on the screen.

Lex was on the sofa when I tiptoed down. I wished him luck. Reminded him to leave a key for Jessica. That it helped to put a Sylvanian badger in the bag with Pearl's packed lunch. He grunted, and grateful, I kissed his forehead, squeezed his warm, broad hand. What if I gave up work? I ran for the Tube, imagining whole days home-schooling Pearl, lying on the carpet, explaining equations with the use of Sylvanian mice.

We were deep below the Channel when school drop-off time came round, and when the train emerged into the flat white light of France, I checked my phone. *How was she? Xx*. I gave in with a text.

Fine! came the reply. My heart sank. Any excuse to use an exclamation mark when an *x* had used to do. It was a theory of Lex's that punctuation was the true reflection of a person's state of mind. An exclamation mark – evasive. The lack of a full stop – aggression. Unease prickled, queasy, until the gridded roof of the Gare du Nord loosened my revolving thoughts, and I lifted my sample bag into my arms and ran. Every sound, every sight breathed freedom, the clang of the Métro, the soot smell of the rails, and by the time I reached the fabric fair, an echoing hall formed into alleyways of stalls, I flung myself in amongst the men and women, presenting my old, new self.

All day I oversaw my stand, making conversation while my textiles were pinched and smoothed, held up to the light, stroked and sniffed and matched. I drank a small black coffee from a booth, ate a brioche without apology as French women do. Later I lapped the room, taking my turn to collect samples, feel for the grains of linen, press wool between my forefinger and thumb. That evening I made my way back to the station, walking with Angelique who specialised in upholstery and who mentioned casually how her husband – her second husband, a reward from God for suffering through the first – would be preparing a celebratory anniversary meal.

'How did you meet?' I expected the usual introduction through friends, but her eyes lit up. 'At this fair. Five years ago, today.'

In truth, Angelique had known Patrice before. They'd been friends, close friends, but had lost touch when he'd gone travelling, and she'd taken up her place at the Sorbonne. Too quickly she became involved with her tutor. Passionate, impetuous, he'd asked her to marry him within a month. Soon they had a child. Then they had two. It was thirteen years before she saw Patrice again. By now she was in the midst of a divorce, had moved with her sons from the family house while her husband ran the place into the ground so that when it was sold, her share, if she ever received it, would be small. It was worth everything, she told me, because she was with the man she loved. She stopped to describe the moment she'd seen Patrice again, the glow that appeared as he walked across the hall, and as she talked she seemed herself to be illuminated by a shaft of light. 'He saw the trade fair advertised, noticed my name, and on a whim he travelled to Paris, knowing nothing of my situation.' We were walking again, our feet in step. 'It was the right time for us. Maybe it was fate.'

We'd reached the Gare du Nord and we stood and faced each other. 'I'm sorry, to go rambling like a lunatic.' She looked into my eyes, adding kindly, 'When the time is right.' She kissed me dizzyingly three times, cheek cheek cheek.

It was late when I slid my key into the lock. Carefully as I opened the front door, Pearl's feet came scampering down. 'Sorry!' Jessica was yawning in the hall. 'I was sure she was asleep.' I thanked her, and paid her, escorting Pearl back up to bed where I lay beside her not daring to ask about her day in case she remembered and refused ever to go to school again. I was in bed myself by the time Lex called. He sounded jubilant. They'd thrown a party, he wished I could have been there. I said I wished I could have been there too, I might have travelled on from Paris, pulled my case over the cobbled streets to his hotel.

'Home tomorrow?'

The line went quiet. 'It's bad form not to support the other speakers. It's a three-day event and—'

'Monday?' I kept my voice cheerful.

'First thing!' The exclamation mark hung above us like a sword.

It was near the end of term when I received a letter from Pearl's school. She'd missed so much they were compiling a report. Would I come in for a meeting? 'We'll both go,' I told Pearl, the meeting was at nine, but she refused – made her body heavy as a log – and rather than enter into battle – drag her, uncurl her hands from the table leg she'd gripped – I left her in the house, alone. 'I'm fine,' she insisted. Her Sylvanians were banked like an army. I turned from images of kettles boiling, my daughter falling, a car crashing through the window, and ran.

The head of the school was waiting, his door ajar. I knew him as a parent; his son had been in the choir, his wife in charge of extracurricular support. How awkward, the mothers whispered, when he left her for a man. 'What's happening?' he said, kindly. When I didn't speak he reeled off a list of reasons why my child might refuse to come to school. Bullying, phobias, trouble in the home.

'She was in an accident.'

He flicked through his notes.

'There was an old piece of machinery, no one imagined it could move. It started rolling ...'

His face was bare, his eyeballs popping.

'It gathered speed ...'

'Was your husband not able to attend?' The head looked round as if he might be saved.

'No.' I'd called him from the ambulance. The siren had been muted, or were we sealed in silence when the doors were slammed? I'd pressed the phone against my ear, listening while he explained the complications of travel from the furthest point in Europe. Two days it had taken. *Stop this!* I told myself. Two days. 'My husband is away.'

The head was waiting, watching me, concerned.

'He should be back ... I'll bring her in. I will.'

'Might it help if occasionally her father were to drop her off?' He said it quietly. 'Pearl may find it easier, the separation.'

He caught my scowl. Had he witnessed me attempting to untangle Pearl at the start of every day? Her spleen was torn. Her liver damaged. One lung had collapsed. Was it written in the notes, how she'd been in my sole care?

The next morning I woke, determined. 'If you're too ill to go to school,' I told my daughter, 'you're too ill to stay at home.' When she refused, even to get dressed, I called a taxi. 'The hospital. I need to get my child to the hospital.'

First I had to catch her. Get her shoes on. Drag her into the cab. She was in her room holding on to the wooden pole of her bed. A curtainless frame, bought in the hope that the floaty lengths of muslin I planned to hang there would make her less afraid to sleep. But the curtains frightened her. Everything frightened her. The bed remained bare.

'Now!' I prised her fingers open, one by one. I had her arms pinned to her side. I was forcing her along the landing, down the carpeted stairs. I pushed her feet into boots, turned to catch hold of my bag, but she was up and off along the hall, had slammed into the downstairs loo. I chased after, and before she could slide the lock I wrenched open the door. 'The taxi's waiting!'

'Miss?' It was the driver. Maybe he had daughters of his own? Mine was curled on the floor, arms around the base of the basin, legs jammed in against the wall.

'Excuse me, miss.' He looked at his watch.

'Wait,' I begged. He was backing away, climbing into his car. 'Please …' But he had gone.

Pearl stood. She kicked off her boots. '*Modern Family?*' She suggested, and wrapping herself in her best blanket, she snuggled into the sofa. I got up and shuffled after, a keening noise rising, strangled, from my gut, and she looked at me, a sidelong glance, curious, before turning to the screen.

It was lunchtime before Lex rang. 'Did you get her to school?'

'Not today.'

There was a disapproving pause. 'She'll have to go in tomorrow.'

'I know.' When I failed to ask my usual questions – when exactly he'd be back – he said he'd see me later, although of course he wouldn't.

I woke in the early hours, my heart galloping, electric tremors running down my arms. I sat up and pressed a palm against my chest. There'd been an article, how heart attacks in women were too easily ignored. I checked for symptoms – cold sweat, shortness of breath, a pain in one or both arms – and deciding it was better to leave Pearl unattended than for her to find me, in the morning, dead, I reached for my phone.

The ambulance slid to a stop in the street. On instruction I'd left the door unlocked. Footsteps crossed the hall. 'In here.' I was on the sofa where Pearl had spent the day. The man was young, the woman older. Both were buckled and prepared. He moved towards me, laden with equipment. She stood by the door, on guard.

'I'm D'Angelo. This is my colleague Noor.' He put a finger to my pulse. 'So what's been happening?' When I told him, he asked had I experienced these symptoms before?

I had. I hadn't. 'Not like this.'

'Are you alone?' He took in the room, the leather armchair, the shelves of books. Photographs, before the accident, and after. The three of us, our wary eyes.

'My daughter. She's asleep upstairs.'

'We're going to do an ECG.'

'She won't leave the house.'

'Could you slip off your top, or would you prefer that Noor attend you?'

I tugged my vest over my head, and with warm hands D'Angelo pressed two dots on the centre of my chest. Four around my left breast, more against my wrists. He attached leads to a black box.

'She was all right, at first. But now … It's been a year.'

A yellow line waved across the screen and the box spat out a graph. D'Angelo knelt beside me. 'Anxiety can cause an excess of CO_2 to build up in your body. If you try and exhale.' He glanced again at the graph.

I took a breath and let it out, and once more he felt for my wrist. 'That's it. Again.' His warmth warmed me, and we sat together in the dark until my heart was quiet.

'You're going to be all right.'

'I just need to breathe, is that it?' I'd suggested breathing to Bea when she'd been panicked. When no amount of meetings, of standing on her head, had helped. *I hate breathing!* she'd snapped.

I laughed.

'You see?' D'Angelo sat back on his heels.

'Sorry to have wasted—'

'It's best to be certain.' He was packing up. 'Take care of yourself, now.'

'And you,' I tried, but my mouth was bunched with tears.

I sat on the sofa and cried, Pearl's blanket soggy where I'd gripped it. Then I climbed upstairs to bed.

The next morning I didn't suggest school. 'Let's dig the pond.' It was what she'd been asking for, to see newts grow and tadpoles transform into frogs.

When the phone rang I didn't answer.

How is she?! Lex texted.

All good

I resisted punctuation. He didn't call again.

V

'Nothing is going to happen.' He stood abruptly – at least that's how I pictured it when I thought about it later – but he couldn't actually have moved because when he next spoke there he was, sitting in his chair. 'It's not as if we're about to jump into bed.'

My face was flaming. I dared myself to meet his eye.

'So ...?' He held my gaze.

Our hour was nearly up.

I'd gone to the therapist on the advice of the woman who'd helped Pearl.

'It might be good for you to talk about ...'

How did she know?

'... the accident.'

'Of course.' What I needed to talk about was my marriage.

'Why don't I leave?' I despaired through the first session, and I detailed how I spent my days, bewailing my passivity, recasting myself as the fiery, outspoken woman I wished I was. I'd sit, my work neglected, and re-enact scenarios – ones in which I threw my possessions into the car, screamed obscenities, roared away. How powerful I felt.

How free. But that was inside my head. On the outside I continued on, the same. 'It's like being in an actual cage.' I gulped water, tissues and tumblers helpfully aligned, and it wasn't long before I started again, listing the myriad ways in which I was trapped. 'I'm so embarrassed,' I stuttered, rising up for air. 'This isn't who I want to be.'

That's the first time I sensed that he'd come closer, although of course he hadn't moved. 'I don't mind.' His eyes were russet brown and warm.

I know you *don't mind. It's* me *that minds.* But I didn't say, because that's why I was there. I didn't, couldn't say.

Each week I dragged myself to see him, compiling lists of things we might discuss – childhood, loyalty, regret – but as soon as I was in his room, had removed my coat and, awkward, another layer, for it was always warm, I forgot about the lists. Instead I started on the story. It was as if I had to get it out – if only I could stop – or at least fall silent long enough to allow him to respond. The next week there was more. 'I'm going to have to tell you every single thing.' I'd start – each affront in order – what I'd said, or not said, how Lex and I had disagreed. Then one day, I paused, and I looked up. I was smiling at him and he at me, and we held each other's gaze for what felt like an indecently long time. 'That was a beautiful moment.' He didn't seem the type to use the word *beautiful*. Not that I'd really looked at him before. Just accepted his presence, moving as it did around the room, so that when I remembered questions that he'd raised, ideas he'd posed, he was always in a different position. Like sex, I thought. And I packed that thought away.

'Tell me,' he took advantage of the pause, 'about your family. How you fit in?' I started, although my chest began to squeeze, how much I loved them, how much I longed for them to get along.

'Your mother and your father?'

'No, my mother and my sister.'

'Why is that?'

'Why is ...?'

'Why they can't get along?'

I swallowed, coughed. 'I don't ...' Or did I know? I shook my head. My throat had closed.

That was the week I had the dream. I woke from it. A light lit inside me. We'd been sitting in a train carriage – the therapist and I – our legs stretched, our feet enmeshed, our backs against the panels of the wall. There was a current running round us, lights revolving in a ring. I saw him as I'd not seen him before. His hair, the green that seams through copper, the flecks of grey, the close shave of his cheek, and something I hadn't noticed, his top lip which disappeared when he smiled. I leant across and kissed him.

Dreaming about therapist!

Radical, Bea texted back.

All day the light stayed on in me, and all that night. I was kinder to Lex. I thought only once or twice of the hurt of his transgressions. I sang along with Pearl as I walked her to school. 'Smile' was the song of the summer: the tune sweetly deceitful; the video, when we curled up to watch it, vicious. Was this the violence I'd been bottling? Beatings and poisonings. Revenge. I held her tight and breathed in the fruit flavour of her hair.

On the day of my next session I was stricken. How ridiculous is this? Last week I would have been hard pressed to describe him to a stranger, and now, even before he appeared in the door, his image was electric. I sat down and he sat down. He looked reserved, his eyes were guarded, his hair savagely cut.

'I've been thinking,' I kept the dream to myself, 'what it means ... love.'

'I've been thinking,' he moved a hand to his heart, 'about you.' Or did he? And the thing is I'll never know, because I interrupted. 'When I said I've been thinking about love –' I found that I was angry '– I mean ...' I drew a circle to encompass all the places we had been '... the love, in this room.' What happened then is still unclear – I'd give a lot to switch it with all the things I do remember – but I must have paled because he asked, 'Why are you so challenged?'

Why? If there was love – if it was real – surely then I'd have to leave? I'd be out on the street, where I had been, alone.

He raised his eyebrows, waiting.

'The way you listen ...' I searched for words. 'The empathy with which you talk, the thread of light between us, that's what I want in my own life. It's what I've always wanted.' I was lying on the grass at Craigmont, the planets spinning, Ted's foot nudging my own. 'That's what I can't imagine that I'll ever have.'

He nodded wisely, sagely, as if he was after all a therapist and not a man, and under his calm gaze, I calmed. We talked about communication, what was possible between two people, a ball, thrown in an arc, and caught, and laughing, dazzled by the depths into which we'd plunged, I asked: 'What happened, it didn't use to be like this in here?'

'I saw you.' He didn't look away. 'I wanted you to know you're loved.'

I might have moaned, or dropped my head into my hands, but I did neither. He caught me anyway. 'It's all right.' That's when he said it. 'Nothing is going to happen. It's not as if we're about to jump into bed.'

Woaaah! My heels were digging in. A few days ago you were no more human than a bear and now we're talking about sex! And dismissing it. Although I dismissed the dismissing part. One step at a time.

On my way home I texted Bea. *Crazy goings-on.* When she didn't call I boarded the wrong train. The light from my dream was blazing; my head, my heart, the blood that sped along my veins, fizzed loud. Grateful for once for Lex's absence, I drifted through the evening, agreeing to every one of Pearl's demands, texting Bea – *Where are you?* – falling at last, exhausted, into sleep.

The next day, unable to concentrate on work, I drove to Hampstead Heath and set off on a walk. Sometimes it seems most people in North London are therapists, or training to be therapists, and it wasn't long before I bumped into a friend meandering along after her dog, who had in the years since I'd seen her, retrained as a couples counsellor for Relate. I asked her how her work was going and then, as if it was inconsequential, about the relationship she had with her – what did she call them … patients? 'What are the rules?' I asked. 'Are you allowed to say that you've been thinking about someone?' I told her how, some weeks before, I'd sighed and said I didn't want the hour to end, and he'd leant his then quite ordinary head towards me and said, 'No, neither do I.'

A look of alarm flashed over her. She was wrestling, I could see it, with her dual loyalties of therapist and friend. I tried her with some more: how he'd stopped mid-sentence to alert me to a blackbird trilling in the tree outside, how he'd recorded the dawn chorus, rising at five to walk to Regent's Park, playing it for me at the start of our session.

'Unorthodox, for sure.'

Before she could condemn him, I jumped to his defence. 'Maybe he's unusually skilled? For the first time in years I'm thinking about things that make me happy.'

'Yes …' She was clearly unconvinced, and later that day she emailed me guidelines on sexual boundaries in the therapeutic workplace. I didn't read them. I didn't want to discover anything that might force me to cancel my next session.

Ten mins till test screening. Chat? Bea's text came through. Ten minutes! I didn't call her back.

As the days passed I became increasingly disturbed. The two of us in that room, meshing, moving, so that I had to remind myself of the photograph he kept in my eyeline, a portrait of his children, a perfect boy and girl, and the references he'd made, in earlier, more tranquil times, to his wife.

I could hardly sleep, was struggling to eat. 'Mum!' Pearl complained when I drifted off during a game of cards, when I put a pan of beetroot on to boil and left it there to scorch.

'Your pulses,' the masseur kept her fingers on my wrist, 'they're jumping everywhere. What's going on?' She was a woman I'd visited before, and so I told her – I couldn't help myself – supplying the therapist's own words: that nothing, obviously, was going to happen.

'Not necessarily.' She waited while I peeled off my clothes, and she confided how her father, an analyst himself, had ditched her mother for a woman who'd come to him for help. 'To be fair, she was younger, richer, and …' she laughed, sardonic, '… nicer-seeming than my mother.' I would have laughed as she did, but she pinged an acupuncture needle into my shin. 'They married, and stayed together for ten years, and then when he retired it was as if overnight the love and admiration she'd felt for him had turned to hatred and disdain. All she could see was some old guy.' The masseur moved behind me and pressed her thumbs into the tight knot of my neck. 'Had her feelings for him been transference? Could he not have managed her attachment instead of responding with feelings of his own? She sought advice, they both did, from a rabbi, but after five sessions she'd upped and left. She'd run off with the rabbi.'

Late that night I looked up transference. *Transference is a common aspect of the therapeutic process and under most circumstances should be discussed and examined. Unless, for instance, you have a phobia of spiders, and this particular therapist is so triggering you're in danger of setting off for a trip into the rainforest untreated. In which case – run.*

Lex called while I was reading, and guiltily I closed the screen. He was in Singapore – there was a professorship open at the university – and although he insisted he had no intention of pursuing it, he'd flown out for a meeting. In Singapore, he told me, there were gardens planted vertically. You could be arrested in the street for chewing gum. 'It might be useful, though, to stay on for another week …?'

When I didn't respond with any bitter or disparaging remarks, he added that he missed me, and for the first time in a long while the voice inside my head stayed quiet.

On Friday I had supper with Nisha. 'I need a drink.' She flagged a waiter. The company she worked for had asked that she transfer to Seattle, and although she was worried – about the children's school, her parents, Tavish, who would have to retrain – she was excited too. 'And you?' She stroked my arm. The last time I'd seen her I was raw with the wounds of my discovery – a text message, white on the black screen of Lex's phone – its yearning, sexually explicit tone, impossible to misinterpret. 'I'm well,' I told her, and I couldn't help myself, I grinned.

'Oh my God,' her face opened. 'You've met someone!'

I waited as our glasses were filled, although I knew I'd have to tell her. About the dream. The kiss. The *beautiful* long look. 'Obviously,' I ended, 'nothing is going to happen.'

'Why not?' She was alive with it. 'Who cares about ethics? It may be destiny, the way you two were supposed to meet.' I tried to interrupt, to tell her about the ties he wore, his ill-cut suit, his wife, but she was having none of it. 'Maybe you'll run away together.' Her eyes were bright with the vicariousness of my living, her own adventures so far in the past. 'I, for one, will be delighted. You deserve to be happy.' She poured us both more wine, and as she did I considered Tavish, kind, devoted – if not entirely bald – and how contented she had always seemed with him. Had I been blinded by Lex? His sadness, the galvanising task of holding on? 'I do think about the therapist ninety per cent of the time.' I gave her what she wanted, and she raised her arm and signalled for another bottle. As we drank, chattering our way into the future, I thought of how his face changed when we talked – a soft look, a sort of melting – and my heart flipped over like a fish.

There were flowers in the room when I next entered. Had there been flowers before? Beside the flowers was a photograph of his wife.

'So, how are you?' he asked when, after some minutes, I had still not spoken.

A cold sweat was collecting, and as the eyes of his wife rested on me, amused, it occurred to me all I had done was swap one unavailable object of obsession for another. 'My work's going well.' I'd hardly mentioned work before, and it was true, through all the recent turmoil, new commissions had been coming in. He smiled his encouragement, and glad to feel him closer, I described my designs. 'I'm branching into wallpaper, I've made a line with wheels, and hearts ...' I stopped when I saw how this had been inspired by my dream. 'Transference. I looked it up.'

His smile remained. 'What did you find?'

I mentioned the spiders and the rainforest in the hope that he might laugh.

'Transference and counter-transference happen all the time,' he said. 'Romantic, erotic … Therapy is about the relationship.'

I gave in and admitted to the dream, the circle of light, how our feet were touching, everything except the kiss. He withdrew a little, as people do when you admit to encountering them in dreams, and I braced myself to feel him get up and move away. He stayed in his chair.

The next day Lex returned. He threw his bag down in the hall and hugged me. To evade him I suggested food, and we moved through to the kitchen where I broke eggs for an omelette, sliced spring onions into a pan. Lex paced. He could accept the professorship in Singapore, manage his work here, be in both places at once. His eyes shone, his leg jumped, and when he pulled me on to his knee, I remembered his pallor when he'd considered himself trapped.

'Are you thinking we'll come with you?'

'That's the beauty, you won't have to, not now Pearl's settled. I'll be able to get back, every other month.' He beamed, close up, and I was nodding when I smelt the omelette burning. I scraped the salvaged remains on to a plate, scattered it with parsley, and watched him, happy to be home, safe in the knowledge that before long he'd be gone.

Pearl had friends visiting. Two girls who raced with her round the garden. 'When will they need you?' I asked as they hurtled into cartwheels, their hair streaming, the tips grazing the ground.

Lex creased his eyes. I knew that look. 'If I make time over the summer I can trial the classes ...'

'Won't the students be on holiday?'

'Not in Singapore.'

Foolish me. Everything was different on the far side of the world. 'Maybe we should come too?' I tried instead. 'School breaks up in the middle of July.'

Again I'd got it wrong. Lex had pushed Singapore to August to leave space for a conference in New York from which he'd fly straight on. 'Anyway,' he squeezed my hand, 'we have our week booked, don't we, by the sea?'

The dates I'd given him flared red. 'Don't tell me.' He scooped up his diary and saw the days run through with work. 'Could you, maybe, find a friend to go along?'

Our eyes locked. There was the iron roller, loosened from its mooring, moving, thundering … I took my cup, and at the moment of collision I smashed it to the ground. Pearl's two friends thumped to their feet. Pearl froze in the splits. 'Fuck you.' I left him to sweep up the shards.

Who even am I? My thoughts swirled as we moved through our familiar routine. To resist would have meant an exile – and Lex had learnt my weakness early. I could not withstand his chill. Eyes closed, I allowed myself to be engulfed, did everything in my power to welcome it, and afterwards, for some little while, we lay together, comforted. In the early hours I woke, alone on my side of the bed. *I'd advise against the larger sizes*, the salesman had warned when, desperate with Pearl's waking, I'd gone in search of the widest mattress there was. *My wife and I kept trading up; when we got to Super King, she left.* He'd stood despondent among the divans, and I saw his stooped shoulders as I looked across the cool divide to where my husband lay, out of reach.

Quietly, carefully, I crept downstairs. I stood in the kitchen and stared into the fridge, and finding nothing that might numb me, I moved through into the carpeted room where Pearl's Sylvanians had been set out in rows. I lay down before them. There were kitten triplets in basket-weave bassinets, a host of pandas in plaid overalls and smocks. A Sylvanian Family magazine lay open, accessories circled, and as I flicked past BBQs and teepees, I did my best to hammer my mind blank.

I was cold when I slipped back between the sheets. I turned to the window, watching for the dawn. 'Hey,' Lex's voice came hoarse, and he manoeuvred himself across the bed, and slid my body against his. 'Are you trying not to love me?'

Tears rose gummily below my lids. 'I am,' I managed, and we lay together as the sky lightened into grey.

'Fuck you,' I reported to the therapist, and he agreed there'd really been nothing else to say.

We sat in silence.

'Do you wonder why I stay with him?'

'I do wonder that, occasionally.'

'It's hard,' I said, 'to leave a man who's never really there.'

Time passed. The minutes ticked. 'How would it feel,' he asked, gentle, 'if you were free to speak your mind?'

I laughed. 'Right now?'

'At any time. Under any circumstance.'

I sighed, my breath released. Was he insane?

Suggesting I speak mind, I texted Bea. *A trick?*

Or therapy? Her message came back, followed by another. *Help! Nothing to wear. Screening in one week.*

Within an hour we were lying on her bedroom floor, shoes and clothes covering every surface. 'You know I invited Mum?'

'I do.'

'I thought she'd be busy. Tangoing. I thought she'd make an excuse.'

'Have you spoken to her … recently, I mean … about …' I was careful as I chose the words '… the past?'

Bea looked at me, her eyes were wary. 'I did try.' There was a pause. 'She said I'd got it wrong. It wasn't sunny, not that morning, and anyway the curtains round the bed were blue.'

I reached across and squeezed my sister's hand.

'We saw a therapist, did I tell you? Me and Mum. One question and we turned. Savage. We were screaming. I ran out. Or she did. Then there we were again, waiting for the bus. The next day she called. "Sorry that you feel this way." I told her to fuck off. Twenty minutes later I called back. "If you can't tell your mother to fuck off," she said, "who can you tell?" We laughed.'

Bea laughed now and so did I, but I could see our mother as she would have been, her hair sticking to her face, her fingers clutching the receiver. Doing her best. Doing everything she could.

'Nightmare.' Bea was rummaging through the chaos of the clothes. 'I'll be going to the screening naked.' She flung away the dress I'd suggested. A camisole landed in the bin.

'Bea,' I had to say it. 'I know Mum can't see the film before the screening, but maybe she could read the script at least?'

'Too late.' Bea was standing at the mirror. Her hair was long, her body spartan. I tracked the scars, silvered as they were across her arms. Each scar had its own story – razor blades, a compass, the needles that she'd used to puncture veins.

'Lucy,' she threw me a shirt, 'any chance this can be mended?'

'I can't help worrying …' I examined the ruffle and its rip '… how Mum will be, how she'll react …' I caught her eye. She was tying a length of silk around her neck, arranging it into a loose bow.

'Hideous?' she asked.

What else was there to say? 'Kinky,' I assured her.

There was no bed big enough. Not now, at 4 a.m., when I found myself awake. 'The hour of loss,' the masseur said when I dragged myself to see her. My chest was caved, my throat ached, the sinews of my neck so tight they stung.

'What about your father?' I was trying for distraction. 'How did he react when his wife ran off with the rabbi?'

'Hard to tell.' Her fingers were up under the base of my skull. 'By the time I got back from college he'd remarried. My mother too, although no one got hitched more regularly than my stepmother who left the rabbi for a more senior rabbi, then for the spiritual leader of a cult.' My face was pressed into a towelling oval, my mouth and eyes forced wide by the pressure of her hands. 'Breathe deep,' she instructed, 'and exhale.'

That weekend my mother arrived.

'It's a story,' I reminded her when she began to fret about Bea's film.

'But what if everyone believes it?'

'They won't. Why would they?'

'"I never felt safe."' The old quote flew bitter from her mouth.

Words rose. I did my best to bite them down. 'Mum, when are you going to stop this?'

'Stop what?'

264

I caught her eye and held it. My stomach dropped. 'I know.'

She looked around as if for reinforcements. 'Know what?'

'About …' The floor, the walls were tilting. 'I've known, for years.'

She frowned. She waved her hands as if to clear away my words, but I was speaking. After all this time. 'When Bea was furious, taking drugs, endangering her life, you kept on asking, "What's wrong with her?" You must have seen me hoping there was something I could do. Longing for you both to get along. It's what I wanted. For the three of us … It was never going to work.'

'What work?'

'You know!' Was she going to make me say it? 'You've always known. The abuse.'

Her mouth fell open. Her eyes jumped, wild. 'There was no abuse.'

A laugh burst from me.

She was on her feet. 'It isn't true.'

'It's not?'

'I was there. I told him. I told him … to stop.'

Stop what? I didn't ask. I couldn't bear to hear. She was pacing, gesticulating, explaining her theory that there were people who used abuse as an excuse. 'I went to a meeting. Did you know that? The dreaded Mel. She said it might help. Everyone was sharing, every other person, about how they'd been assaulted. About how what happened led to their addiction, led to slashing at their arms.'

'But, Mum—'

'It can't be a coincidence …' She was talking, louder, faster, about the lengths people were prepared to go. 'All those men and women, avoiding responsibility. Avoiding blame. It was like some kind of punishment. Being forced to listen to their stories. I wanted to stand up and shout: "Convenient, don't you think? It's not your fault?" But I said nothing. I said nothing to Bea. The thing is,' pain suffused her, swelled her face, 'I'd never have allowed it. I'd never have let it happen. Not to my own little girl.'

The worst thing, Bea said when she'd first told me, wasn't the man, or what he did. It was her mother refusing to believe her.

'How could she remember anyway?' Mum was shouting. 'She was only six years old!'

There was silence. I wanted to run, to keep on running, but instead I went upstairs to fetch the quilt, to check on Pearl who lay, her arms outstretched in sleep.

On the day of the screening I was so relieved to see the therapist I couldn't speak. We sat quiet, for some minutes, while a bird, our bird, as I thought of it, sang, delirious, in the tree outside.

'It's so good to be here,' I exhaled.

'Yes.'

'An actual, physical relief.'

'We're lucky.' His eyes, once brown, had turned to blue. 'To have found this connection.'

'But if we can't …' I fought against the yearning. To leap over boundaries. To climb into his lap. 'What use is it, really? What's actually the point?'

'Ideally…' he was searching '… you harness the love … you've …' he swallowed 'we've … discovered in this room, and take it into your marriage, or ...' he must have seen me shiver '... if that's not possible, then out into the world.'

Wildly I searched for a solution, skipping ahead down corridors, doors slamming as I reached them, reached him. Exhausted, I gave in, describing the night with my mother, re-enacting for his benefit every disconcerting word.

'So how was it the next day?' He leant forward.

I told him that neither one of us had brought it up. We'd had our breakfast, walked Pearl to gymnastics, idled through the market as if nothing had been said. 'What if I'm back where I started?' I pressed a hand to my throat.

'You won't be.' He shook his head.

The session ended, and the time ticked on. 'Next week, then,' he said, and when I gathered myself to leave he stood and lifted my jacket from the chair. He held it out, a hand at each shoulder and I turned, leaning into the shelter of his frame, allowed myself three heady seconds before stepping out into the street.

Lex was free, for once, to accompany me into the West End. The cinema was in Soho, small, with red plush seats and a padded velvet bar. I'd read the script, but even so, I watched, transfixed, as a young woman, alone, in Florence, wakes in the grandeur of a crumbling hotel. As she rouses we see the floor is carpeted with cats. Eyes flick open, green and copper, hazel, blue, before she sinks back into sleep. Now we descend with her into a dream – her child self, running across a beach. Mum! she shouts. The sun is setting, shadows stretch along the sand. She stops and looks around and we pan out to see the ridges and the stacked stone cliffs, a lighthouse in a walled enclosure, caravans in a field.

In the next scene she is grown again, and scavenging for food. A chef appears, cursing, and she sprints away along the alley, turns a corner, dashes through a square where a man, his shirt cuffs starched, his watch heavy on his wrist, lowers his newspaper as our heroine flits by.

The hotel is deserted. The cats have taken over every room. Sometimes as she lies in bed we hear the sound of drumming from the floor above. One night she climbs the staircase, there are portraits rising with her up the walls, ancestors that could be Colquhouns, but as she nears the attic the drumming stops. She is face to face with the child. The child is wearing wellingtons, and there's a cat held in her arms. She's staying right here, she says, her cat, he needs her, and anyway, her family, her mother and her sister, they'll be coming for her, soon.

The cinema was warm. I glanced across at my mother, sitting at the end of the row, at my father in a seat by the door. The next section I watched through the grille of my fingers. The Lost Months, as I'd thought of them, although until recently I'd thought of them as mine. A caravan in Scotland. (Morocco was considered too expensive a location.) The child waving as the mother and the sister set off on a journey south. At first she lives contentedly with her mother's friend, but soon they are joined by a man. They sit round the table, playing cards, drawing pictures which they pin on to the walls, a happy family of three. Then one night a fight breaks out. We see the child in her bunk, the covers pulled up to her ears as crockery is broken, pictures smashed. The following morning everything is quiet. The woman sloshes water in a basin, the man sits slumped by the door. From then on the rows are frequent. Clouds draw in. The rain comes sleeting down. Our girl roams the clifftops. She finds a kitten mewling in a hedge, and tucks it into her jacket, feeding it with milk from the tip of her finger, slipping food from her own plate to where she's stored it in a box under her bunk. We see her at the bus station, the cat peeking between the toggles of her jacket, watching a coach as it pulls in, but she's not there when the mother and the sister scramble from a car, thanking the driver, hoods up against the rain. The wind is up, the coast is lashed, and the field where the caravan once sat is nothing but a lake. The mother rushes, as the child has done, along the beach, her younger daughter clinging to her hand, climbing the cliff to the lighthouse where she bursts open the door. From above, the girl watches as they peer into the dark. They call her name. They search the rooms where the lighthouse keeper and his wife once lived. She doesn't speak, even when her mother collapses sobbing on a step. And then in the silence, there is the sound of a miaow.

'You OK?' Lex reached across and took my hand, and I wrenched myself from real life, the one in which we'd searched for Bea in Marrakech, where the couple with the baby had packed up and left before we'd managed to return. How long before we found her? We'd scoured the square, the souk, we'd run from one Riyad to another, calling, and when we did discover where she was, it was a home, for boys with polio. The woman who ran it had taken her in. We'd expected celebration – at least I had – but Bea was steely. Changed.

Applause rose with the credits. The director stepped on to the stage, calling for Bea, who appeared in a suit, the shirt ruffle mended, the bow framing her face like a flower. There were cheers, and whistles, and the actress who'd played her in flashback, skittish in a feather boa, threw her arms around her waist. 'Myself!'

Drinks were served in a velvety room beside the screening theatre. I fought my way through to find my mother at Bea's side. 'I'm so proud,' she was saying, and I wrapped my arms around them both.

'I don't know how to …' I began, but Bea was whisked away.

'Love her,' I said to myself.

Dad was standing by the bar alone. There was no mention of a father in the film. 'Do you know,' he shuffled, awkward, 'I haven't been inside a cinema for forty years.'

'Mum!' I'd left her, stranded, and not caring that she'd threatened my father recently with court, I took her arm and pulled her forward. They greeted each other, wary. 'Congratulations.' He ducked his head, and she smiled, both shy and defiant, the girl she must have been when they first met.

When I next looked round Lex was talking to a woman, familiar as a film star, their faces so close they blurred. I turned away, threw myself into conversation, sought out Max who was devouring crisps, but even as we spoke I could see their outlines overlapping, and as Max described the progress of the engine he was building, I felt my head fill up with cloth. 'Sorry.' I backed away. 'I need to …' I descended on the enraptured couple; stood by, ominous, to be introduced.

Lex turned. 'I was just saying to Gabrielle, how well it works, this collaboration.'

Gaby! My vision cleared, and I held Bea's producer in a grateful hug.

We left the party late. 'Wait for me,' I called as Lex stalked ahead and without slowing he let it be known my suspicions had been noted. He'd not be punished for mishaps from the distant past.

The next day I wrote to Bea, a fan letter, illustrated with cats. Mum – I wanted to set it down in black and white – had told her she was proud.

But never sorry, Bea said, when she rang.

'It's not that distant, is it,' I asked the therapist, 'five months?' and he agreed that it was not. I took a breath, lightened as if I'd set aside an actual load, and I allowed myself to watch him without swerving while he offered an evaluation of my night. 'There's so much to unpack with the film's focus on abandonment, on damage, the entanglement of the three main characters ...'

I challenged myself to stay with him, not to look away, and then, with no warning – what warning could there have been? – I was lifting up and out of myself, was falling through his eyes. A second passed as I touched down, and we were travelling together now through space and time until with the narrowest creasing of each pupil, he in turn swooped into the centre of my gut. I felt him land, as I had, with a stroke. 'Loyalty, division ...' He was still talking, although what he said was impossible to hear. And he was up again, and out. I couldn't help myself, I laughed.

He stopped and laid a hand against his stomach. 'It's so physical.'

I placed a hand against my own. 'It is.' We were grinning, words inadequate. Falling, meeting. All pretence was gone.

That week I skipped through London, traffic blaring as I stepped off kerbs, scattering possessions, leaving my key hanging in the door. I wasn't alone! I wasn't crazy! And if I was, I didn't care. Lex remained silent. Was he expecting me to beg?

I wrote a poem, scrunched it up, sketched the mystery of our connection – a wave, a quaver, filled it in with colour. I sorted through the cupboards, resurrected my red dress, took a mismatched stack of Lex's socks, and instead of searching, as I'd done too often for a pair, threw them in the bin.

'What's this?' He was standing in the kitchen, fishing them out, one by one. That's when I told him: I couldn't go on.

'Go on, with what?'

'I need something to change.'

He let the dustbin lid snap shut. 'By *something*, you mean me?'

I nodded. How often had I argued: *No. Not you. It's probably me.* But now, even if he had to travel to the desert, whisper to horses, grieve his father, throw rocks into a fire, I needed him to change. 'Try. At least.'

He slumped down at the table. 'I'm not sure that I can.'

'That was a long week,' I said when I next sat in the therapist's small room.

'It was an age.'

We smiled. The sky was azure, the tree outside in leaf.

'Have you thought about what happened?' I was free to ask the questions now.

'I have.' He had the face of a boy. 'And you?'

I gave him my theories: suspense, a phenomenon caused by yearning.

He laid a palm across his stomach. 'I think it may have been our souls.'

Souls. Was that where they resided? 'Now what do we do?'

'I'll be entirely honest,' his eyes looked washed, 'this wasn't covered in my training.'

I waited, smiled. What was I in hope of? That we combine our energy, engage in an experiment, show that love could break through walls?

'I worry I'm no longer the right person to help.'

'No!' It was impossible. He must have felt it. He glanced around. 'Maybe if we stopped, continued our relation-ship … as friends?'

I leapt up and raced along a cobbled street to where he waited, arms outstretched. 'I'd love that!' But he was tussling with an image of his own. 'That wouldn't work.' He shook it out.

Another minute passed.

'Last night –' there was nothing for it but to revert to the old story '– I told Lex I needed him to change.'

'What did he say?' We were back on our safe ground.

'He said he wasn't sure he could.'

'If my wife –' we both startled '– told me she was unhappy—'

'The thing is,' I interrupted, 'if Lex really wanted to …
Sorry, you were saying?'

He raised an eyebrow.

'About your … wife.'

'There's nothing in the world I wouldn't do.'

I reached out my hand. There wasn't any plan. It sprang
forward of its own accord. He hesitated, then he offered
his, curling my fingers with his palm, encasing it with the
other. How often had I longed for this? To feel his touch.
To feel him. But there was only duty, no promise travelling
along my arm. Slowly, politely, we withdrew.

The seconds ticked, and then the minutes. The clock
reached our hour.

I stood, snatched up my jacket.

'Goodbye.' He was unrecognisable. A therapist, professional. I didn't thank him. To thank him would have meant
an ending, and desperate as I was to leave, I needed, for as
long as it would take, to pretend that I'd be back.

On the way home I called my mother. She was wary of
me. I felt it now every time we spoke. I told her there was
something I needed to say.

'All right.' I heard her tremor, and I said I loved her. It
was as easy as that. I said I always would.

'Oh,' she sounded dazed. 'Thank you.' We hung up.

I texted Bea from the bus. *Sorry for trying to cheer you up your
whole life.*

It has been quite annoying, she came back.

The night before Lex left for Singapore I crawled across
to his side of the bed. He turned to me, and I saw him as

I'd first conjured him up, wandering past my market stall – he was as lonely now as he'd been lonely then. 'Hello.' He pulled me against him, an end to our long freeze.

The next morning he held me on the doorstep, never more tender than when he was about to leave. 'I hope it's good there.' He wouldn't guess, till later, that I was saying my goodbyes. 'Let me know how you get on.'

'My love to Pearl.' He kissed me, sad, and he was gone.

Still dressed, I climbed back into bed. *Chat?* I texted Bea, and while I waited for her call I thought about the masseur and what she'd said. 'The mistake we make,' she'd lain a finger on my pulse, 'is to think that love must be about possession. You can love someone, you can hold them in your heart, and nothing has to happen.' I felt my own heart, pulling free.

Acknowledgements

The first chapter of this book was originally published in the *New Yorker* as the short story 'Desire', written in response to homework I set the students of the writing group I run: an assignment called The Journey, which – as always – I attempted myself. I'd like to thank the participants of this group, past and present, for the warmth and inspiration over these many years. Thank you also to Tracy Chevalier for the use of a room to write in one winter when my own house was full, and to Kirsten Hecktermann and Virginia White for advice on all aspects of textiles and design. I'm most grateful to my early readers Emma Hewett, Kate Weinberg, Natania Jantz, Xandra Bingley, Kitty Aldridge and, in particular, Gerry Simpson. Also my editors Alexis Kirschbaum and Allegra Le Fanu for their invaluable notes, and to the ongoing support and generosity of my agent Clare Conville. My most ardent thanks to my sister Bella Freud.

A Note on the Author

ESTHER FREUD trained as an actress before writing her first novel, *Hideous Kinky*, which was shortlisted for the John Llewellyn Rhys prize and made into a film starring Kate Winslet. After publishing her second novel, *Peerless Flats*, she was chosen as one of *Granta*'s Best Young British novelists. Her other books include *The Sea House*, *Lucky Break* and *Mr Mac and Me*, which won Best Novel in the East Anglian Book Awards. She contributes regularly to newspapers and magazines, and teaches creative writing with her own local group. Her first full length play, *Stitchers*, was produced at the Jermyn St Theatre in 2018, and in 2019 she was made a fellow of the Royal Society of Literature. She lives in London.

A Note on the Type

The text of this book is set in Bembo, which was first used in 1495 by the Venetian printer Aldus Manutius for Cardinal Bembo's *De Aetna*. The original types were cut for Manutius by Francesco Griffo. Bembo was one of the types used by Claude Garamond (1480–1561) as a model for his Romain de l'Université, and so it was a forerunner of what became the standard European type for the following two centuries. Its modern form follows the original types and was designed for Monotype in 1929.